The Changeup

Emily C. Childs

Editing by Sara Sorensen

Cover design by Clara Stone at authortree.co

For rights and inquiries please reach out to agent Katie Shea Boutillier at The Donald Maass Agency here: ksboutillier@maassagency.com

Dedicated to those who love a little nerdy with their sexy.

Author Note

I'm so glad you're here.

For your information on triggers this book deals with someone with a traumatic brain injury overcoming a bully, and there have been deliberate liberties taken with MLB procedurals for story purposes.

(The last note is for my brother, Landon. I did things on purpose, Lan. On. Purpose.)

Chapter 1

Parker

MY SISTER HATES ME.

I'm good with it. There's nothing I take more seriously than babysitting Alexis and my nephew who is about to smash his way into the world.

She says I hover. I disagree. I'm efficient.

When Bridger, my best friend turned brother-in-law, needs to run to the recording studio with his band, and asks me to make sure his living room doesn't turn into the Labor and Delivery Department, I will step up to the plate no matter how many glares are shot in my direction.

Bridge called in a frenzy this morning, saying there was a last-minute fix needed on Perfectly Broken's latest album before the final production could begin.

If I didn't think he'd basically be the coolest dad in the world, I'd probably hate him a little for taking his family on tour this spring. Then again, if they stayed behind, I wouldn't be here to help out anyway.

Alexis insists her birth schedule is not dependent upon the Vegas Kings' game schedule, but . . . it is.

Deny it all she wants, subconsciously she wanted her big brother around for this little guy.

"Lex!" I shout over my shoulder. "Garlic butter, or no?"

"I can butter my own sandwich, Parker," she yells from the living room. *Three. Two* . . . "But, yes to garlic."

Thought so. I grin and flip the grilled cheese over in the skillet. I won't rub it in Lex's face that I see through her grouchy charade about being coddled; she gave it all up when I told her we could have the three-cheese sandwiches I made us as kids.

There were definite tears in her eyes.

Maybe she hates me for encroaching on her stubborn independence, but at the same time, I'm basically her hero.

She's mine too, so it evens out. Naturally, it's easy to babysit her and take her snippy tone. The truth is, Lex is my person as much as Bridger.

We've sort of established a hodgepodge family. The entire band of Perfectly Broken is made up of my closest friends, but we have a few of my teammates tossed in the mix too. Rock and roll and baseball. It works.

I load one of the sandwiches on a plate with a few chopped veggies because, as mentioned, I take the duty of making sure my sister and nephew are healthy seriously.

Alexis hasn't moved from where I left her fifteen minutes ago. One pillow against the beachball she calls a belly, another between her knees, and an old, tattered edition of *Wuthering Heights* in her hand.

She groans and closes the book. "That smells so good."

Hero.

Alexis wiggles her fingers, hands out for the plate.

"Knew you'd be happy I came over eventually."

She narrows her eyes. "I'm not. Between you and Bridger I can barely take a breath without one of you flipping through a baby book to make sure it's the right kind of breath."

I'm not even going to deny it.

Look, there are a handful of people who mean my world keeps spinning. Alexis is one of them. Since my nephew is part of my best friend and part of my sister, he's basically the golden egg to me.

I haven't even seen his face and he's got me wrapped around his finger.

Big plans are being made in this head of mine on all the ways we'll pull pranks on his parents, or play way too much catch in order to steer him away from the guitar Bridger will try to brainwash him with.

So, yeah. Sue me. I've read a few pregnancy and baby books.

"Want to watch the Collin Firth *Pride and Prejudice*?" I ask.

Alexis stops midbite, a quizzical lift to her brow. "Who are you?"

"Hey, I'm here to make sure you are comfortable. I don't know how long Bridger is going to be, so we might as well waste time."

"First, watching that will never be a waste of time. Second, yes, I want to watch all six hours. Third, I need to pee first."

I roll my eyes when she shoves the plate against my chest, stumbles out of her pillow nest, then hobbles to the bathroom.

Halfway through stealing a bite of a pretty perfect grilled cheese, Alexis squeaks in surprise. "Um, Park?"

"I'm not coming in there, Lex. We have to draw the line somewhere."

"Well, you picked a bad time to build boundaries," she says. "I'm pretty sure my water just broke."

A rush of adrenaline clamps onto every nerve in my central nervous system. But, funny enough, each movement is collected and controlled. Gently, I put the plate on the end table, stand, and head to the bathroom door. "You sure?"

"I didn't have an accident if that's what you're thinking."

I pinch my lips together, pull out my phone, and dial the go-number. "Hey, Griff. It's time."

Do I sound like a secret agent? Yes.

Is it necessary? Also, yes.

When you live a public life there are vultures waiting to pounce. Rumor has it cameras and paparazzi have been camped out at the hospital for two days after Alexis's due date came and went. With a famous husband and a brother who is way more famous, she doesn't stand a chance at avoiding paparazzi without some leg work.

"Did you just call Griffin?" she shrieks.

The catcher for the Kings is one of those buddies you can count on. A charmer, a bit of a goof, but he's solid. And holds a lot of affection for my sister since she feeds us all the time during the off-season.

"No worries, Lex. What I need to know from you is if you're having any contractions yet."

She huffs a few times. "No."

"Okay. I don't believe you," I say, firmly. "This is not a drill, Alexis. We are doing this."

She hiccups. "I need to call Bridge. He'll freak out, and rush, and get in a car accident, and—"

"Take it easy. Griff is on it. And I've got some of our rookies to play the shiny objects outside the hospital. You call Bridger. I'll get the go-bag."

I know exactly where it is because two weeks ago I packed it with Bridger when Alexis was sleeping.

She hisses, then half-cusses before she flips her tune. "Sorry, baby."

I snort. This kid is going to be on tour busses with Tate Hawkins, the drummer of Perfectly Broken. He'll hear plenty of words before he's two, but it's cute that Alexis thinks she can cover his unborn ears.

"Sounded like a big one, Lex. What number on the pain scale?"

"Um . . . maybe a fouuurr—" Another groan follows. "Six. A six. Park, why are they coming so fast? Am I a wimp? I didn't think I was a wimp, but these are only the beginning ones. I have forever to go. How am I supposed to do this when they already feel like something is ripping out of me?"

"Nothing wimpy about you." I dig in one of the coat closets and pull out a black duffel bag. "Need me to call Bridger?"

"No." The bathroom door opens and she's wearing a bathrobe, trembling. "No. I'll call him. I n-need to get dressed."

She needs her big brother. I see it in the glassy shine of her eyes. We've seen each other at our worst more times than I can count, and right now she needs her brother reassuring her she's superwoman.

I curl my thick arms around her skinny frame minus the basketball middle. "Hey. You've got this."

"I can't be a mom, Park." Her chin quivers. "What if I'm the same as—"

"Nope." I grip her shoulders. "Don't even go there. You are going to be awesome. This kid will be quoting Brontë by the time he's three. Want to know why? Because he's going to love his mom so much he'll want to be just like her."

A tear drips down her cheek and she hugs me back. "Thanks."

I kiss the top of her head, then unravel from her arms. "Go get dressed, and we'll get out of here."

When she comes back out again, she's dressed in loose pajamas and has her hair tied up in a high ponytail.

My body stiffens when she stops and braces against the wall. *Come on, man.* Discomfort is to be expected. Not exactly a day at the spa pushing a kid out of a body.

When it passes, I'm there to take her hand. "Did you tell Bridger to keep cool?"

She sniffles. "He didn't answer, Park. I called four times. If they're recording, he won't hear it."

No problem. A hitch in the plan is all.

We can do this.

"It's all good," I tell her. "I'll keep trying. You focus on those breathing exercises."

"I don't want to know how you know about my breathing exercises," she mumbles and slips on a pair of flip flops at the front door, then grips my arm as I lead us to my truck parked in Bridger's spot in their massive garage.

I know about breathing exercises because all my focus since the season ended has gone into this moment. Focus which included falling down a YouTube hole on different breathing techniques during labor.

There are some images I'll never unsee.

Maybe people think Lex and me are weirdly close, but the truth is, we helped raise each other. Bridger and most of the guys in Perfectly Broken were there, but they didn't see all the nights I built tents in my room for Alexis to sleep in when she was scared. Or the way she looked at me like I was the person who could protect her from anything when too much yelling filled our house.

By the time we've made it halfway to the hospital, I've dialed Bridger's number once. Twice. Finally, on the third time he answers, a little breathless. Alexis sighs in relief when his voice fills the truck.

"Parker. Why is Griffin here? What—"

"Bridge," Alexis says, gripping the armrest. "I . . . my water broke and—" She clenches her jaw.

"Lex, open your mouth," I say, and demonstrate dropping the jaw. "Don't clench. Remember, it'll help keep the rest of you relaxed."

"Al," Bridger says even more frantic. "I'm coming. I'm on my way right now." He curses, but she's too busy to call him out. "I'm so sorry I wasn't home."

"I've got her, man," I say. "Just get to the hospital because I'm pretty sure you're about to have a baby."

"I'm on my way." Bridger lets out a haggard breath. "I love you, Al. I'm coming."

"I love you," she whispers.

I feel as if I've invaded a private moment. It's not weird my sister married my best friend. Not anymore. Can't say I reacted with the same attitude at the beginning, but now anyone can see they're perfect for each other.

And for some reason, I feel like an outcast here. This should be their thing. Not the Parker and Bridger, with Alexis tagging along thing.

For once, I'm the tagalong.

I grip my sister's hand the rest of the way to the hospital.

I'll be honest, I'm rocking this birth partner thing. Ice chips, light dimmer, wet washcloths, nurse caller, I take on all the roles.

The only part I can't take away is the grimace on Alexis's face.

"Starting to think you weren't being completely honest earlier about your pain level," I tell her. "Probably why you were on the grumpy side."

"I am not discussing my moods right now, Parker!"

If there was a way I could take away the pain, no question, it'd be gone in one second. I'll do the next best thing, at least.

"I'm going to get that shot for you, Lex." With care, I pry her steel-locked fingers off my hand.

"I want the stupid shot, but—" She winces and lets her head flop back on the pillow, a tear in her eye. "I *need* Bridger."

Does it jab knowing she doesn't need me? A little. But if I could've passed the torch to anyone it would've been Bridge. Still, it's almost a slap in the face. The one person who always needed me . . . really doesn't.

"Working on it, Lex." I show her the text from Griffin. "Bridge is finding a different way in. They ran into some paparazzi outside. Someone must've spilled."

Her eyes flash in something dangerous as the nurse comes into the room. "Those rookies of yours need to get out there now and tell those idiots if my husband misses the birth of his son, I will personally break every camera they own, and I will not feel bad about it!"

Alexis is about as vicious as a goldfish. I'm going out on a limb to say pain level has jumped up a notch if we're planning attacks on paparazzi.

I look at the nurse. "She wants her shot."

The nurse draws in a breath. Maybe she recognizes me, maybe I came off too briskly, I don't know. What I know is my sister is about to foam at the mouth, and I'm not here for that.

"The anesthesiologist is coming. Let's check you, Hon," she tells Alexis.

Alexis points her finger at me. The only signal I need to look away and face the wall.

A minute later, the nurse says, "Oh. Sweetie, you're ready."

The nurse takes off her gloves and Alexis looks at me with a wash of horror. "Park. No. No, I can't do this."

In another second the door opens, and Bridger rushes in, flustered and wide-eyed. He only has one of his trademark black onyx studs in his ear, and his long sleeve shirt covers most of the ink all over his arms.

"Al." He doesn't even look at me before he's trading places with me and pressing Alexis's knuckles to his lips. "Sweetie, I'm so sorry I wasn't there."

The look she gives him says a thousand things, but the one I take away is how he is her orbit. He's all she needs right now.

I clap him on the shoulder. "They're getting the doctor now. She's ready."

Bridger lifts his eyes to me for the first time. A healthy dose of fear is there, but even more there's a thrill I can't describe. "Thanks, Park."

"You guys got this. I'll be out there waiting."

"Park," Alexis says through a gasp. "Call Mom. Will you?"

Oh. Didn't plan for that hitch in the game. I want to remind Alexis our mother has been rather undeserving of the word. But this isn't my day. I simply give a little nod and step out into the hall.

I feel a little guilty I don't call and send our mom a text instead that simply says, *Baby is coming today.*

In the waiting room, Holly Cole, Bridger's mom, gives me a huge hug. If anyone was a mom to me growing up, it's her.

"Mission distract cameras is underway." Griffin materializes from an alcove with vending machines, and pops a peanut from a packet of trail mix into his mouth. We're often mistaken as relatives with our height, chronically messy hair, and we're often spotted together.

Griffin and I joined the team the same year, and just clicked.

"Good."

"Rookies love camera time," he says, offering me a peanut. "How's it going with our girl?"

"She's going to birth the heck out of that kid." I rub my hands together and glance up at the clock over the doorway.

In the thick of it, time sped by. Now, waiting, it's a viciously slow crawl. I pace. Eat Griffin's trail mix. And fight not to replay everything that could possibly go wrong today.

After another agonizing hour, Bridger finally comes out into the waiting room, a huge dopey smile on his face. "He's here!"

My heart returns to my chest.

I let out a long breath and follow Bridger and Holly back into the room. Alexis looks like she was hit by a bus. I'm her brother, I can think those things, but she also has a new kind of beauty to her when she touches the dark fuzzy head of the baby in her arms.

We're overwhelming, no mistake. But I love it. Watching the people who practically raised me love on my nephew.

"Do you have a name?" Holly asks, pressing a kiss to the baby's head.

Bridger and Alexis look at each other.

"Garett Parker Cole." Alexis winks at me.

Great. Just great. She got me with a double hit to the heart. Garett—after Bridger's dad who passed away when we were teenagers. The loss of him still bites like a hot fire stoker. But I didn't know I'd be part of any name, and it means more than I'll ever get my stupid mouth to admit.

"That's a good name," I say, voice rough.

Holly smiles and passes the baby over to me. He's tiny and perfect, and I'm ready to meet epic uncle status.

I'm only halfway through my manly bonding moment when the door opens with another face. My frown comes instantly.

Probably not the reaction most people should have when their mother steps into the room, but in my opinion she hasn't earned more than that.

Clearly, she's uncomfortable, the way her gaze skirts to everyone in the room. But I'll give her a little credit when she goes to Alexis and tells her she did a good job, then gives Bridger a stiff hug.

She lifts her eyes to mine, and I fight the urge to curl away with my nephew. She won't dismiss him like she dismissed us. I won't let it happen.

"Park," she whispers. "May I see him?"

I look at Alexis. She tilts her head, a furrow to her brow, almost pleading with me not to ruin this with bitterness.

I clear my throat. "His name's Garett."

My mom looks to Holly, then smiles as she takes him out of my hands. "He's perfect."

Soon, Holly tells us the new parents deserve some quiet time to rest and bond with the baby. With a bit of reluctance, I head back to the waiting room to Griffin. He could've left, but he didn't. I smile and clap his shoulder. "Thanks for sticking around, man. Want to go to that baseball museum thing they set up at the expo center?"

There is a traveling exhibit set up on The Strip for the next few days stocked with baseball relics. It'll be a top five sin if MLB players didn't pay homage to their livelihood.

"Can't," he says. "Remember, my mom is staying with me while she's recovering from her knee. She's weird with anesthesia and I still don't like to leave her too long."

"That's right. Yeah, you should go. Thanks for helping today."

"Always." He tosses his trail mix bag. "I'm going to sneak a peek at the kid, then head out."

"Lex will want to make sure you're fed even though she pushed a human out. Tell her to sleep."

Griffin laughs and waves before he heads toward the room.

I consider sending a text to the guys in Perfectly Broken, but they're all married or about to be married, so nights are usually taken. Plus, they're about to go on tour. They're busy.

Dax and Ryder, two of my teammates, both have excuses. Dax insists he's busy. Guarantee he's not. He's borderline antisocial. Ryder is out with a date.

Fabulous.

Outside, I stand on the curb for too long. Alone.

I have a new nephew. My friends are happy, most of them are in healthy, awesome relationships with amazing women. I'm happy for them. Really.

Sometimes, though, I'd like to be happy in the same way.

Chapter 2

Skye

ANOTHER ONE BITES THE dust.

Outside the restaurant, among the flashy, vibrant lights of the Las Vegas Strip, I am nothing but awkward, jerky movements as I give my date a horribly uncomfortable handshake-hug.

He moved in. I read the body language all wrong and went in to hug it out. He had other plans and stabbed me in the stomach with his extra-long fingers. So, here I am, a twenty-eight-year-old woman with my hands on some guy's shoulders like we're going to slow dance, and his hand rammed in my gut like an Old Western hold up.

Beautiful.

"Um, it was great to meet you, Vincent," I say, sort of arching my back out like a cat to avoid his fingertips, then peeling my fingers off his shoulders one by one.

By now, the damage has been done. I should've let the handshake go, but to add to my glamour, I drop my hand just as he's pulling away. Before he's fully recoiled, I manage to curl our fingertips together in a dainty finger-shake.

Lovely.

Vincent clears his throat; he smooths the front of his shirt. "Yeah, it's been . . . interesting."

Wow. Swoon. No, really, stop with those sweet nothings, Vince. Not exactly the sort of word that brings all the tingly feelings.

I'll restate my previous assertion: another one is biting the dust. Teeth bared, snapping up all the dust as we speak.

If I kept track of all the bad dates I've had in the last few months, I'd be up to twenty and a half. All right, so I'm counting, and no I did not miscount. Getting a date is not the problem. It's keeping them.

My brother calls them rebounds, so they're destined to be bad. I'm not sure I agree, but the description does make me feel a little better.

One of the guys in my train wreck of a dating ledger constituted a half date because dinner was cut short when he insisted there was a medical emergency and he needed to rush away.

He was a podiatrist.

Unless those bunions were turning feral, I can't imagine what constituted a podiatry emergency on a Saturday night.

The point is the common denominator is me.

"Do you, uh, need me to call you a car?" Vincent asks.

"No." I hug my middle. "I think I'll head back in, maybe finish the exhibit."

A deep groove pulls at his brows. The sort of look a man gets when he's truly frightened. "You sure that's a good idea?"

I look over my shoulder at the bright, flashing billboard announcing the exhibit to the Strip. "Yeah. I think it's a fabulous idea."

In there is where I'll find a bit of reprieve from this odious, failed date.

Vincent takes a wide step toward his Uber. "Well, okay. If you're sure."

"I'm sure. Good luck with your plants."

"Myxomycota," he clarifies, which doesn't really clarify at all, simply makes the rest of the population feel rather insignificant in their vocabulary levels.

"Right," I say. Because that's a word I'll certainly be using again. "Slime."

He huffs, clearly unimpressed by the tone I used for his precious slime. Listen, he went on for a solid hour on the stuff, and I smiled politely while he lit up over the prospect of little slimy amoebas.

"You staying or going?" the Uber driver asks.

"I better . . ." Vincent jabs his thumb over his shoulder.

"Yeah." I smile, waving him into the car. "Go. Be free."

I snicker, but only snag a quick brow flick before my slime-loving date slips into the backseat.

Total. Bust.

This is what I've become—a woman on a lonely curb, a little ashamed for being shattered that the guy who grows slime in petri dishes found her intolerable.

There was no spark with Vincent, yet I'd wanted one success, one flawless night to prove I wasn't a total dating disaster. I figured a specialized slime botanist might be a little on the quirky side. Thought we might commiserate for being on the deeper side of different.

Turns out I'm way out to sea and Vincent has barely made it beyond the waves of weird.

With a heavy sigh, I turn back toward the building.

My eyes scan the glowing billboard. Opening night on the traveling exhibit I've only been waiting to see for the last four weeks, and I'm slouching in frustration, not prancing with glee. What made me think I could manage this kind of thing with a plus one when I know—*I know*——how I get?

I'll blame Mike, my pushy, annoying, big-little brother. The guy stands at six foot three and looks like a football player. Not the sort of person you'd think would dream of numbers and algorithms all day for our dad's empire. Mike is three years younger than me and has rose-colored lenses when it comes to his older sister.

To him, I'm delightful. Witty, too blunt it makes him laugh, and the perfect match for some lucky prince out in the world.

Love him for it, but his urging to get out there, meet people, and get my feet wet in the Las Vegas vibe has officially crashed and burned.

No. It exploded.

I wonder what part of the evening became the final straw for Botanist Vince. The tears and streaky mascara, or the heated debate on the way to the third room in the exhibit?

Doesn't matter. This night is my turning point. No more hopeless daydreams of white knights and delicious heroes coming to carry me off into the casino-tinged sunset.

Let us declare this day as the day Skye Anderson is no longer interested in love and romance. On this day, I will live vicariously through fantasy, whether via TV or book, and I will live a fulfilling life with a new career, a new place to call home. A new chapter.

Maybe, just maybe, I'll get a dog. A little creature who will turn inside out the second I walk through the door, and greet me with unhindered kisses. A dog will snuggle next to me even when I cry at the same movie scenes over and over, as if the scene might finally get it right.

Who needs a man when you can get a dog?

I give a mute nod to nothing but the night, as if sealing my declaration into stone, then hurry back inside. This is how I should've handled this night all along. Alone. Now I can perseverate on certain things without botanists looking at me like I'm loose a few screws.

I'm passionate. Nothing wrong with that.

Inside, the crowds are beginning to filter. The exhibit will be closing within the hour, and I only made it to the first-class dining room.

With the card in hand with a name of a real passenger, I hurry through the black and white images of crowds bidding farewell to the RMS Titanic, to the glass cases of replicas of staff uniforms, of the lifebelts people wore.

By the time I get to the speckled displays of real Titanic relics that were dragged from the bottom of the ocean, tears are once again in my eyes, and I'm gripping my passenger card like it's a lifeline.

The scene before me is tragic. Photos of the expanse of the Atlantic, the frigid ice bobbing in the waves, and paintings of the reimagined infamous death of the Titanic.

"Did you think the baseball exhibit was still in town too?"

There is a rumbly voice somewhere behind me. Powerful, deep, a little rough underneath. No such voice would be directed at me, so I don't turn around. A shadow casts over my card, and the hair lifts on the back of my neck. Someone has stepped into my bubble, and I'm keen to build a wider berth.

I whip around, slamming into a wall that smells a little too much like a pine forest to keep my head focused on sinking ships and death counts. I sort of fumble on my own feet

"Sorry." A man takes up my path of retreat and I just kissed his sternum.

Fabulous. In truth, he's not a man. He's a Viking. A reincarnation of some impossible lovechild between Thor and either Tarzan or Hercules. My eyes tilt up, and up, and . . . geez Louise he's tall. Broad, and . . . "You're very attractive."

Oh. Oh, Skye, for shame.

Another one of those pesky brain misfires that really hurts the bottom line in my dating success statistics—I have a wretchedly broken filter between the thoughts in my head and the path to my mouth.

My face is a boiling pot of embarrassment. To make it all worse, he laughs. It's a delicious sound. Something deep inside that king-sized chest of his.

"Feeling's mutual." He winks. Because of course a guy with eyes like someone tossed sapphires, emeralds, and gold coins into a blender would use them in a weaponized wink.

I clear my throat, force my body to calm the fire roaring in my veins, and unravel my arms from his waist. Shivers dance down my spine when one of his big hands slides off the small of my back.

No wonder I blacked out. His arms were holding me like one of those bodice-ripper romances on supermarket shelves, where the hero has the heroine smashed against his bare chest, her neck painfully arched.

This guy has delightful arms. The kind I'd like to reach out and squeeze to see if those muscles are as firm as they look.

Ugh. This is Exhibit A on why I don't do public places often. One should not dream of manipulating a sexy stranger's arm, or any place on this bomb of a body.

"Sorry," I say, tucking a stray lock of hair behind my ear. "Sometimes I just blurt things out."

"I like it," he says. "I think most of us should blurt out what we're really thinking more often."

"Right?" I open my arms, as if it makes the declaration more legitimate. "It would clear up a lot of misunderstandings, to be honest."

He studies me like I've amused him, maybe annoyed him. Hard to tell, honestly. Before I'm fully recovered from touching him the first time, he holds out one hand. "Parker."

Why did he say his name so slowly? Like he's testing me.

I hold my breath and take his hand. "Skye."

When his eyes drop to my chest, I clutch my imaginary pearls, and consider slapping him until he points to my shirt.

"So," he says, "did you come for the baseball exhibit that apparently ended yesterday?"

I drop my focus to the Vegas Kings logo on my T-shirt. The wooden bat tucked against the shimmering lights of Las Vegas might not be date attire, but these new shirts my cousin, Alice, spent so much time designing are butter for the skin.

It takes a few breaths, but finally I take note of the Vegas Kings ballcap on his head and it clicks.

"Oh." I flick my finger between our matching logos on our attire, chuckling nervously. "Uh, no. But I did come last week, you know, when the true fans knew it was open. I'm here for the Titanic intentionally."

"True fans?" He places a hand to his chest, as if I've wounded him. "You think I'm a lukewarm Kings fan?"

"Pretty much."

His glass-chip eyes burn like a turquoise flame.

Uh, yes, please. All at once, warning lights flash in my head and my inner voice puts up bright, neon reminders that we have just declared our singlehood and future hunt for a canine companion.

Now is not the time to quit the dream.

My Viking adjusts the hat on his head and leans against the iron bars keeping us from touching a set of restored silver forks.

"Okay, number one fan," he says with a sly curve to his mouth. "Tell me this, who was the Kings' first baseman when they won the series in—"

"Ninety-nine? Hal Strickman. Made a double play, then assisted at home, which would bring the Kings to victory, two runs to one."

"Who'd they play?"

I snorted. "Easy. The White Sox."

Parker narrows his eyes. He rubs his chin. "Year the team was organized?"

"Nineteen seventy-one."

"First pitcher?"

"Martin Lee."

"Team owner?"

"Past or Present?" I step forward, like a challenge. My competitive nature is triggered and it. Is. On.

"Present. He doesn't flaunt himself. It'll be harder."

Ah, if only Parker knew how easy this one was. I could give him the owner's favorite brand of coffee, and if he prefers white or wheat toast. My dad is the only current team face I'd recognize, though.

Ask me the history of the team, past players, and I'll score big every time. Question me about the current team faces, names, positions, and I'll overheat.

I'm still studying them from a stack of flash cards on my nightstand.

My ability to retain information has never been the same since my accident. But I, at least, have this answer in the bag. "The team owner is Dallas Anderson."

I've stunned him, and I'm not sure if it's a good stun or bad. All I know is Parker has lost his words.

My fingers tingle. I take a step back, ready to beeline it to the exit if this gets weirder. I wanted a night with the Titanic, nothing more. First mistake came by inviting a slime botanist. Now, I'm heading into round two by coming on too strong about the way I bleed for the Vegas Kings with a complete stranger.

I clear my throat. "I'm not the number one fan, I just live with them."

My voice snaps Parker back to the moment. "Boyfriend? Husband?"

I bite the inside of my cheek to keep from smiling. Sly way of finding out if I'm single.

Ha! What am I saying? Maybe I could think a delicious man like this would be trying to find out my relationship status if I didn't promptly recall I am the antithesis of romance. He's probably asking because Parker is clearly a frequenter of Burton Field, and Kings' fans stick together. He's digging to see if he knows the fans that I live with.

Not because I interest him.

But I'm certainly not going to make it uncomfortable by admitting the owner is my father.

"I just moved here from California," I say. "So, I'm crashing with my dad until I find a place. My brother and dad are season ticket holders."

Not a lie. We just all sit in a big fancy suite during the season. Well, I won't anymore. A squirmy rush of excitement tugs at my stomach. This upcoming season I'll be right there in the thick of it, keeping our guys in top-notch shape.

I can hardly keep the thrill of it contained and force my hands into fists to keep from shrieking.

Parker flashes a tantalizing grin. "Well, Skye who lives with the number one fans, would you mind if I stuck with you through this tragedy?"

He waves his hands, gesturing at the display cases.

I snicker. "I'm surprised you stuck around if you came for the baseball exhibit."

"I was distracted," he says with a shrug. "Didn't realize I'd stepped into the disaster that made me cry in sixth grade world history. I was already through the turnstile by the time it was obvious there would be no jerseys here."

Did I just find a soulmate? He doesn't need to be a romantic soulmate because I'm not being romantic, but I, too, sobbed in a school bathroom after my teacher showed a thirty-minute documentary on the sinking of the unsinkable ship.

"So, care for company?" he asks again.

He'll regret it. When I spontaneously break into tears, he'll regret it. But I'm not going to be rude and tell him to get lost.

He's too beautiful for that sort of thing.

"Sure," I say. "But I should warn you, if you think I'm a Kings fan, you have no idea how much I love the Titanic."

Parker gives me a quicksilver smile and nudges me onward with a searing touch to the small of my back. "I can handle it."

We'll see, Viking. We'll see.

Chapter 3

Parker

I'VE EITHER MET THE coolest girl I get to mess around with, or my wife. Since I'm never going to have a wife, I'm so here for this.

I'm thirty years old, there is nothing wrong with enjoying the company of beautiful women. Add on a woman who knows the backstory of the Vegas Kings, and I'm sold. This day has gone from awesome to epic. I've got my Gare-buddy, and now I'm ending the night with a woman like Skye.

She's tall with perfect curves for my hands. Her hair hangs long over her shoulders like drapes of roasted almond satin. It's glossy and keeps catching the light of the expo center. I have to shove my hands in my pockets, at first, to keep from touching it.

Sexy and knowledgeable about the game of baseball. Not sure there is a better combination.

Part of me thinks she knows who I am and is playing ignorant. How does anyone know that much about the team and not know the players? But she's hinted at nothing, no stats, no pitching terms, nothing. There is a part of me that really thinks she doesn't recognize me at all.

Even better.

A lot can be said about spending time with someone authentically. Most of my dates—if that's what we're calling them—are jersey chasers who are wholly interested in my bank account, and not me.

It's worked perfectly for me this far, but I'm all for new challenges. Can Parker Knight, the man, get the girl who doesn't know anything about his contract with the Vegas Kings?

I'm just arrogant enough to think I can.

She's making it easy. I've hardly had to think up conversation starters. Most of the time my dates are filled with a lot of, "whatever you want, Parker", or "why don't we skip dinner". I have a feeling if I'd planned a night beyond expensive meals and ending evenings with more than one kiss to remember me by, they wouldn't be game for anything.

Like batting cages. I've always wanted to take someone to batting cages, but never have. It's too personal. I'd probably have too much fun. Baseball has a way of lowering my defenses, and I'd hate to give anyone the wrong idea. No strings. Ever.

I bet Skye is the sort of girl who'd go to batting cages.

My gaze kicks to her as we meander our way into the section of the exhibit that talks all about the iceberg and the fateful night of the sinking. Her eyes are alight with fascination as she pauses to read the plaques with information.

I think what I'm most intrigued by is the sheer boldness radiating out of everything she says. Maybe it's because I'm ninety-two percent sure she doesn't know who I am, but I've also never had a woman go toe-to-toe with me in a battle of Vegas Kings trivia.

Passion for the game is probably the hottest thing I've seen in a long time.

Then, there is the Titanic. Every image, every trinket, every turn Skye's eyes sort of glaze over, and I'm oddly jealous of a ship.

Look, is this a place straight out of a history buff's dream? Absolutely. Will Griff and the guys torment me if they find out I spent a Saturday night looking at decaying silver and listening to historians drone on about the size, shape, and speed of a ship at the bottom of the ocean?

Maybe Dax won't, but yeah, Ryder and Griff will eat me alive.

Yet, I'm enjoying myself and it's unsettling.

I take a step back, putting some space between me and Skye. Better keep watch on this one, or she might make me like her for more than one night.

She pauses at a sign that has sepia images of the crow's nest. I don't know what happened to my precautions, but I shove my hands in my pockets, then settle a half step behind her shoulder.

Her head tucks under my chin with the perfect amount of space. How lucky is that? I can breathe in the ripe strawberry smell of her hair, but she's still low enough the fly away pieces don't tickle my face.

We're the moment in a jigsaw puzzle where two missing pieces lock in place and bring the satisfaction of the full picture.

"I heard somewhere the binoculars for the crow's nest were locked up and no one had the key," I say. "Made it so the crew wasn't able to see as far."

I don't know where my little fun historical facts came from, but I'm walking a fine line here. Skye looks at me like I'm some kind of hero. No mistake, I'd be content to bring out the same look again and again.

Something is off with me tonight, and I think all the emoting and loving over Garett is to blame.

"I've never heard that," Skye says. "Where'd you snag that little snippet of knowledge?"

I shrug. "Some documentary, probably."

Her face lights up ten shades as her smile cuts over her mouth.

Two problems here—first, her smile is captivating. It's doing things to me. Second, I don't know what I've said, but I have a feeling she likes it, and I like that she likes it, and I need to seal up the vault inside immediately.

"I didn't have you pegged for a documentary guy."

"I've been known to indulge." I wink, then change course. "So, you said you moved here from California?"

"Yeah." She sighs.

"Not a good thing?"

"Oh, no. It's fine. Most of my family is here, so it's good to see them more."

"What spurred the move?"

"Oh." She hesitates and looks away. "Um, my mom passed away."

I know how to offer sympathy, but I'm not supposed to build a tight, hard knot of it in my chest for someone I've just met. For a mother I never knew.

"I'm sorry, Skye."

She waves it away, but there is a tremble to her chin. "Yeah. It hasn't been my favorite part of life. But before she passed we talked about this move, and I think it made her happy to know I'd come back home. I was born here."

"Yeah?"

She nods and pushes a button to start a clip with some expert on temperature and oceans and how the air added to the distortion of the berg. "Yeah. After my mom and dad divorced, my grandpa's health failed, so Mom moved back to California. I went with her."

"Got it," I say. "Are you close with your dad?"

Why am I asking family questions? I don't dig below the surface. There isn't a point when I always put an expiration on every date.

"I'm really close with my dad," she tells me. "My parents were basically the poster children for amicable divorces. Never spoke poorly to or about each other. Held a united front in co-parenting. The works. My dad didn't like me living so far, but he called every night to read me stories when I was little, then just to bug me when I was a teen."

I laugh. I've been fatherless long enough, I didn't think it was a big deal. But the way she describes her dad, I'm almost envious.

"I spent every summer here," she says, moving on to a tunnel carved through a massive iceberg. They even made it cold to the touch. "And Mom and I would come out for Christmas."

"Wow, they were amicable enough to spend Christmas together?"

She nods. "Yeah. Sort of weird right?

Her family sounds like the divorced Cleavers.

"Or awesome," I say.

"It was nice. I mean, I wish they would've stayed together. At Mom's funeral, my dad sort of blurted out she was always the love of his life. They just couldn't figure out how to make it work. I think my grandpa had something to do with it, but you didn't hear that from me."

"Your grandpa?"

She grins with a touch of slyness. "My dad's dad. He was basically a king. All money and shiny things. Pretty sure he didn't like that my dad picked my mom. I suspect he might've caused strife. But again, you didn't hear it from me."

I laugh softly. "Okay. Your secret is safe."

"What about you, Parker who loves documentaries? Tell me something about you." Skye grins and my blood heats.

Not a problem. Heated blood is just a preshow for what I hope comes later. I'm quick to bury the rogue surge of . . . *something,* and guide us to a room plastered in paintings of the sinking, and photos of the *Carpathia* rescuing survivors.

"I became an uncle today."

"Really?" She nudges my arm with her elbow. I jolt at the touch. It wasn't anything sensual, nothing seductive. It was more friendly than anything, and I'm reacting? Skye walks backward for a few steps, grinning back at me. "Congratulations."

"Thanks, he's pretty awesome."

"I've always thought newborns looked like prunes with a face."

The laugh takes me from behind and is out before I can stop it.

Skye groans. "Sorry. Was that rude? I'm sure your nephew is adorable and not prune-ish."

"He's pretty cute." I lean into her, taking too much enjoyment in the way her pupils dilate. "But he was wrinkly."

"I'm sure he'll grow out of it," she says. "Is he from your brother or sister?"

"Both." I laugh when she grimaces in horror. "My sister married my best friend, so it's sort of like both."

"Oh, good." She presses a hand to my chest, bracing herself when a long breath escapes. I'm not positive she knows she's touching me, but I'm fine with it. Skye chuckles and pulls back without a word. "I was about to plot an inconspicuous escape route away from you before we finished the tour."

I lift my gaze ahead. "Huh. We are finished."

Skye's smile fades as she points her attention at the wide exit. She flips around, tracking the exhibit at our backs, then squares her shoulders to the front again. "We are."

"Yeah." My mind is three steps ahead. How to keep this night going? I'm about to suggest we go get a drink, but I stop when she makes a funny snorty sniffle.

"I didn't even realize we were done," she says, laughing like she's stunned. Those big eyes kick to me. "You're a good distraction."

"Did you want to be distracted at the exhibit you paid to see?"

She snickers and shakes her head. "Maybe a little. I get heated over Titanic."

I quicken my step to keep up with her pace. The scene has shifted. Where a second ago we meandered lazily through the pedestals, now Skye is a woman on a mission to abandon the building as soon as possible.

"What's to get heated about?"

With the heel of her palm, Skye slams the thick exit doors open. "Because she could've let him on. And when I see all the fear and suffering that went on . . ." She lets out a grunt of frustration. "She was just being selfish."

I take a long stride and make it to the outermost door first, opening it before she can punch this door too, and wait for her to storm past, out to the street.

"Who was selfish?" I ask once we're outside. Casino lights, a thick plume of cigarette smoke, and a blast of dry air slams into my face. I aim for a bench on the curb, away from the bustle of Las Vegas nightlife.

Skye follows my lead and plops onto the seat with a huff. "Rose. She didn't even try. If you love someone as much as she was supposed to, don't you think she should've tried a little harder? I'm sorry, but those doors were large enough for two people."

She is fuming.

"Wait." I hold up a hand. "What are we talking about?"

"*Titanic.*" Skye flips a hand in the air, gesturing at the big Titanic exhibit banner. Her right fist curls over her knee. She mutters under her breath and stretches out her fingers with the left hand, rubbing out the tension.

My jaw pulses. Not out of irritation or anything, I'm merely trying not to laugh. "Titanic . . . the movie?"

"Yes." She frowns. "Tell me I'm wrong. If you loved someone, you'd fight for them to get on the door. You saw all those pictures in there. What a terrible way to die."

"The movie?"

Skye crosses her arms over her chest. "I have a thing for the movie, okay? Some might call it an obsession, I call it scrutiny. I keep hoping she'll wise up the next time and let him on."

This woman is . . . unexpected. She's nerding-out over a movie. We might have more in common than I thought.

I lean back against the bench and extend my arm behind her shoulders. "I see it differently."

"Do tell."

"What if Matt—"

"Jack."

"What if Jack loved her so much, that he didn't want to risk trying to load up together on the door?"

"That is obviously what he did."

"Okay, so if I loved someone, I'd do the same. Give up my place on the door for them to live."

She narrows her eyes. "I'll see your self-sacrifice, sir, and raise you one loving someone so much you would fight until the bitter end to save their life. Once, Parker! They gave it one go, then she hogged the whole thing."

When I woke up this morning, I didn't see the night ending with a healthy debate over the logistics of fictional survival in a movie, but here we are.

Skye slouches. "Sorry. I get weird about that scene. I'll stop being so intense."

She curls away, like she's bracing for a lash from me. It's not coming. I take her hand. She stiffens, but doesn't pull away. An invitation to keep this rolling in the good direction. I use my index knuckle, give her chin a little nudge up, and lower my voice. "Hey, Skye."

"What?" Her voice is rough, a little breathless. Perfect.

One side of my mouth curves into a grin. "You're weird. But I like your weird."

"Oh. Oh, no." Skye licks her bottom lip, pulls back, then jolts to her feet. "Are you going to suggest we go somewhere, get a drink, or am I off base?"

"Not off base," I say, confident and collected. "I'm not ready for the night to end. Come get a drink with me."

"Why?" She scrunches her nose.

What am I supposed to say to that? "I, uh, I'd like to spend some more time with you."

Skye pinches the bridge of her nose. "We just met. You're Herculean gorgeous. Now you're making me feel all cozy about my quirks and intensity."

It sounds like she's spouting off a checklist from her head. As if she's puzzling through steps and forgot I'm here.

I did like the Herculean part, though.

"Is there a problem with all those things?" I ask.

"Yeah," she scoffs. "The problem is you're being sweet and romantic and I'm, well, I'm taking a break from that sort of thing. I came here to focus on my career and a new chapter in life. I promised myself I wouldn't jump into anything because I jump too much."

I hold up my hands. "That's the best part, no strings attached."

"Oh, see, I like the strings." Skye wrings her hands together. "Tangle me up in the strings. But most people don't want *my* strings, and I'm tired of untangling myself. Alone. You seem like a really nice guy, but I'd get so tangled in you, it'd be exhausting to unravel again."

"Skye—"

"No," she interrupts, smiling nervously. "Thank you for keeping me company tonight, but I think . . . I'm going to head home."

My mouth parts a bit. What is the step to take here? This, well, this hasn't happened before, and I'm at a loss.

I'm disappointed.

Not because the chance to taste those bubblegum lips is being ripped off like a bandage, but I think I really didn't want the night to end.

Oh, no.

I like spending time with her.

Skye lifts a hand and gives me an awkward wave. "Thanks again, Parker. It was nice meeting you. Be sure to check the dates for any baseball related stuff, yeah?"

I force a quick smile. "Yeah."

Then, Skye heads for a parking garage near the expo center, leaving me stunned, confused, and weirdly at odds with the thing in my chest.

I don't know how to deal with this.

Normally, I'd text Bridger, but he's busy being a new dad.

I pull out my phone and send a message to Griffin. ***I think I just got rejected. How do you handle this?***

It takes him less than two minutes to respond.

A curse slips out in his honor when I read the message.

His wise, help-a-guy-out response is nothing but ten consecutive Gifs of different people roaring in laughter.

Chapter 4

Skye

"FOR THE LOVE, SKYE." Mike groans when he steps into the family room, half an orange slice hanging out of his mouth. "Not again. I beg of you. Nothing's going to change. He will die. Every. Time."

Mike crumbles dramatically on the loveseat. I guess it's his way of acting out a death scene. He's a mathematician, not an actor, but it makes me snort all the same.

I pause the movie as Rose kisses Jack's frozen, lifeless hands before she lets him go to be fish food because she's a jerk.

"Still in *Titanic* mode." More like I'm having a hard time shaking the memory of a delightfully attractive Viking I shot down, and this movie is my connection to the moment I almost gave in.

I'm still deciding if ditching Parker was the right thing to do. He'd have broken my heart. I've had enough of that—another huge reason I packed up and moved to Las Vegas. Even with mom gone, I thought I still had something in California to stick around for.

I was wrong.

Still, I can keep the sizzling memory of my exhibit stranger alive while watching this movie.

"Want to know what I think?" Mike lifts his head. "I don't think it's the ending your brain likes, it's Celine. Admit it."

One brow rises, and I look down at the flashcards spread over the mahogany coffee table. He might be onto something. The song, *My Heart Will Go On* is my chocolate and fuzzy slippers. Sad, excited—it's my jam. One of my old therapists used to have a Celine Dion playlist during my sessions. Maybe my head sort of latched onto the sound when it was healing.

"I've got you thinking," Mike says, whipping his feet around until he's sitting right on the sofa.

"A little." I give him a wink. I jab one of the cards at the TV. "Sometimes it helps me focus to have it on in the background."

"I thought you weren't going to worry about memorizing names until you see their faces."

"I'm learning their stats right now. Weaknesses, strengths, what position they play, that sort of thing."

Mike finishes another orange slice. He has a boyish face. A spitting image of our dad in his younger years with big storm gray eyes and thick lashes. Mike lived with Dad while I lived with our mom in California, yet he's my best friend. We lucked out.

My brother settles on the couch at my side, eyes roving over the player flashcards. Cards were how my tutor in college told me to practice retaining information. Handwrite notes. Read through them. Handwrite them again. Read. Repeat, repeat, repeat.

It helped then, figured it would help now.

Mike points to the shortstop's card. "I predict Huntington will have his batting average up to .302 by the end of the season. He's the best hitter on the team."

"Does it excite you?" I tease. "Do you just drool over his numbers?"

"Same way you'll drool over his body later today. Yep."

I snicker and look back at the cards. Mike needs a hobby besides baseball statistics. Then again, I might need a hobby outside of Titanic and knowing body structure, gait patterns, and endurance in baseball players.

I pick up the catcher's card. Marks. The one with a weird first name. The only first name I have a glimmer of a memory for due to the strangeness. Hippogriff, I think.

I'm wrong. I mean, I have to be wrong. That isn't a first name, and if it is, I have questions for his parents.

Sweat starts to gather on my palms with nerves. I'll meet the team today. For me, waiting to face people, to hear their voices, helps me with the recognition more than any picture.

The best way to get to know the guys of the Vegas Kings is to wait to meet them. Still, the nerves are heady. What if I see them, speak with them, and still can't recall their name or background?

Through the whirlwind of Mom's death, her funeral, getting hired, and moving I've hardly had time to focus on much more than abilities to help develop a new regimen for the team. It'll be my job to help shape them around their strengths, while improving where they lack.

I'll be fine. So what if it takes me triple the time to remember a name or face as Mike? So what if too many new people all at once is overwhelming and makes me want to shut down?

I have a plan. I'll chat up the players, maybe crack a few jokes with them, shadow them for a few days. I'll memorize one unique factor about each player, like I did with Parker who loves documentaries. To be fair, the man had several memorable qualities.

But with the team, if I do the same, I'll start to just know things. Right? Please, be right.

He must notice the way I'm rubbing my tight fingers because Mike's hand falls to my shoulder. "Hey, you're going to do great. No one will give you trouble, or they'll get fired."

I roll my eyes, grinning. "Thanks."

He knows I hate the idea of special treatment over being the owner's daughter. Both Mike and I have worked for our positions. He's not the lead statistician, in fact, he has junior in front of his title. Mike isn't even the one to go to the meetings with coaches and Dad's board.

I've worked with athletes for nearly six years, earning additional certificates and endorsements to be able to claim I have some knowledge on how to keep our boys in top shape. I plan to shake a few things up, of course; it's why Dad hired me.

I have new ideas, and I think they'll help the overall outcome of the approaching season.

Mike shoves my shoulder, stands, and reaches for his car keys in a community bowl by the front door. We are both crashing here, the cool adult children who never leave, but the house is massive. If we didn't want to, none of us would have to see each other.

"Meeting them is going to help," he says. "You were smart to wait to use all those senses."

I grin. "Look at you, remembering all the therapist spiels."

"Hey," he jabs the end of his key at me, "it makes sense. Shake their hands—don't be weird and sniff them or anything—but by talking to them, putting a voice to their faces will help."

Exactly why I planned to wait before I stressed out by trying to memorize names and faces from pictures, or ESPN.

"Don't overthink it, okay?" Mike goes on. "I know you think you're awful at remembering people, but you're not that bad. You'll connect the dots."

"Hopefully."

"You will. Be nice to yourself, Skeeter. It's the first day."

He's a good brother. Always seems to know what to say. I give Mike another wave, but once I'm alone again, I stare at the cards on the table like they might burn me.

We knew it would be difficult, but I can't seem to adjust away from the players of a decade ago to the players of today. As if my head wants to hold onto all the memories before life changed.

I'm making progress. I think I've memorized the first baseman's numbers, at least. Name: D. Sage. One hundred fifty-seven games played last season, eighty-six runs, and a .262 batting average.

I'm slowly making my way around the infield.

I pull out the pitcher card. Dad's been bragging about 'his kid' for months now. Name: P. Knight. Former closer for the Kings, now moving his way up in the bullpen with the other relief pitchers. He's favored to start on the mound. Impressive and unusual. Closing pitchers aren't usually pulled into long inning stretches, but Dad has admitted more than once if Knight does well at spring training, he could be the starting pitcher, maybe the ace.

He has a lower batting average than Huntington and Sage, but pitchers aren't drafted for their skill at bat. It's impressive to see the clear upcurve of his stamina and speed by the numbers. Moving from relieving Jovi Green, the former pitcher, in the ninth inning, to taking the game from the seventh, the fifth, then at the end of last season taking three games on his own.

I blow out a soft whistle. At the latest report, Knight's fastball clocked in at ninety-one miles per hour.

Bet his arms are like iron rods.

This guy is interesting to me. I might not know numbers like Mike, or the deep strategy of the game, but I know enough about the expectations of a player's body, and how the league will expect their draft picks to perform.

Closers are amazing, no mistake, with their fierce accuracy. The pitchers responsible for a save in the ninth, the best relief arms in the league. But talent and skill aren't the trouble; it all comes down to arm endurance.

I'm curious what training Knight underwent to increase his game. I pull out a golf pencil from a mug on the table and make a note to review Knight's previous training regimen.

He could prove to be difficult.

Pitchers, from my experience, are notorious for keeping their tried-and-true routines. Superstitious types. Understandable, and I have a little bit of baseball superstition in my blood too. Not to the point it will outweigh my education and professionalism, but superstitions are all part of the game.

I smile at the index card, tracing the letters in *Knight*.

Poor guy.

His world is about to be rocked. But if he'll let me, I think I could help his already impressive stats and make him one of the top pitchers in the Cactus League.

If not the entire country.

THE KINGS' CLUBHOUSE IS packed with people. I zip and unzip my official jacket. It's thin and breathable. The same uniform the other trainers and therapists on staff wear, except mine looks too new. No blood, sweat, or tears in the fabric from injuries yet.

I hope there won't be too many, especially if the players heed my warmup techniques for stiff muscles, but I can count on a few strains and pains, no doubt.

In the cement corridor leading to the locker room, the air is cool and clean. The walk is like stepping into a museum with pictures on the walls of past players making epic plays across Burton Field.

To keep my nervous hands from twitching at my sides, I tug on my high ponytail, tightening it to my head until my skin pulls back a little.

Buck, a gruff man whose official title I don't know, leads me through the crowds toward the team room. I've aways named him as the guy who makes sure there are no problems with the team, the fans, or the stadium. His official title to me is the fixer.

Buck is like a growly uncle and has known me since I was eleven. His handlebar mustache is straight out of the Wild West, and the way he glowers frightens away anyone who might stop and annoy him.

With me, with Mike, though, he's one big frowny teddy bear.

"This way, Skeeter."

I'm not sure when the nickname came to be. Something about always catching the water skeeters whenever we went to the ponds in the hills.

Buck takes a sharp left. I'm free of the busy people scurrying to and from their duties making sure the field is in top shape before opening day, but my nerves kick up a notch when I catch sight of my dad huddled with the coaches outside the door to the team room.

I hold my breath.

Buck has a sixth sense and wheels on me, scowl in place. "You're the best these ninnies are going to see." With another grunt he gives me a curt nod.

I blow out a long breath. "I'm filling some big shoes."

"Well, those shoes needed to retire. Toddy boy had been here a solid twenty-five years. He was done wrapping and massaging all these smelly guys."

"Oh, you're making me tingle in excitement for my new job, Buck."

His mustache wiggles. I take it as a sign he's grinning underneath all that scruff. "You've got the backbone to handle all these boys, but don't let them mess with you. Let 'em know what you expect."

"Think there'll be pushback?"

Buck shrugs. "They're all good guys, I suppose. But they don't like their routines shook, you know what I'm saying?"

"I mean, who really does, right? They call it a comfort zone for a reason."

"Exactly." Buck taps his head, then takes a step behind me. "She's all yours Dal."

My dad halts midsentence and lifts his grey eyes that always look like a snowstorm at me. He smiles, the sort of smile that makes you feel like you're the only person who could ever matter in the world.

My parents married young after a whirlwind romance. I joined the family before Dad hit twenty-one, then Mike before twenty-four. Owning a baseball team before fifty is remarkable unless you inherit said baseball team from a grouchy father. Dad is savvy with money, already had a solid investing firm before Grandpa died with a frown on his face, but owning the Vegas Kings was always his dream. The one thing Dallas Anderson connected with his own father over.

We've breathed and bled baseball since the day he got the keys to the field fifteen years ago.

"Hey, kiddo," Dad says, curling an arm around my shoulders and pressing a kiss to my temple. "Ready for this?"

"Ready." I'm lying through my teeth. Based on the chuckle my dad gives me, I'm going to guess he's fully aware my stomach is inside out.

My dad adjusts his suit coat sleeves, gives me a wink, then says, "All right. Let's roll."

Such a Dallas thing to say.

I follow him into the team room after the third wave of faces. The room is rife in masculinity. A collision of way too many different aftershave flavors. None of it is helping my nerves.

A comfortable space, lined in leather couches and chairs. A fridge and freezer, kitchenette, and a coffee cart in the corner. Each step I take, I give the room a few nervous flicks of my eyes, trying to peek at the team, trying to gather my guts for when I'll be expected to speak to them.

Murmurs die off when Dad steps to the front of the group and lifts his hand with wave. "Hey, guys. Thanks for coming in."

I'm hiding behind Buck's broad body, counting to ten. I've wanted this job. I've earned this job. I'll rock the heck out of this job. My fingers dance at my sides as I think each word.

Men shift around, some take their places on the couches, some lean against the wall as dad continues.

"As you know, we've hired a new team therapist and trainer. She's worked the last six years as a minor league trainer with the Scorpions."

The Kings minor league team was perfect until it wasn't. Until it turned rotten and heartbreaking.

"She knows her stuff," my dad goes on. "Now, I know there have been rumors about her. Some have even managed to niche it down to my daughter, which is impressive." That draws a few rumbly chuckles. "I can tell you guys these are all true, I managed to convince my daughter to come work for her old man in the heart of the Vegas Kings world."

He looks over his shoulder, searching for me. "Skye. Come meet the guys."

Here it goes.

Chin lifted, shoulders back, I repeat the words my mom always told me when I was reluctant to try something hard. *Fear is the coach for regrets still in training.*

Yes, even Lydia Anderson used athletic euphemisms. I'm not going to let my fear of being rejected, or fear of letting people down, or fear of biting off more than I can chew hold me back.

One deep breath. Two. The smile starts to come naturally by the time I glide through the coaches and come to my dad's side.

I smile at the front row of dewy-eyed Kings. No doubt the rookies still on the draft high.

"Hi. It's wonderful to be here." My smile widens. "I'm really looking forward—"

Spluttering and choking and a bit of gurgling stops my speech. Unfortunate, because I finally hit a brave, bold stride, and I was about to deliver an epic introduction.

My eyes lift to the coffee cart where a tall, behemoth of a player is coughing into his elbow, a water cup tipped over on the cart. A groove forms between my eyes. Is he really choking? I'm about to call for someone to help the poor guy when he pulls his arm away and I get a perfect glimpse of his sharp, beautifully carved face.

My eyes pop out of my skull. Our gazes lock. They stay that way until the hair on my arms stands on end.

"Oh." My voice is hardly a whisper. There and gone. "Parker who loves documentaries."

Chapter 5

Parker

I'm HALF CONVINCED WHAT I'm seeing isn't real. Skye is in the front of the room wearing a black Kings' trainer uniform.

Skye, the woman who argues about movie endings, who rejected me. The woman I reluctantly thought about all day yesterday.

My throat is closing in on itself.

I didn't mean to inhale my entire tongue, but she knocked the wind out of me. She says something, I'm pretty sure it was my name, and I'm not sure what step to take.

Dallas Anderson—*my boss*—gives me a strange look. "You okay, kid?"

"Yes." My voice comes out all wrong, hoarse and raspy. I clear it away as best I can. "Yes, sir."

"Skye," Dallas says. The owner of the team. All around cool guy. Father of the woman I tried to . . . I swallow back a knot. I don't want to think about what I'd planned to do Saturday night. Dallas beams at me like I didn't almost stab him in the back. "Seems like you already knew, but this is Parker Knight, one of the pitchers in the bullpen this season."

He gives me a wink that says a thousand things. Dallas Anderson and Coach aren't shy about their hopes for me this season. They've already informed the rest of the relief pitchers, based on my performance last season, I'm favored to start this year. The Kings have three more relief pitchers, all good players, good guys, but I'm the one who's worked endlessly building my stamina to last seven or more innings.

Hopefully.

The look Dallas gives me, like I can do no wrong, only builds on top of the knot of guilt for the thoughts I had about his daughter.

I can't worry about Dallas right now. There is another Anderson who has my full attention.

With her left hand, Skye stretches her right fingers. Her mouth opens and closes a few times. Don't look at her lips. What sort of man am I? This shock comes out of nowhere, and here I am once more staring at the shape of her mouth.

Teeth clamped tight enough they might crack, I force my eyes to hers.

Finally, Skye forces a smile, breaking our gaping stare with each other. "Knight. Parker Knight."

She does the worst thing she could possibly do for my stress level. She laughs.

Not a little, polite snicker because we have an elephant sized secret. No. She's red in the face, snorting, chortling, all the laughing words, and everyone is looking at me like I've done something to break the owner's daughter.

Griffin catches my eyes and mouths *What?*

I shrug and plot how I can escape without anyone noticing I'm missing.

"Sorry," Skye says, wiping tears—tears at my expense—from her eyes. "I had a funny thought."

Dallas shrugs like random laughter is a normal thing and turns his easy grin back to the team. "Parker is who you'll need to look out for," he tells her. "We've been gearing him up for the changes, and I don't think he's sold yet."

All at once I'm reminded of how much I hated the idea of this meeting. My eyes narrow. The new trainer has a slew of new ideas, new exercises, new group work as I'm told. For three months all I've heard is how we're going to try new age exercises, limber up, and change my routine that has taken me this far.

My shoulder begins to ache. A reminder of how little baseball life could possibly be left, and now is not the time to flip the world upside down if I'm going to make it to thirty-four in the MLB.

I don't want this. Don't want her here.

To discover the trainer I've been dreading is the woman who won't escape my thoughts is unsettling.

I cross my arms over my chest, desperate to try to make her the new enemy. Unfortunately, it's proving to be an impossible task, and I'm not sure if that's a relief or if it sucks.

For the next ten minutes we listen to Skye and Dallas give her rap sheet of qualifications. Next, Luke, our conditioning coach, steps up and describes how Skye's focus and expertise in flexibility and meditation has improved performances team wide with the Scorpions.

We're going to meditate now?

"Why don't you go get acquainted with Parker," Dallas says after they finish. Oh. He's pointing at me. No. I don't want to get reacquainted, or she'll never leave my head. The man gives me a sly grin. "Since he's the pitcher you're set to look at today. Might be good to get over the formalities."

If Skye is discomposed, she's hiding it well. With slow steps she backs away, letting her dad and the field management finish a few admin things about what we can expect before spring training.

My teeth grind together. My body is a board. I don't budge as Skye sidles next to me, wholly prepared to remain unmoving and mute until the end of this meeting.

But I have a weakness, it seems. Skye Anderson's voice.

"You left out a fun fact about yourself," she whispers with a touch of irritation.

Poses matched, jaws tight, eyes straight ahead. We look like we're reaching the same level of annoyance, but don't have the willpower to step away from each other.

"Seems you did too."

"You were a fan of the team! I'm not going to introduce myself by saying, oh, by the way my dad owns the Kings."

"Exactly," I hiss back, doing my best to avoid looking at her. "Same reason I held back a few things too."

"Fine," she snaps under her breath.

"Fine," is my brilliant, well-thought comeback I can be proud of.

We fall into a tense silence. For ten seconds.

"You could've at least said your last name," she says. "I might've put it together with the name."

"Right back attcha."

Skye clicks her tongue and huffs. "Fine."

"Fine."

As if locked in the same vein of unease, we both draw in sharp breaths, eyes narrowed at the other. We're behaving like petulant children. A little entertaining, a little disconcerting too.

Skye shifts at my side, her gaze locked on Bill, one of the fielding coaches, as he discusses spring training details.

"I didn't trick you," she says. "People look at me differently when they know."

"Same."

"Fair." She swallows. "I still think you could've said something, but . . . you should know I had a good time on Saturday."

A weird dip takes my chest. I rub it out with my hand. "Well . . ." There is a slight bite in my tone, as if I'm reluctant to speak, "I had fun too."

"Good."

"Good."

This is what we're going to do, spin and spin in circles until one of us gives up and walks away. I think the culprit behind all my unease is that at the sight of her again there wasn't aversion. Not even when she was named the therapist who is going to be a thorn in my side. The ground tilted when it shouldn't have. This new thing my chest keeps doing with the rushes of blood and cinching took hold when I should've felt nothing.

I'm someone I don't recognize around Skye Anderson. She's one of those funhouse mirrors. A reflection is there, but distorted.

With shoulders squared, Skye faces me. She broke first, and I'm pretty satisfied my stubbornness can still win something.

"We're getting baselines today. I'm going to evaluate each player, so I guess I'll see you in the gym."

"I guess you will."

"Good."

"Great."

"Perfect." Skye gives me a cute little nod before taking a step to leave. The trouble is, I take a step at the same time. She plows into my chest, my hands go to her waist, which is never a good place for my hands to be on a woman like her.

"Sorry," she grumbles.

I step again, curse under my breath when she does the same, and we're locked in our awkward waltz all over again.

At long last we break free. She steps one way, I go the other. A bit of pink stains her cheeks. Skye flicks her ponytail off her shoulder, clears her throat, and hugs her middle like she's barring herself away from me.

"So, the gym. Later."

"Yeah," I say, voice rough. "I'll be there. Later."

"Okay." She hesitates, then makes an abrupt turn with a hurried, "bye."

She half jogs, half walks toward the door where she slips out into the hallway.

Only once she's gone do I breathe again. I'm all discombobulated and it's not like me. I need to dunk my head in cold water, or head to *Rocco's Sport's Grill* for some nachos. All I know is Skye Anderson did something to me on Saturday night, and she's still doing it.

I'll need to put an end to whatever haze is in my head. And quick.

A slow building applause breaks my stare on the door. Griffin, red in the face, comes to my side, laughing. "That was the worst thing I've seen since I tried to ask Amy Mills out in the seventh grade."

I frown and turn my back on the catcher. Griffin is my closest friend on the team. Always up for anything, slick with fans, my partner in a non-profit charity we set up, and dubbed the charmer.

He's all those things, but also nosy and annoying. I could do with less laughing from him right now.

I fill the cup with water again, swallow without choking on my tongue this time, and focus on the door where Skye disappeared.

"Park," Griffin says, leaning one shoulder against the wall. "What was that? You guys were bouncing around like you kept shocking each other."

I can trust Griffin with this. He'll torment and tease me until the day he dies, but he'll tell me how to handle it too.

I lower my voice, check to make sure no one else is listening, then lean in. "Remember what I told you on Saturday?"

His face scrunches as he digs through a million of his random thoughts. "A lot happened on Saturday. What are we talking about? Lex and the baby, or when you—" His eyes widen. I can practically see the stupid lightbulb over his head. Griffin's smile is slow. It builds like a crescendo, and he looks at me like I've given him a gift he'll never repay. "*No*. Parker Knight did not hit on the owner's daughter. She's the woman who finally, *finally* kicked you down a notch."

"Shut up," I say through my teeth, checking to make sure no one else is around.

Griffin doesn't listen. It gets worse.

His stupid head falls back, and he barks a laugh. One felt throughout the bones of the clubhouse.

Ryder and Dax are nearest to us and look up from something on Dax's cell phone. I swallow another chug of water, my face practically melting off with embarrassment.

"Good talk, man. Good talk." I toss the paper cup in the trash and start to walk away.

"Wait, Park. Wait." Griffin takes my arm, tears in his eyes, and he sort of shudders as he keeps from bursting into laughter all over again. "You good? Did she know who you were?"

"No," I say, folding my arms across my chest. "How does the owner's daughter not know the team?"

"Maybe she's not that into it."

"She's been working for the Scorpions. If she wasn't into the game, why work with athletes?"

I leave out the fact that Skye Anderson owns the top spot in Vegas Kings trivia. She knew plays from thirty years ago, but didn't recognize a current pitcher? Either I've been played big time, or she's terrible with names and faces.

Griffin shrugs. "I know it's hard to believe, but not everyone memorizes our faces, man. It should be a requirement, I know, I'm with you, but unfortunately, it's not."

I roll my eyes. "She's not an every day fan."

"Is that what bugs you? That she didn't fawn over your ugly face, then took it a step further by making you go home alone on Saturday?"

"No."

I pause, checking to make sure I'm not that big of a douche to be upset at a woman for not being interested. Sure, my puffed up ego was bruised, but I'm not over here holding it against her. It's deeper than all that. I'm resentful because we'd connected. A thief in the night, Skye snuck up on me, gripped me like I haven't experienced before, then she left me wondering if it had been completely one-sided.

I run my hands through my hair. "No. I didn't expect to see her again. Definitely not as the new trainer."

Griffin's face sobers. "But you're going to let it go, right? You're not going to try for attempt two? Seriously, I know you like to win, but this is Dallas Anderson's daughter."

We knew Dallas had a daughter. But no one on the current roster has ever caught a glimpse of her. Some of us were starting to wonder if she existed. All this time Skye has been part of the Kings through our sister team, probably watching games from the family box.

She simply never had an interest in meeting any of us, I guess.

"Parker," Griffin tries again when I go quiet. "Tell me you're not going to be dumb and try something that could get you in trouble with the guy who owns your arm."

I smile, but it's forced. "Quit worrying. I'm not an idiot. This has crossed the line into being professional. I'm not that insecure that I need my ego stroked from every woman I ask out."

I clap him on the shoulder and head for the door. Griffin watches me through a narrowed stare. "Seriously, man. It'll be nothing but drama and paperwork if you try."

"Relax, Griff. I'm not interested anyway." I'll keep saying it until it becomes a reality. "I don't need to spend time looking for a second shot when there are other women waiting for their first."

I flick my brows, grinning at the door, but the second I step into the hallway it fades. I'm a jerk, but what I said wasn't a lie a month ago. Once. That's the extent of my time spent with women. I've always been upfront and clear in my expectations, never risked a second or third date since with those, new expectations are set.

I should hope for the same aloof disregard when it comes to Skye Anderson.

But with her, I'd take a second shot. No question. If her name were anything but off limits, I'd try again. Griffin doesn't need to know. Honestly, no one does. It's like my own dirty little secret that isn't dirty since nothing happened.

Nothing. Not even a peck on the cheek, a close hug that promises there's more to come.

How ironic, the first woman I'd like to get to know a little more is a woman I one hundred percent shouldn't want.

Chapter 6

Skye

Two hours later, my hands still haven't stopped trembling. Parker Knight is Parker from Saturday.

A fan. I thought he was a fan of the Vegas Kings, not the hope of the team!

The click of the keys on my keyboard speeds up the more I think of it. How many times has my dad talked about 'his kid', the up-and-coming ace? Dad's been pulling for Parker to take over as his starting pitcher for the better part of two years, and I made an utter fool of myself in front of the man. Not only with my rant over a movie I can't get my brain to forgive, but the way I walked away from him. I'd admitted I would be tangled up in him from the first drink, the first touch.

A kiss? Oh, a kiss from him would undoubtedly knot my body like a pretzel in unrequited want, and hope, and desire.

Good thing past experience can be the greatest teacher. I learned my lesson when it comes to talented ball players and their ability to love.

I finish typing the last line of my note, then abandon the alcove set up with computers for the therapy and training staff to keep notes and routines.

"Dax, I think that's all," I say, repeating his name and his attributing characteristics in my head. Dax is his preference instead of Daxton. His last name is Sage, and his eyes are the sort of pale that almost looks like sagebrush. Dax lives in the desert with a *ton* of sagebrush. So, he's Dax-ton Sage.

It's lame, but it works for me.

Out of the players I've evaluated this morning, Dax Sage is the quietest of them all. A good player. He's handsome, sort of the messy hair, lean tone type. Polite, respectful, but he looks like he'd rather be in a hole than chatting me up.

"I want you to watch that elbow, though. Bursitis can be incredibly painful. You were wise to nip it in the bud the second you felt something off," I tell him as I manually flex and extend his right elbow. Inflammation in the bursa of his joint impacted his throwing arm at the end of his last season, but that's what I think I'll like about Dax—he doesn't have such a puffed up head to grit his teeth through the pain. The second something felt wrong he went to the old team trainer and has been on a rest, ice, and stretch program since.

"It's feeling right again," he says, and hops off the padded exam table.

"Would you be open to wearing an elbow brace?"

Dax shrugs. "If it keeps it from inflaming again."

"It'll help. But you'll need to really focus on not overworking your arm. No pain, no gain doesn't exist in my world." I give him a little smile as I hand over his Kings hoodie.

"Will do," he says softly. "It'll help if that guy doesn't let people hit off him and they never make it to my base."

My heart flares like a stupid, heated sunburst when a deep laugh fills the room.

"You'd get bored if I didn't let some get to you, man."

Dax smiles. A shy, reserved grin. I like the first baseman. He almost seems horrified that his job has given him a public image, and it's endearing when humility is raging through a rich, attractive athlete.

A shift happens in the big open space of the training room. As if the aura of Parker Knight is too big it spills into every corner, capturing everyone in its path. He's a guy. Nothing more. Parker is a player on the team, and I will give him the same level of professionalism as I offer the other players.

"Welcome to my lair, Mr. Knight." I nearly let out an evil laugh, but grit my teeth, clamping it back down my throat.

So much for giving him the same level of professionalism. It's almost like my mind insists on dishing out a bit of dork because it knows I've already shown him the odd behind the curtain.

Dax scoffs and waves at his teammate before striding out of the room, leaving me with the heady presence of a man who is more off limits now than he was when I turned down his offer to extend our night into . . . whatever Parker had planned.

I lift my gaze to his. He's a tree. Not a skinny aspen. Parker is a redwood. Thick, strong, those eyes that remind me of a magical forest with all the green and brown and gold. A Viking. One who has caught me staring.

A smug sort of grin tugs at his mouth. "So, where do you want me?"

"Shirtless and as close as you can get." I pick up a tablet and start scanning notes Todd left on Parker's musculature, strains, and his past guide on how he taped the shoulder before and after each game. I think I'll add some stretches to help keep the muscles limber. I turn around, expecting him to be on the table, but he's still standing there, gaping. I point the corner of the tablet at the table. "Do you need a stool to get up? No shame in asking for help."

He blinks. "I'm trying to decide if you were being sarcastic or serious."

"About what?"

"The shirtless, getting close thing? I mean, I would've been down for it before, but I doubt your dad would—"

"Oh, my gosh," I say, smacking his arm with the tablet before I can think to stop. "I'm not asking you to strip just so I can look at you, Creeper."

His face heats red for a split second, but the man is good. He's quick to cover it with one of those stomach twirling smiles. "Shame. This is an impressive thing to look at."

I roll my eyes. "While I'm so grateful you have a plethora of body positivity, I need to look at your shoulder because I am your *trainer*. So, shirtless, and as close as you can get."

Okay, the second time saying it, yeah, I can see how it might've been a weird shock to his system.

Parker pinches his lips, but does as asked.

The moment his shirt is abandoned on the edge of the table, however, I'm considering this was a horridly stupid idea. My tongue sticks to the top of my mouth. How is this man not used as the model for anatomy books for perfect muscular structure and definition?

Professional. I'm a professional. I'm going to be so professional he'll be wowed off his feet.

I clear my throat and gesture for him to find his place on the table. Parker is compliant and judging by the satisfied look on his face, I have a feeling he knows exactly how fast my mind is whirling right now. No doubt he's rather satisfied with himself. He's probably giving himself mental high-fives for making the girl who turned *all this* down get hives from too much attraction.

"Never had to strip for Todd, you know."

"Would you stop saying strip," I mutter, grinning.

"I'm just saying."

"For the initial evaluation, I like to see and touch to get a good baseline." I lift my eyes and catch his. He's not so smug, more like he's interested in my process. I'm not sure he meant to be, but such a simple look is encouraging. Like he's not entirely against me or my new methods. "Your reports say you had a slight muscle tear on your humeral head two years ago, correct?"

He nods. "Yep, but nothing a little ice and heat didn't fix."

My fingers touch the top of his shoulder where the joint connects with the top of the bone. While I touch, I move his arm, studying his range of motion, his movement, and any catches in the joint. Satisfied he has full range, I move onto the wrist.

"And you had a sprain here?"

"Dumb mistake. Tried out a new pitch without warming up. No big deal."

"Damage is damage. I want to cover all the bases. Pun intended." A snort escapes before I can choke it back down. No. No. I'm laughing at my own dad jokes. But funny enough, Parker chuckles too. I don't even think it's forced.

"Nice," he says.

Silences drapes over us as my hands wander—in an entirely therapeutic way. I return to the right bicep, then back to the shoulder cuff, and rotate the arm like a pendulum. My forehead wrinkles when I go the opposite direction.

"What's the look for?" he asks.

"How long has your inflammation been there?"

Parker's face falls. "I'm not inflamed."

"Beg to differ, Knight."

For the first time, the cocky, too sexy for his shirt pitcher stiffens. "There isn't anything there but basic wear and tear. I'm not exactly young by MLB standards."

True enough. I rest my palm on the joint and move it through a few controlled motions. Clearly, this has bothered him, but he's probably the guy who grits his teeth through any ache, any pain. "I missed it the first time, but moving your arm to the back—" I demonstrate by guiding the elbow toward his spine. "There is definite inflammation where your old tear was. Has it bothered you at all?"

"Nope."

"Great. Want to try being honest with me this time?"

"I am. I'm fine. There are not going to be any problems this season."

A small curl tugs at my mouth. I get it, and I'm going to call him out on the *it* right now. Releasing his arm, I pull a wheeled stool in front of the table, and sit down, eyes narrowed. "Mr. Knight."

"Getting serious, huh?" He's trying to be playful, but there is a shadow in those eyes that rams a sliver through my heart.

"Very." I flip my ponytail off my shoulder. "I can feel the inflammation. It is significant enough I'd be marching my way to a massage therapist or bathing in medicated muscle rub."

His face turns to stone. "So, what are you going to do? Tell your dad I can't pitch? I better stay in my lane and keep closing the games? Leave the starting to the rest of the bullpen?"

"Wow, it's like you can read every thought." I roll my eyes and scoot the stool closer. "Parker, I'm not saying any of that. If you think I'm not going to do everything I can to help you take this shot of leading each game, then you're way off base."

"Pun intended?"

"Always."

He shoots me with a cautious smile. "I've worked for this season since I became a King. I'm not going to let a little heat in my muscle keep me from it."

"Agreed." I pull out my tablet, take a few notes, then meet his eyes again. "But I want you to trust me to give you a specialized plan to decrease that inflammation, and keep that muscle from being reinjured."

Parker's jaw tightens; his grip clenches on the edge of the table until his knuckles turn white. One of the benefits of being raised an Anderson, of working in the minors first, of being someone who thought she'd lose the ability to do things she loved most, has given me empathy for the fear these players have of leaving the game.

I forget about boundaries, and fall into the connection I had with this guy when I didn't know his name. My hand falls to his knee, and I keep it there until he looks at me. "I'm good at my job."

"So am I," he says. "I've been working out a certain way for years to get to this point. Obviously, I have fewer pitching years ahead of me than behind me, but I'd really rather not shake it all up with something new."

"I can appreciate the vulnerability, but I'm stubborn. And I'm right. What if I can extend those pitching years?"

His brow arches. "I'd say you're trying to sell me to get what you want."

"What if you trusted me and gave me a shot to prove it to you?"

He doesn't answer, more growls in response.

"Come on," I say, smacking his knee. "You've got to give me a chance to prove it to you."

"I don't have a choice, huh?"

"Nope. It's literally my job to keep you oiled and ready for the field." Skye flicks her brows at me, then scoots closer, voice low. "And remember, I can tell my daddy his 'kid' tried to seduce his daughter."

Parker coughs like he did in the team room, eyes wide.

I can't help it. My head falls back, and I laugh with enough force my whole body shudders. My elbow jabs into his ribs, like we're twelve. Sometimes I wish I could not step over the line like this. Jokes, sarcasm, stubborn. It's all part of me, and I don't always read the room well.

Still, I think—now that he's recovered—Parker is starting to get my odd sense of humor. He smiles, shaking his head.

"You went there, Anderson?"

"Oh, I went there, Knight. You should've seen your face. Whoosh." I swipe my hand down my face. "Ghost pale."

"I didn't try to seduce you. I asked you to go for a drink. There's a difference."

"Is there?" I balk. "The Scorpions practically worship you."

"And you still didn't recognize me?"

"I didn't worship you. I knew the name Knight, your batting average, and all the saucy rumors about the Kings' former Closer and his way with women. What's the number of broken hearts now?"

For the slightest moment, hardly a blink before it's gone, his face flushes like he might be ashamed. Then with a crooked smile, he leans in, voice soft. "All that talk about me, and I just don't know how you didn't recognize me."

As my own embarrassment builds, so does tension.

Tension leads to the fingers in my right hand curling in tone and stiffness. On instinct, I reach over and pull at the hand, giving each one a good stretch. I'm sure anyone else would've recognized the Parker Knight straightaway. Maybe I owe him a bit of an explanation. "I, um, I wanted to wait until I met you all in person. I'm not great with names and faces. In fact, I'm terrible with them. I thought it would be overwhelming to memorize baseball cards and Wikipedia pages, and the last few months have been . . . difficult."

Parker closes his eyes, and lets out a little groan. "Skye, I'm sorry. I didn't even think of your mom."

"No, no." I wave him away. "It's okay, really. I didn't say that to make you feel bad, only to make my case on why I've been a little distracted."

"You don't need to make your case with me."

"Feels like I need to make it with everyone," I admit. Why am I spilling about this? This is basic Mike's ears only stuff. Yet, words keep coming. "Like I need to prove I deserve to be here, and I don't know why I'm admitting this to you."

I hold the sides of my face, sort of mutter at myself under my breath.

"Hey, I know your dad," he says. "We all do. We know he makes everyone earn their place, including his kids. I'm not thinking you're some princess who gets a free pass here."

I blow out a breath. "Thanks. I'm invested in this position, and I don't want special treatment. I really need to meet people in person to make them stick." I tap the side of my head. "The team has changed so much in the last few years, but even if I hadn't waited, you're not famous enough to me to recognize, so there's that."

He makes a motion of a knife stabbing into his chest. "Now, you've taken it below the belt, Anderson."

"Noted." I grin. "Don't punch the cocky pitcher's ego."

"Shatter everything else, but not my ego."

I wring my hands a bit, building the courage to say what I want to say. "I'm going to shake a few things up by coming here. I realize changing routines is the first sin of baseball."

"It is," he says with a little nod. "Don't rock the boat. Find the system that brings the wins. Leave it. Caress it. Cherish it. Don't. Touch. It."

"Exactly. I'm fully aware how ridiculously unreasonable ball players can be. Especially pitchers."

How our conversations go from serious, to snarky, to playful on a whim, I don't know. But I like it.

Parker tilts his head. "What one of my superstitions are you trying to pulverize, Skye?"

"Nothing. I promise. I'd like to add some things, though. I know a thing or two, but these are the major leagues. I'm the owner's daughter. Even if you're being nice about it, there might be some who think I'm here because of special treatment and won't take what I say seriously."

"They will. You'll be respected." His eyes shadow in a sensual darkness, and I'm not even ashamed of the swirl in my stomach. Any woman would react the same.

"They will for sure if I have a friend they respect on my side." I wince like he might hit me when I lift my eyes.

"What are you saying? Why are you looking at me like that?"

"The team respects you, looks to you. They'd follow your lead when it comes to my changes." My shoulders slump. "I'm glad we met before today, okay? You're a nice guy who . . . well, I felt comfortable with you. I'd

like to be friends. I'd like you to trust me and have my back."

Parker crosses his arms over his bare chest, and he really shouldn't

weaponize his body in such a way. "The only women I'm friends with are

married to my best friends."

"Is that all it takes? Great. Get someone in here to put a ring on it, and

we'll have some playdates, Knight."

I don't know what I expected, but the deep, delicious rumble of his

unhindered laughter wasn't it. I sort of think I'm lame when it comes to

my humor, but I'll say a thousand ironic punchlines if Parker Knight keeps

laughing like this. I have mighty plans to find a way to record the sound

and listen to it at night like my white noise.

"You're weird, Anderson," he says. "But I like your weird."

"Parker," I say with a resignation that gives up I'm putting down the

sword and tossing away any armor. "You're nice, you're fun, and you're an

incredible pitcher. I'm not here to mess with all that. But I do like the idea

of being your friend. It'll benefit you, I promise."

"Hmm. How so?"

He's being annoying on purpose. Bring it on, Knight.

I roll my shoulders back and hold his stare. "When I'm your friend, you

can trust me to be totally honest. I won't sugar coat anything for your

tender little feelings. If I think something I'm doing is going to hurt you,

I'll pull back immediately. But I'll also tell you straight if I think something could improve the longevity of your arm. Because as my friend, I care about you and what's important to you. I know your arm is your livelihood and your passion."

"And do I get to do the same? If I think something you try to change isn't good, I get to tell you?"

"Sure. I love honesty." I shrug. "Doesn't mean I'll listen, but by all means voice your truth."

"Maybe I won't listen to you then."

"You will. Because I'll be right."

Parker proffers up another half grin. It's tantalizing and sweet, delicious and soft. I can be friends with a man I'm fiercely attracted to. I'm a recovering romantic, a little jaded, stitching up a broken heart. It'll be fine to know my new bestie locks my head in a spin when he smiles.

It's. Fine.

"All right, Anderson. I'll have your back." He slides his shirt back over his head and hops off the edge of the table. With one knuckle he nudges my chin, urging me to look up at him. "But I expect you to always be honest and really listen to the team. Todd was great, but he didn't give much thought to our own instincts with our own bodies."

"I'm all about listening to the signals in our bodies."

"Okay then. Friends."

"Friends." I give him a smile.

Before he leaves, Parker gives me a last look. A hundred unspoken things seem to beat against his skull, and he says none of them as he fades into the hallway.

Strange, but Parker seemed more at ease with the fact that he'd tried to hit on the owner's daughter than the thought of being my friend.

Chapter 7

Parker

"I DON'T LIKE IT." Ryder pouts and stretches an arm over his chest.

"Surprise," Griffin says with a snort. "Ryder is grouchy at something."

"I'm not. This is weird, and I really need to work on the dead lift." Ryder smacks one of his toned thighs. "These babies are out of shape."

I flip my hat backward and scan the rest of the field where the team is starting to line up. A week after the big reveal that my impromptu Titanic expo partner is now my new trainer, we're gathered again for surprise workout.

No weight room.

No jog.

We're doing some workout Skye has been quiet about all week.

I've asked, and the woman is a vault. More than a vault, Skye Anderson is relentless. I've added her routines to my workout. Nothing outrageous. A few new stretches and weight exercises, but the bit of inflammation in my shoulder has her flustered even if she pretends like it doesn't.

She's called me into the gym three times to massage my shoulder. All three times I let her, ignoring how much her touch sparks heat in my chest that lingers for at least a day.

Every time I leave our sessions with the promise she's overreacting about my shoulder.

And every time she responds with some retort about how she knows best and she's not going to wait for the curveball, or changeup, or some other baseball reference.

Then it ends with one of us trying to beat the other with "pun intended".

I'm not sure when it happened in earnest, but Skye Anderson is my friend. As in, I look forward to texting her, seeing her, making up the best lame joke. Is she the sort of woman I'd do a double take to look at again? Yes. Have I kept my promise not to make a move on the owner's daughter? Also, yes.

We can be friends. It'll be enough.

I've been repeating it to myself all week.

I smack Ryder on the chest with the back of my hand. "Hey, let's keep an open mind. She knows her stuff."

Ryder scrunches his forehead. He's constantly scowling, but if you're Ryder Huntington's friend, it's for life and probably after death. He's that loyal.

"I'm surprised you're on board, Park." Dax's soft toned voice pipes up as he rises from a hamstring stretch. "You're the most superstitious out of all of us."

"It's because they're best friends." Griffin hooks an arm around my neck, laughing.

"We are friends."

"With benefits."

I shove him away. "Griff, did you ever mature beyond the eighth grade?"

"Oh, yeah." He winks. "Just ask my date from last night."

I roll my eyes and speak sharper. "Will Skye and me getting along be an issue with you guys?"

"No," Ryder grunts. "It's just that this is you. We're surprised."

"I can be cool with her without trying to take it further." Griffin chuckles, but has the brains to keep his mouth shut this time. My eyes narrow. "What? You guys don't think I can be her friend without making a move?"

"Again." Never mind. Griffin doesn't know how to shut up. "Don't leave out the part about her shutting you down."

"Good thing," I snap. "Or we wouldn't be such good friends."

"We'll see, man. We'll see." Ryder says with one brow lifted. If the guy wasn't the best short stop in the Cactus League, he'd do well as a detective or interrogator.

I roll my shoulders back. "Bottom line: you guys will be cool with whatever we're about to do. Be examples to the rookies."

My friends share an extended look, loaded with a thousand things they won't say out loud to me, and quietly finish stretching. Skye is up in the sound box doing I-don't-know-what, and there's a woman on the pitcher's mound in tight spandex and a sports bra top with too many ruffles it makes me think we should've brought maracas.

By the time Skye returns to the field most of the team is watching the woman on the mound run through tricky footwork as if we aren't there.

"Okay everyone," Skye says. "Thanks for coming out to the great mystery workout."

Murmurs filter through the team. I'm getting the feeling the Kings are either wary for what is about to happen, or they're planning to put up a bit of resistance.

Frankly, part of me wants to resist, then Skye catches my eye and smiles. The shadow of her vintage Kings cap hides those thoughtful eyes, but I know she's looking right at me. I crack my neck side to side, ready to pummel any pushback into the ground if it means she keeps smiling like that.

"I know this is going to be way off the norm, but trust me, you will all leave here sore." Skye glances at the woman. "You'll make sure of it, right Genie?"

"I promise," she responds.

"What are we doing?" I don't know who shouted it, but the voice carries from the back of the group.

Skye takes a deep breath. "Has anyone heard of Zumba?"

Immediate groans. Deep, keening sounds from grown men. You'd think someone told them baseball sucked the way some are curling inside out.

"What's Zumba?" Dax whispers.

"I don't know," I say.

"Dancing." Griffin looks pale. "That's what it is. We're going to be dancing. I don't dance, guys. I don't dance because I have all girl cousins. They made me dance. They dressed me up."

Ryder chuckles in his weird way that doesn't even crack a smile. "Some trauma there, Griff?"

"You have no idea."

I turn my silent scrutiny back to Skye. She's making us skip the weight room for dancing? Based on the reaction, she's also losing command of the ship here. Baseball players are in a mutiny, and the way she keeps tugging at her hand in the odd nervous habit, she knows it. Skye is looking for a friendly hero, a silent plea in her eyes for him to have her back.

The same way I dealt with my bossy, pregnant sister, I can deal with a few baseball players.

"Hey." My voice booms over the team. "Quit with the moaning. We're going to listen to our trainer's advice, and we're going to do it without acting like spoiled douche bags. Now shut up and listen to her."

Pulse racing, I turn back to Skye, give her a wink and a nod when the field quiets. "We're ready for you, Anderson."

She gives me a look like I hung the moon.

Mission accomplished.

"Thank you, Mr. Knight." Skye claps her hands together. "One day, guys. Only one day a week, remember? I promise stepping outside regular routines works wonders for muscle fluidity and strength. Today, this is going to work on coordination. I promise you'll feel it by tomorrow."

With a gesture to the sound box, Burton Field blasts in upbeat music that instantly gets Genie shaking her hips.

I'm going to regret doing this. No mistake.

As Genie barks her orders on the footwork we're going to be doing, I steal a glance at Skye who settles in near the front. She must feel my stare because she flips her eyes around. No smile is on her face for a few breaths. It's like she's looking straight into my head. My palms sweat, but I fight the urge to look away.

Thank you, she mouths.

Scratch that. No regrets. Make me dance as much as she wants. Making Skye's day, having her back, that is something I'll never regret.

My body aches. When Skye promises we'll feel a workout, she means it.

An hour of pretending like I had any rhythm at all had my thighs and core burning. Not one King went into her meditation finish without sweat dripping into his eyes, and funny enough, it was the lightest I've ever felt in the clubhouse when it was all over.

Even Ryder cracked a smile when Genie praised him for his technique.

I went over to visit my Gare-buddy after, endured Bridger mocking me for dancing, then played games with my sister, the guys from the band, and all their significant others. It was the first night I'd realized how alone I was there.

I ended up spending time with Garett while they broke off into teams. Not a bad way to spend the night since the kid is awesome, but I was unsettled, and I blame Skye Anderson.

All her grins. Her appreciation for stepping in to have her back. She's been in my head since I left the field, and I don't like it.

For the ten thousandth time I walk across my front threshold, but for the first time the house is cold and empty. A spark of annoyance builds in my chest since the only thing here to greet me is a coffee table strewn in Lego bricks.

The house is big, open, and comfortable. Plenty of room to fill with people, but . . . it's just me.

I toss my keys onto my table next to an ugly clay pot I've kept since elementary school. Bridger made it. I gave him my project; he gave me his.

It's probably one of my favorite things in the house. Reminds me of the people I do have. The ones who know me inside and out.

I don't need more than I already have. A little distraction and I'll be back to normal.

On the coffee table is an unfinished Lego set, the pieces arranged in organized clusters. A vice of mine, a way to calm my thoughts. But I'm too fidgety to even work on it.

I pin my gaze on the bookshelf surrounding my TV. Tattered spines of classics stare back.

No. Reading is out. My mind is too busy trying to avoid what I really want to do. With a loud sigh, I flop onto my couch and stare at the ceiling. Alone is what I wanted, it's what I've always wanted. I have my family, my friends, I had grand dreams of being the eternal bachelor, and I've been satisfied with every second of my choices.

One thing has changed, and no matter what I try to do my head keeps spinning back to her.

I don't want to read, don't want to build, don't want to watch anything. What I want is to talk to her.

Why shouldn't I? Friends talk. I have the insane group texts to prove how much friends talk about nothing.

It's innocent, and maybe it will sate this constant spinning since leaving my sister's house with her happy marriage and perfect baby.

As friends do, I pull up the text, add her name, then hover my thumbs over the keyboard for half a breath.

Me: *I can't believe our trainer made us twerk on the field today.*

I bite the inside of my cheek. Lame. I shouldn't have sent that, but I'm new at this. I don't midnight text women. How do you start one when you really don't have a reason to talk, you simply want to?

My breath catches when my phone lights up with a new message.

Skye: *She sounds amazing. I wish I knew someone as cool as her who gets a bunch of manly men shaking their hips.*

Me*: Oh, sorry. That was supposed to go to Griffin.*

Skye: *My response still stands.*

I grin.

Me: *How were the meetings after the dance off? Everyone on the board approve of your diabolical plans for the Vegas Kings?*

Skye: *Muahahaha yes. I've got them all suckered into my evil overlord plot. I have a particular interest in making a pitcher keel over.*

Me: *Give him everything you've got, Anderson. He can take it.*

Skye: *Doubtful. The poor sap has no idea what I'm about to throw his way. Zumba was only the beginning.*

Me: *Maybe he's looking forward to it.*

I close my eyes. Stop. Flirting.

Skye: *Can I be honest?*

Me: *Always.*

Skye: *I was so nervous today. It was the first time with the entire team doing something so different. Sort of sets the tone for the season, you know? There is a method to my madness, I promise.*

I sit up. Unbidden, a smile breaks over my mouth. I like when she does this, when she drops the shield and confesses something personal.

I want to play the hero and chase her self-doubts away. It's a need that takes me by the lungs and squeezes until I don't draw in a full breath. Like the other moments of stray thoughts about Skye Anderson, I'll push this one down, too, until it's forgotten.

Eventually.

Me: *Want to know something?*

Skye: *Something is my favorite thing to know.*

I chuckle.

Me: *You were great. Everyone stalked your background with the Scorps right after, and they're impressed. Yeah, that's right. We read about Sam Channel and the way you helped not only his throw, but his anxiety. Show us your ways.*

The dots dance for what seems like forever. Maybe I freaked her out. We did read up on Skye. A lot of the guys wanted to know exactly what she didn't want people to assume—was she here only because her dad owned the team?

Her reputation speaks for itself. Skye has massage endorsements and conditioning certifications on top of her master's degree. The proof is there with the wins and decreased injuries—she helped a lot of Scorpions reach a new potential

Skye: *Thank you. You had my back today, Knight. Like you promised.*

Me: *I do have your back. Helps that I can't move, so you were right about the workout.*

Skye: **laughing emoji* ice and heat, big guy. And stretch!*

Me: *I'll just make my trainer give me another massage.*

What am I saying? I shouldn't be allowed to text.

Skye*: She wouldn't mind.*

Skye: *I mean to keep that arm limber. I only like your big arm.*

Skye: *Can you pretend I didn't write the last two texts?*

I laugh, the sound fills my empty house. She's as awkward as I am.

Me*: Can't. They're out there now, Anderson.*

Skye: *You know what, good. Better to say what you're thinking anyway, right?*

Me: *I do like the way you think.*

Skye: *You should've been a therapist in another life. I should warn you, I'm getting loopy, so if I say more things about your face or any other part of you, just pretend it isn't happening.*

I look at the clock on the wall. It's late. I care more about her being rested than me.

Me: *As much as I'd like to see it, I'll let you get some sleep. See you tomorrow.*

Skye: *Goodnight, Parker.*

I fall back on the couch again and let my phone sit on my chest. I can be her friend. I just rocked the heck out of befriending her, and I keep telling myself the same lie until my eyes grow heavy and I fall asleep in my living room, all at once excited for the morning.

Chapter 8

Skye

WEEK TWO, AND MOST of the guys keep looking around for a ballerina or hip-hop dancer to pop out of the woodwork.

Not this week. They killed it with Zumba, but my goal here is to keep their bodies utilizing movements and calisthenics out of the ordinary. I've seen fabulous results before, and the board approved the techniques. In fact, a few of the people most invested in the Vegas Kings insisted on coming today to watch.

Deep breath in. Exhale out.

I shake out my hands and keep setting up the team room. The lights are dim, the air is spiced and pungent, and foam mats litter the floor. Because he is a good little brother, Mike came today. He's dressed in sweats and a T-shirt, and helped me set up.

Part of me always wants to blurt out everything I know about gaining control over your muscles and movements and the reasons I know it. But the origin story behind my passion is a little heavy and usually causes people to look at me strangely. Like I might break any second.

In the back of the room, I place the last mat as the door opens. My back stiffens, and I brace for the mutters, or curses, maybe outright refusal to do whatever weird thing I have planned.

"See, now I thought I was going to keel over. But I feel like I'm walking into a group nap. Should I have brought a pillow?"

Still facing the window, my smile breaks. His voice is deep. It's silky, and soft, and safe.

I glance over my shoulder as Parker pulls off his hoodie, taking in the setup. He greets Mike with a nod. I'm sure he's seen my brother around. Mike isn't star-struck with the players and responds with a quick wave before choosing a mat.

Parker's eyes find me, and I'm too satisfied the way his mouth tugs at the corner, the way the green brightens in his gaze, as if he might like seeing me the same way I like seeing him.

Ugh. I'm bad at this friendship with a sexy Viking thing.

"If you fall asleep, then I know I've done my job," I tell him. "Of course, you'll be forced awake for the workout after, but hopefully you'll be perfectly rested."

He comes to stand beside me. I fight the urge to lean over and sniff him. Tempting. His skin is the perfect balance of spice and smooth. When I met him at the exhibit in his jeans and tight T-shirt he was delicious. But Parker Knight dressed for a workout in his black Kings warmups and a shirt that shows off the divots of his muscle is practically edible.

Naturally, it's the perfect moment for my no-filter brain to have its say. "You shouldn't be allowed in public, Parker Knight. I'm probably going to stare at those arms the entire time, and it's not fair to the other guys."

His eyes brighten with more amusement. "Then I know I've done *my* job."

My hand has a mind of its own and I squeeze his arm. "Hopefully one of your teammates comes in looking better, or I'll make a fool of myself."

"No." His face shadows, and he leans in. "You make a fool of yourself with me, Anderson. A new friend rule."

"It's sort of sweet how you think you can make rules for me to follow."

"Good. I'm amazing at pretending I have control here."

"As long as we know who really has the reins."

"I'd never forget. Eyes here, Boss." He points two fingers between us as his signal to keep eye contact with him.

"If they stray, I promise they'll never be gone for long. They like you too much."

By now I should at least feel like I'm dipping my face in boiling water. But here I am blurting things out because I'm almost comfortable doing it. Like it's our thing. Do we have a thing? From the first night he discovered I'm blunt, but I didn't anticipate a man like him to play along.

But Parker has this way about him. He's my home plate. The safe zone to be me.

Unexpected, but certainly welcome.

We're not one on one for long. Griffin Marks and Ryder Huntington step in next. Then, the outfielders, a handful of rookies. The last to arrive are the basemen, with Dax Sage as the final piece to our big team puzzle.

Parker looks to me. My heart jumps in my chest when he takes my hand and squeezes. "You'll be awesome. Just like last week."

That's it. A simple reassurance before he's gone to join his teammates who all look rather befuddled by the setup.

It's all I need. With a quick roll to my shoulders, I step to the front of the room.

"Hi everyone," I say, hoping my nerves aren't as noticeable as they seem. "If you'll all find a mat, I'll explain what's going on here."

Murmurs rippled through the room. Some of the guys shot wary looks in my direction. I'm sure this is nothing like what Todd did, but my dad wants changes. Mindfulness and calm can make or break a game. High stress leads to injuries. This is part of my process for muscle fluidity, and it's worked well in both professional and personal experience.

When each mat is taken by a King, I start to weave my way through the rows, voice soft. "Maybe some of you have practiced meditation, maybe this is new to many of you. Either way, it is going to be implemented into our routine this season."

A few grunts came at that. The rookie section. I can usually spot the new guys on the team. They hang tight to each other, and some—not all—but some can be rather cocky.

My heart backflips when Parker shoots the two younger players a scathing look when they start humming like stereotypical meditation.

They shut up right away.

He has my back.

"I'm talking fifteen minutes added onto workout regimens," I go on. "Time to bring your mind into focus, your body into relaxation, and I promise you'll notice a difference in your game."

"Wait." Griffin raises his hand. "So, before every workout you want us meditating?"

"Griff," Parker warns.

"What? I'm seriously asking."

I nod. "Fifteen minutes. Every workout, whether it be team workouts, or personal."

For a moment I think Griffin might balk, maybe make fun of the process, but the catcher merely shrugs and says, "Got it."

"Trust me on this one, guys," I say. "You'll notice a difference. But regarding group workouts, part of my process is challenging your mind and body to push limits and, well, step outside of the box."

"Sounds dangerous, Anderson." Parker winks from the front of the room.

I smile. My pulse is racing, but he's helping set a playful, easy mood. The players are responding to it.

"It could be, Knight. Ready for this, my superstitious friends?"

A multitude of groans follows, but most of the guys are smiling.

"Are you making us dance again?" Ryder asks, a brow lifted.

"No. Not today. Have I freaked you all out?"

"Freaked."

"We're good."

I get a few answers, but it's helping me calm down. Even the tension is leaving my hand. I wave them away and take my place on the mat mirroring the room. "Well, freaked out or not, you're going to do it. Once a week workouts my way, remember that's the deal. Now, I'm adding meditation. One morning a week, a few pauses to stretch and connect with your body, and I promise you'll be buying me chocolate when you guys up your game."

"I'll buy you more than chocolates," one guys says.

"We could call it a dinner," says another.

My face heats.

"Hey, chill," Parker says with a little growl behind it. "Let's shut up and meditate." He faces me again and winks. "We're all yours, Skye."

I give him a small, cautious smile.

Honestly, if we weren't friends, I think I might want to start falling for Parker Knight.

CAPOEIRA. BRAZILIAN MARTIAL ARTS were the surprise group workout. I even had a trainer from a local studio come in and lead the choreography.

Meditation went as good as can be expected. A few guys looked uncomfortable, but by the end it looked like a lot of them were into it. The most important thing was the guys were relaxed by the time I plopped them into the outfield where they used their bodies in kicks, strikes, and footwork, fluid like an underwater dance.

I'm pleased to see more than one Vegas King a little breathless as they gather their bags and tip back water bottles.

The members of the board who came to observe wave from the stands before they disappear. A surge of relief cinches in my chest. This is working. I'm on the precipice of finding my place and stride here.

"Well, second workout, count it as a success," Mike says, slinging his gym bag over his shoulder.

"Thanks for coming. You didn't need to, but it helped knowing you were here."

He smacks my shoulder, grinning. "Anytime, Skeeter. I better get up to the office, though. Gary thinks we already need to be analyzing opposing players who are going to be at spring training."

"Your job sounds incredibly boring."

"Your job sounds incredibly sweaty."

I scoff and shove him away. Mike leaves me with a little wave, and one weight I'd let climb my back all day dissolves into nothing. A successful—I think—second group workout is done. The players are treating me with professionalism, I know more faces on the team, and no one ran me out with pitchforks and cries of nepotism.

Now, I can focus on the other weighted thing on my spine. Adulting.

Back inside, I start to clear the mats away in the team room, then pack up the incense. The door opens. I don't turn around, and cliché as it is, I breathe Parker in before I even turn to look at him. All the rich, heady spice of a shower and rugged soap overwhelm my senses, and I need to close my eyes to get my brain to stop spinning.

"I've got to hand it to you, Anderson, that kicked my butt."

I whip around, grinning over my shoulder. "What'd I tell you, Knight? I am not a woman who messes around with her workouts."

He drops his duffle bag and rolls the mat beside him, then takes the one in my hands. "What's the method? Why insist on these out-of-the-box group workouts?"

"We all get into our routines, right? Tell me you don't do the same thing over and over again."

He shrugs. "It's worked, so why shake it up?"

"Don't get me wrong. You guys all likely have fabulous routines. You all know a lot about what works for your bodies and what doesn't. But there is a lot to be said about throwing a wrench in our bodily comfort zone. It pushes muscles and keeps the brain flexible to different movement."

"Makes sense. I definitely got a workout."

My teeth pull my bottom lip between them and bite down. "You think it went okay?"

Parker hesitates; his eyes scan my face once, twice, then he smiles. "Yeah, Skye. You killed it. Everyone in the showers was going on about next week, wondering what you'll throw at us. And I think Dax is ready to propose since the meditation forced us all to be quiet."

I snort a laugh. "Good. I'm glad it went well."

"I've known my share of trainers, but no one has used these techniques. Did you learn this stuff through one of your certifications, or what?"

My stomach tumbles in a harsh knot. I don't know why I make this such a thing. Maybe it's just the last curtain I let others see behind. I clear my throat and take the mats from him. "Um, I was hurt in a car wreck. My physical therapist used a lot of these calming techniques and a lot of calisthenic exercise. He thought it was important to use the body as the resistance more than anything. Then, yes, during school I earned a few certifications."

Parker stares at me for two, furious heartbeats. Will he ask more? Will I give up more?

It's not a dilemma I need to face yet, because eventually he looks away. "Well, I feel a bit like a douche for being so anti-new-trainer all this time."

"You were anti-me?"

"Oh, yeah. Hey." He whips his hands up when I shove his shoulder. "You said you'd be honest with me. I'm being honest here. We didn't know what to expect. All we knew was we were getting a new Todd."

"I'm not so bad, right?"

Another breathless pause. Parker has the ability to look at me and see me. As if his eyes can peer deep into my guarded heart and pull out the best parts of me all at once.

"Yeah," he says, voice soft. "You're definitely not so bad."

A bright spark of heat flashes through my chest. My fingertips tingle. I'm teetering on a line I do not have any business crossing. One might learn her lesson after having her heart blended into oblivion by a man who is not so different than this one not so long ago.

But here I am. Thinking things. Things like how it might feel to have his hands on my skin. Or if his kiss would be a soft as those smiles. I bet he'd be the perfect balance. Sweet and spice, a sensual kiss, but gentle.

With a jerky motion, I turn around. "Okay, well, I need to get going. I'm officially rental house hunting and have an appointment with a realtor."

Parker takes a step back and shoves his hands in his pockets. "Sounds fun. Make sure you read up on the neighborhood."

It's adorable how serious he sounds. Concerned about me is a good look on Parker Knight. Enough that my mouth, once again, flies on its own accord.

"Would you want to join me?" *What have you done?* "I mean, it's just, you grew up in this area a lot longer than me. If you want. You don't have to. You know what, forget I asked, it was—"

Words are cut off when his hand grips my palm. Parker leans close. Too close. I absorb too much of him and he doesn't even realize it.

"I'd be happy to come," he says in a terribly husky whisper. "I am the all-knowing voice when it comes to the Vegas housing market, so . . ."

I chuckle. "Should've known you would somehow turn this into an ego trip."

"Always, Skye. Always."

With one hand, I lift my bag, with the other I hook my arm around his. "Fine, ego maniac. Let's go, but if I rent the wrong house, I will blame you extensively."

He grins, tightening his arm against his side, so my hand is smashed to his chiseled core. "Guess you'll have to trust me, Anderson."

I don't think he notices my smile as he leads us toward the parking lot.

Odd as it is, I think I trusted Parker Knight from the moment I met him.

Chapter 9

Parker

TRUTH IS, I WASN'T ready to step away from Skye Anderson.

There. I can absolve myself of the weirdness of my reality. The workout ended, a workout that was strange, and insanely awesome all in one ninety minute morning. The other guys scattered as soon as they cleaned up.

Me? I kept finding reasons to linger. Took my time in the showers. Chatted up some of our maintenance guys. Finally, I went back to the team room and tried to ignore the jolt in my chest—I think it might've been exhaustion from the workout. Alexis would probably call it something lame like butterflies—and pretended like I wasn't thrilled Skye hadn't left for the day.

Now, I've somehow inserted myself into her house hunting.

I'm not clueless. I've got an unrequited attraction to my trainer. No problem. In time it'll fade, and we can be the friends she is adamant we be. Until then, I'm going to stick around and try to puzzle through why this woman has me captivated the way she does.

"What do you think?" Skye whispers at my side.

We're both staring at the vaulted ceiling. It'd be impressive if not for the tiny chandelier that doesn't come close to filling the space.

"Sort of . . . small."

She snorts. "My thoughts exactly. Buuuuuttt . . ." Skye shuffles toward the kitchen and splays her arms over the enormous granite countertop on the island in the center. "This kitchen is what dreams are made of."

She looks like she's going to start petting the counter.

I lean over onto my elbows next to her and look around the area. "It's big, for sure. Do you like to cook?"

"Yes," she says firmly. "I'm terrible, but I still love it."

"I bet you're not that bad."

"Ah, now I'll need to cook for you to prove it."

I've never had a girl offer to make me anything—unless I count my sister, but that's not what I'm talking about here.

"I wouldn't make you do that."

She nudges my ribs. "Never said you'd make me. I'd do it just to do it, and to prove a point, of course."

Skye leaves my side and checks out the pantry again. It's tall and large enough I can fit inside. My palms are starting to sweat, and whenever I get too close my chest tightens until it's uncomfortable.

Time for some space until my stupid head can get on straight.

"Okay." Her voice comes up behind me. "My mom always said there were a few things needed in order to make a house a home. I'm torn, so we'll need to go down the list."

"What's the first thing?"

"Kitchen." She jabs a thumb over her shoulder. "Can you imagine mornings watching the sunrise."

"I think you established your love for the kitchen the way you were kissing the countertop."

She pinches the back of my arm, laughing. "Number two. Can you dance in the living room?"

We're standing in the middle of the room, a few staged couches in place. There isn't a lot of room. I don't know who took over my brain this morning, but at once, I shove one of the loveseats aside, creating a larger space, then tug on Skye's hand until her body flattens to mine.

Her eyes go wide, giving up all those shimmering pieces of sunlight she keeps inside. There. Those eyes are what capture me, drag me closer, upend every previous notion there will never be a person who could burrow into the thing in my chest. Playful, bright, kind. All these things make up Skye Anderson, and I want more.

Too much more.

"Hot Shot," she whispers, "Are you dancing with me in my living room?"

"Purely experimental," I say. "We need to find out if this is the place, right?"

Skye smiles, bright and full. Her arm drapes around my shoulder, her fingers tickle the back of my neck as if she can't help herself. "Right. Show me your moves."

"They're minimal, but skill isn't what this is about."

"I think uncoordinated living room dancing is the best kind of dancing."

I grin and spin her around, drawing out a yelp-laugh. A sound somewhere between a scream and toss-her-head back laughter. Skye spins back in, curling into my chest.

All I can do is pray she doesn't feel the race of my pulse.

Time bleeds out. The realtor murmurs something about needing to take a phone call. I don't even care. Truth be told, I forgot the woman was in the house. I don't dance. Never have, but here I am swaying my hips, dipping Skye until her face turns red from trying to keep a serious expression, spinning around like we know what we're doing.

By the end, Skye's face is buried against my shoulder, she's snorting, arms around my shoulders. Those fingers are sly. She keeps tickling the bottom of my hairline. Unbidden, a shiver pulses down my spine.

I pull her closer.

Her eyes flutter up and her voice cuts off. I get it. A simple stumble has turned into her body being pressed to mine, my hands on her waist, her palms over my chest. All of her burrows into me before I can stop it. I fight a groan when the sweet fruity hint of her hair fills my lungs. When her hips, shoulders, everything aligns with mine. My palm overtakes the small of her back, like an instinct, my fingers draw slow, gentle circles over the divots of her spine.

Her eyes widen. Maybe she's feeling the same current of heat as me. Maybe she's wondering how this could feel so peaceful, so right, as if another human was designed to fit right here.

The final thought jolts me awake.

Catching feelings was never part of my life plan. It never can be.

I clear my throat, and with a touch of reluctance pull my hands back.

Skye lifts her head, her smile fading a bit.

"I think we can check off dancing." Her voice is soft.

We're stepping too close to the line. There is no question I want to teeter over the edge, but it'd be complicated. No doubt something Skye doesn't want or need with all the changes in her life right now.

My hands fall away from her body. I force a smile. "What's next, Anderson?"

She indicates toward the backyard. "It'd be out there."

I head for the small yard, my hands still burning for a chance to touch her again, and that is the problem here.

She's undoing me, piece by piece.

A little distance might do me some good.

Outside, I shove my hands in my pockets and take in the yard. It's one of the rare houses that has grass. A small patch, but it's still green. Summertime might be a different story. I stand in the center of the yard inspecting the red, pink, and white rocks of the xeriscape edges. There are plenty of date palms and spiky yucca plants to make the yard interesting. It's a nice house on a quiet road. She could be content here.

The question is why am I here?

Why am I letting myself dive into this infatuation with Dallas Anderson's daughter? One night. We had a few hours together and I didn't even touch her. It should've been something utterly forgettable. But here I am like a hormonal fourteen-year-old boy wiping his sweaty palms on his pants, hoping the girl doesn't notice how uneasy she makes him.

The glass door glides open, and Skye swings her arms, taking a deliberate stride away from me. "So, thoughts?"

"It's a good house," I say and sit in a porch swing set up against the back wall. "Good area, close to Burton."

"I like it." Skye's gaze finds me. She does the sexy lip biting thing and I'm positive she doesn't know it's sexy. "The last thing my mom said was a house is four walls and a roof, but a home is a place you can sit outside, barbecue, and have conversation and laughs with the people who matter."

"You think this is a place you can do that?"

"Let's find out. I don't have burgers to grill, but we can talk." Skye sits next to me and starts swaying the swing. "What was it like growing up here?"

She's trying to have a conversation with me. Meaning, I matter.

Don't read into it.

I slump back in the swing, staring at the deepening orange of the sun as it prepares to set behind the hills. "I didn't live in Las Vegas. I grew up about forty miles away. It was fun. Spent every day with Bridger—my brother-in-law—and Tate and Adam. Two more guys in Perfectly Broken."

"Perfectly Broken?"

I lift a brow. "You know, the band? My brother-in-law is the lead singer. They're pretty big, and regulars at the field."

"Oh, yeah." Skye rubs her forehead. "I remember reading about your connection to a rock band when I was stalking you on the internet."

I laugh because she's not trying to be funny. Guaranteed Skye looked me up and she's admitting it with abandon now.

"I think I heard some of the team blasting their music in the gym yesterday," she goes on. "Hard rock?"

"Yeah," I say. "They're loud, but cool guys. When they aren't touring, they'll always be sitting behind home plate."

"Sort of sweet how your sister married one of them. Do you have any other siblings?"

"Nope. It was just me and Lex."

"You two sound close."

She has no idea. "We are. Alexis and I took care of each other growing up."

I grit my teeth. That sounded too personal. I look away, hoping Skye didn't catch it. Wishful thinking. Skye seems to catch all the moments I don't want her to.

"Where were your parents?" She smiles. "I'm sure there was a better way to ask that, but I think by now we've established sometimes the questions just come."

"As I said, if we all said what we were thinking a little more, maybe misunderstandings could be avoided."

"Unless you're a jerk and blurt out every rude thought."

"A caveat." I sigh and cross my arms over my chest. No one outside of my friends and reporters desperate to learn a little about me and my closed mouth has ever asked about my life. I think if anyone else sat beside me, I'd be a vault. Skye has a way of pulling things out of me, and I don't like it. Yet I keep giving in. "My dad died when I was three and a half. He just went to sleep and didn't wake up. They think it was an aneurysm."

"I'm sorry, Parker."

"It's fine. I barely remember him. My mom worked a lot to keep food in the fridge. So, it was Lex and me alone most days."

I'll leave out the part where my mom was lost in a drunken haze whenever she was home. How she resented having mouths to feed. I'll leave out the string of boyfriends and one awful stepdad who came in and out, screaming and throwing things. Sometimes to the point I made Alexis sleep in my room with my dresser pressed against the door.

"I'm glad you had your sister then," Skye says. "But you must've had baseball, too, right?"

"Baseball was my escape." I clench one fist, hurrying to fix that. "An outlet, you know? From school, or to escape my little sister when she was bugging me."

Skye laughs at that. I let out a breath of relief. Saved. We can claw our way back to the surface. Exactly where I want to be.

I think.

"That's Mike." Skye shakes her head. "We didn't live in the same house growing up, but still managed to annoy each other."

"Mike seems cool."

"He's a nerd," she says. "Total math guru. Who gets excited over calculus?"

"Smarter-than-me people. I get the opposite sibling thing, though. Alexis is the definition of a bookworm. She has a master's degree in Library Studies if that paints a picture for you."

Skye chuckles. "I do love a good book."

"Well, if you ever meet her, don't get her started or she'll never stop talking about her books." Not that I'd ever stop my sister from rambling. I'm the one who fostered her own escapism as a kid, after all. Always picking up secondhand books from library sales, reading to each other after dark.

"I'd like to meet her," Skye admits. "She'd probably tell me all the nitty gritty on her brother."

"I'm an open book." Skye snorts a laugh like she doesn't believe me at all. I nudge her thigh with my knee. "What about you? Tell me what it was like to work with the Scorps."

In an instant, Skye's body tenses. Her knee bounces. But I'm going to go out on a limb and guess she's trying to cover it with her white smile. "It was a great opportunity. I got to know some amazing players."

Surface. Keep to the surface. Impossible.

I can't explain it, but I want to dig to the deepest places of Skye Anderson. I don't want to offer the same in return, but with her, I can't help but want to know more and more.

"Skye," I say, a sly grin on my mouth. "That was the most vanilla answer to hide what you're really thinking."

She lets out an irritated sigh. "For once, I'd like to hide just a little bit of what's going on in all this." With a sweeping gesture, she signals to her entire body.

I laugh and drape my arm behind her shoulder. Without a nudge of encouragement, she leans into me. Friends can sit close. And I'm a massive fan of sitting close to this friend.

"I like knowing what's going on in all that. What is said on the swing, stays on the swing."

"That's the motto of Vegas, isn't it?" Her body relaxes into me a little more. One more motion and her head will be on my shoulder. "I committed a cardinal sin. I dated a player."

A lead brick lands in the pit of my stomach. Should've kept it to the surface, because this plot twist in the conversation sucks.

"Really?" I keep my tone aloof, but I'm pretty sure she'll soon hear my teeth grinding. "Bad breakup?"

Skye sits up and leans over her knees. "Here's the thing you should know about me, Parker. I'm a bit of a hopeless romantic. When I fall, I fall hard. Then crash and burn hard. I should've seen some of the signs, but I couldn't look beyond the ridiculous heart eyes."

"Signs of what?"

She flicks her gaze back at me, there is the constant playful mischief I can't get enough of, but there is a bit of pain there too. "Who is my dad?"

I already hate this douche and don't even know who he is.

"He was using you for your connections."

She shrugs. "He wasn't invited to move from the Scorpions to the Kings, so he had an outburst, and his contract wasn't renewed at all. He's lucky, though, and received a trade offer to the Utah Gulls. So, when he broke up with me the day after my mom's funeral, yeah, I got the vibe he was only sticking with me because he wanted to be on the Kings."

Yeah, the d-bag is going to die if I ever meet him. "The day after your mom's funeral?"

"Yep." Skye plays with the ends of her hair. "He made it seem like I read too much into our relationship. I mean, he literally told me since he didn't need to focus on growing with Dallas Anderson's team, what was the point of us? My mistake."

"He's an idiot." My voice is all wrong. Less tone and more growl. I'd say it all again, though, because she sighs and finally leans back with her head on my shoulder.

"Thanks, but he was probably right about me reading into things too much. Like I said the night we met, I get tangled in all the strings, but I'm usually the only one."

I want to shout at her that I'm here, tangled in her strings, and it's a blow to the throat.

With a severe swallow, I choke the knot back down. When did this happen? I *like* her. Beyond one night. Beyond frivolous physical affection. I like Skye, and I've liked her from the moment she flipped out over the ending of Titanic.

The truth is, I'm in uncharted waters and I don't see the lifeboat. She'd probably like that adage.

Great. I'm relating everything to her, thinking of things that would make her smile, wanting her to lean in closer.

This is what she was talking about, being tangled.

I've never experienced it and can't decide if this is the best feeling, or a stab to the chest because it can't happen.

First, she's the owner's daughter, and her heart is healing from loss and a jerk of an ex.

Second, no one has stepped into this thing in my chest. For good reason.

If I let it open, what will I become when they step back out? I know—to the marrow of my freaking bones—I know I'm shiny on the outside because of my bank account, but on the inside I'm just . . . I'm just me.

A mess of baggage and sharp edges and nerdy hobbies.

"You've gone quiet," she whispers. "Did I plop too much in your lap and your brain shutdown?"

"No." My voice is stern, hoarse. I hold her stare. "I'm just trying to wrap my head around how a guy could be that cold."

"Come on, Parker," she says. "You're you. Don't tell me you haven't broken a few hearts."

"I've always been straightforward." Blood heats my face. "I might not have wanted to settle down yet, but I never played anyone like that. What's his name?"

"Nope." She shakes her head and pinches my leg. "Not going there, Rambo."

"Just a name. A simple name, Skye."

"No way. I have a brother to defend my honor, I don't need to sic my Viking on him."

"And I already have a sister. This isn't like that."

Skye laughs and traps my face between her palms. I hold my breath. It's surprising and intimate in a way I've never experienced before. She hardly seems bothered when she levels me in her scrutiny. "I'm lucky to have a friend like you at my back."

Friend is such a dirty word. I hate it. The whole stupid syllable.

"But I'm over it," she goes on. "So, we're not going to bring him up again."

"You know I can look at trade picks, right?"

"Yep. But at least I wasn't the one to give it up like a woman scorned. My pride is on the line here, Knight."

I make a note to look who was recently drafted to Utah later. "Fine."

"Fine." She sort of strokes my cheeks before releasing me, then stands. "Ready to go?"

"Yeah." I bury the bite of disdain I have for a nameless guy when I should be thanking the man for being an idiot. If he'd held tight to Skye, she wouldn't be here with me.

I shove my hands in my pockets as she talks with the realtor who has remained a silent observer the entire hour we've been wandering around.

"I think it's the one," she announces.

"Conversation sealed the deal, huh?"

"Couldn't have asked for a better one," she says with a little wink.

I'm undone. As Skye chats with the realtor about applications and deposits, I start to suffocate and career out of control. My fists clench and unclench. Why am I allowing myself to spin so far out of sync? Then again, what is so wrong with liking a woman like Skye? Maybe I could do the whole dating-relationship thing.

Boyfriend stuff? I could do it. Like knowing her favorite movie. Done. Titanic. I'd even recreate the ending to make her laugh. Favorite food. I'd learn it. Maybe even try to make it for her. Holding hands in public, kissing—I think Skye and I would rock the heck out of kissing—but there is more to being in a relationship.

A lot more.

Gross words like vulnerability and fears.

My eyes flick to Skye. She laughs at something the realtor says, and my body reacts. A rush of blood to my head, the need to swallow before my throat tightens. Skye Anderson is the sort of woman who deserves all the gritty, deep things in a relationship. The guy she deserves is someone who won't hesitate to let her see inside, who won't hide behind reputation and his bank account.

Someone who is willing to do that will be a lucky idiot.

With a quick glance back at me, before she signs the rental agreement, she grins like I make the room a little brighter.

Yeah, the guy who earns her heart better realize he's handling gold.

For the first time in my life, I wish I could be that guy.

Chapter 10

Parker

"WE'VE DOUBLED THE FUNDS from last year," Griffin says with a touch of excitement.

He points out the spreadsheet on the screen, filled with accounting documents sent over from our financial overseer of our non-profit we started a few years ago. Charity games with celebrities to raise money for low-income families who can't afford competitive sports for their young athletes.

To-date we've placed over a thousand local kids on scholarship to play in their favorite sport. But the last year we've expanded to most cities with Major League teams since the league loved the idea so much, they started to sponsor us.

It's amazing, and gives me hope that kids like me, who don't always like being home, might have a place they can grow, learn discipline, grow a skill. Be safe.

"This is amazing, man," I say and grip Griffin's shoulders, giving him a weird little shake.

"I know. Earning our sainthood one freaking donation at a time."

I snort. He's joking. Griffin has his own stuff from the past, his own reasons he wanted to partner with me in this idea. He's as passionate about it as me, and our combined reasons, drive, and grit feels like it's finally paying off.

"Think the guys will play the game this year again?"

He's talking about Perfectly Broken.

"If I ask them, they will. Their record label CEO is pretty eccentric, and if family has a request, he usually forces them."

Griffin chuckles. "I remember the last game they played; the entire label had to come out."

"Exactly. If we can't find anyone willing, we'll ask them again. I warned Bridge they'd always be the back up every year. He seemed to pretty much expect it."

Griffin smiles and closes the computer. "Speaking of rock stars, do you have a date for their concert tonight? Is it still on? Or is Bridger going to fall asleep at the mic?"

"Probably will, but their manager will find a way to play it off like it was supposed to happen."

Silence gathers around us.

Then Griffin clears his throat. "Dude. Date?"

A date. Whenever I can—which is a lot—I attend every home concert Perfectly Broken puts on. The same way they fill the seats behind the plate every home game they can. There are always those times I'm at away games, or they're touring, but tonight we're going to a metal festival. They're the headliners, and it's the last show before they head out on the road and the season begins.

I'm going.

The thing is, usually we all take dates and sit in a suite, unless I'm trying to throw Bridger off as he sings. In that case, I'll belly up to the stage.

Tonight, it was supposed to be a suite situation and I haven't even thought of a date.

My thoughts can't seem to escape one woman, and it's becoming a problem.

"I haven't found anyone," I say after a long pause.

"Have you looked?"

No. "We've been busy." I gesture at the closed laptop.

Griffin arches one brow. "Okay. Well, find someone. I've got that cute barista from the new coffee place going with me."

He winks with a touch of slyness. I roll my eyes. There isn't anyone I want to go with except . . .

My eyes drift toward the training offices. I mean, friends attend concerts together, right?

Obviously.

I clap Griffin between the shoulder blades. "I'll get it done, man."

I swear he groans when he notices the direction I'm heading. Let him.

Skye has the door open. The space is empty but for the click-clack of keyboard keys. A grin twists on my face as I slip through the clean gym. She's tucked in an alcove writing her notes for the day.

Like at the rental house, a cinch in my chest tightens. A rush of attraction.

Friends. We're cool. This will be something outside the realm of baseball we can do together. Like I do with Ryder, Dax, and Griff. Skye will now be tossed into our lives as rock and roll junkies.

I knock on the wall, startling her from her concentration.

"Hey, big guy. If you're here to tell me you've torn your meniscus or broken something, I quit."

I plop into a second office chair and laugh. "I'm golden, Anderson."

"Good." She turns back to the computer and finishes the last few words of her sentence. "Because don't think I haven't missed the inflammation in that arm, Knight. One direct hit, one bad slide, and you'll really feel what's in that shoulder." She glares at me. "I will tell Grant you are not allowed to be on the batting roster, and are to sit in the dugout with an ice pack while a DH bats in your place. I have the power, Knight. Don't test me."

I have no doubt she'll go straight to the batting coach if I do so much as wince wrong. My fingers drum over the arms of the chair as I lock her in a narrowed gaze. "You're scary."

Her eyes brighten; she ruffles like she's been praised. "Thank you."

"I did come in here for a reason, though."

"I love reasons. What's up?" Skye leans back, and crosses one knee over her leg.

"I wondered what you thought of rock music?"

"Is this a trick question since I know you're basically blood brothers with a rock band?"

"It might be."

"Then, I love it. Always. The more screaming the better."

She's . . . I can't even explain. She does something that lightens the air around me. As if every breath is easier to take, my body is more fluid, more at ease.

"Good. Although, Bridge only screams sometimes. I was wondering if you'd want to come with us tonight to one of their concerts. We have a suite we usually watch from because we're impressive, then we always go backstage because, again, we're pretty impressive."

Skye's lips part slightly. "Backstage. You . . . you want me to meet your friends?"

I never took the time to consider it. In the past I've brought dates around the guys. They never cared to get to know them much, but this is different. A notion that slipped past my notice. I want them to get to know Skye, and initially they probably won't even try. They'll think she's a passing face they'll never see again, but . . .

She's not.

What is wrong with me? My throat is thick like I've swallowed honey. When I look at tomorrow, I want Skye Anderson involved in my life. Whatever capacity that means, I do.

I've slipped into an alternate reality. All this back and forth, catching feelings stuff is spinning my head into a fog.

Not saying I love it, but it's not like I hate it either.

"I'd love to introduce you, if you want," I say, trying to conceal the throaty rasp in my tone.

It takes a few more seconds, but soon Skye's eyes light up. She nods. "I'm in."

"Great. I'll come grab you tonight then."

A quick nod, a fleeting smile, then I'm on my feet. I need to figure out what my endgame is here and quick. I want Skye, I like her. No question. But in the same breath, I value her friendship, and for the first time I don't want to do anything that might cross the line and ruin it.

A NEW FAVORITE THING in life: watch Skye Anderson enjoy a rock concert.

Her hands are often covering her ears, but she hasn't lost her smile once. Usually by the end of the songs, she's starting to mouth the words and bob her head a little whenever the words wrap up.

The concert is filled with bright bursts of light, massive sound, and a different sort of energy than at the ball field.

When the guys play, the beat rolls to my bones. There is an addictive tension, waiting for each beat to deepen, to build. I love it. Could be because I'm connected to every guy on the stage, but I think even if we didn't know each other, I'd be a fan.

When the final, luminescent white flash ends, and the stage darkens in the final note, Skye slumps back in her chair, a little breathless.

"I feel like I've been running all night." She presses a hand to her chest, laughing. "That was amazing."

"Yeah?" I take a drink from a glass. The suite is always filled with drinks and food. Again, makes us feel like we're pretty impressive when I doubt very many of their fans even care we play professional baseball. I nudge Skye's knee with mine. "I'm glad you liked it."

"Are we going to meet the band yet?" Ryder's date, I don't know how they met, asks. Ryder was attentive at first, now he's gone back to his growly disinterest. She taps his shoulder. "You said we could meet the band."

Ryder shrugs. "Up to Knight."

I scoff. "We're going backstage to say hi, yes."

The woman beams and gets a hungry look in her eyes. I'm about to mention the guys won't take it well—their significant others even less—if she tries to get too touchy, but Skye must've noticed too.

"Isn't everyone in the band married?" Skye asks me, in a tone louder than before.

I smile. "Yeah. Or close to it. Their girls will be back there, except Lex."

"Your sister, right?"

I give a quick nod. "For some reason she thought a newborn didn't belong around loud music and germs. I don't get it."

Skye snickers and stands with me. Almost like an instinct she links our arms together. I don't mind.

The guys filter behind us. Griffin hasn't stopped schmoozing his barista. She's gobbling it all up, looking at him with pearly stars in her eyes. Dax was forced to step into the sunlight by Ryder. He's here stag, but I think the drinks and food have him loosened up. He's even chatting with Ryder's date about his position on the team since Ryder looks like he's forgotten about her.

He's not a jerk, merely . . . unemotional.

I'm not sure what happened in Ryder Huntington's back story to make him such a growl-fest, he's closed-lipped even with us, but he's the most honest man I know. Loyal. Albeit a little intense.

We make our way through security with our passes. They lead us behind the stage toward the greenroom where the band gathers.

The security guy at the door is dressed in a pressed, fitted suit. He's familiar. I smile and reach out my hand. "Quinn, how's it going man?"

Quinn is probably a few years older than me. A total boss when it comes to intimidation. Nicest guy ever, but he looks like he'd crush your bones and sprinkle them over his cereal if you tried to hurt anyone in his care.

"Hey, Park." Quinn gives a nod to each of the guys, glances at Skye, but again, probably doesn't think she's someone to commit to memory. "Enjoy the show?"

"Always."

Quinn opens the door to the greenroom, and gives us a smile. "Head on in. Take your time unless Bridger starts to fall asleep. Your sister told me that's my cue to take him home."

I laugh, curl my hand around Skye's without thinking, and lean close as we step into the room. "Quinn works for Bridger," I whisper. "He met my sister by her trying to crack his skull with a book. Guess it won him over."

Skye's nose scrunches up. "What?"

"It's a whole story," I say, waving the thought away.

"There he is!"

I face the room. Tate Hawkins, the drummer, stands from a couch. Already he has a homemade peanut butter and jelly sandwich in one hand, his fiancée, Ellie's, in the other. His two favorite things.

I scoop him up in a guy-hug. A lot of slapping and congratulating each other on being masters of our industries. At least that's how Alexis describes it.

Adam Stone, the lead guitarist steps out next. His wife is absent, but he's quick to let me know she's out of town with her sister.

Rees, the bassist, is with his girlfriend, and breaks away to greet us. I didn't grow up with Rees. He joined the band a few years ago when their last bassist quit in a shady way. Since then, he's become a close friend.

Bridger stands in the corner, sweaty, black eyeliner darkening his eyes, with his phone pressed to his ear. I'd bet anyone he's on the phone with Alexis catching up on all the things with Garett he missed.

He catches my eye and gives me a quick chin lift.

Let him be for a second. My hand on the small of her back, I nudge Skye forward toward Rees. "Rees, this is Skye Anderson."

He gives me a befuddled look. It strikes me I'm a bit of a jerk, because I realize I've never really introduced anyone to them before.

I've never been anything but honest with women. Always upfront about what to expect from me, but the idea that I didn't even bother to introduce them to my friends, to remember their names, causes a grimy sick heat to coat my skin.

No more. I clear my throat. "She's the new trainer for the Kings."

"She's kicking our butts," Griffin says, clapping Tate's hand and giving him a quick hug behind us. It's not strange anymore to see the two sides of me be friendly.

Honestly, it's my favorite thing.

"Good to meet you," Rees says. "I hope you're letting this guy know he's not as awesome as he thinks."

Skye chuckles. "He's pretty impressive, but he's also going to admit my changes aren't going to supernaturally ruin the season because I change something up. He's learned I'm in charge."

"Good. About time."

I whip around. Bridger is off the phone and comes to my side. He studies Skye longer than he normally does, then looks to me.

This guy has known me since I could barely walk. We're closer than brothers. If anyone is picking up on the unrequited feelings in this room, it'll be Bridger Cole.

"I'm Bridger," he says, shaking her hand.

"The brother-in-law best friend," Skye says aloud, like she's memorizing his face. "Got it. You're very talented. I didn't think I was a rock fan until tonight."

"It happens to the best people," Tate says, winking. He spins one of his drumsticks. "They come in as doubters, and leave converted."

Bridger smirks, then faces me, lifting his brow as if to say, *What's going on here?*

I flick one shoulder. *Nothing.*

A simple eyeroll is my answer. *Right.*

We do this a lot, and it drives Alexis nuts. She always tells us to stop speaking telepathically, but it's just what happens with Bridger.

I make a move to stick by Skye, feeling like she'll need me to break the ice with the band and their girls, but when I look again, Skye is sitting next to Tate and Ellie. What is . . . is she looking at their wedding colors?

Ellie isn't shy about showing off her plans to us. As in the people she considers family, but even Dax drifts next to them when Skye rushes him over, explaining Daxton Sage has a good eye for detail.

Does he? Detail to what? I've been Dax's friend for years, I know he's smart, but I haven't noticed his impeccable attention to detail enough that I'd have him review wedding colors to see if they mesh.

I'm a little stunned.

Tate is even smiling. My guy doesn't trust anyone until he puts them through what I call the Hawkins Gauntlet. A process of Tate glaring and observing until he determines if someone is a dirtbag or not.

He's talking to Skye like they've known each other for years.

"So," Bridger says, snatching a bottled water off a table. "You going to tell me what this is all about?"

My fists clench once. Unclench. Then, tighten again. "Us coming to your concert, or how you look like you're sleep walking?"

"Good redirection, d-bag." He nods at Skye. "You thought you could bring her in here and I wouldn't notice?"

A prickle of unease teases my arms. "Notice what?"

Bridger grins. It's not exactly friendly. A little wicked, like he's planning something. "That you finally fell for someone."

I look away. There is the option to lie, but what's the point. I know the truth; Bridger knows me too well not to know the truth. With a slow step closer to him, I lower my voice. "We're supposed to be just friends, but . . ."

He snorts through another drink. "Yeah, I had that happen to me once and I married her."

"I've never done this. I've tried not to like her, man. She wants to be friends, so that's what we'll be, but—"

"It's not easy to turn it off." He nods with understanding. And he does. Alexis is my sister. By default they were a pair of antagonistic friends who eventually fell in love and fought tooth and nail not to. "Want advice, or want me to show you pictures of Garett?"

"Both."

"Done." Bridger squares to me, leans in. "Let it ride, man. If you like her, I automatically like her, because she must be pretty incredible if she got you to look twice. And if she's the one who's keeping you at a distance, I like her even more."

"Is this supposed to be a pep talk?"

"Yes." He grins. "Be her friend, but follow your gut. There might come a point where it tells you to take the risk to become something new. Listen to it, or you might miss an opportunity."

I flick my gaze back to Skye. Now she's chatting with Adam and Rees. She's a missing piece I didn't know was missing. A perfect fit with the people who matter most. Griffin, even Ryder, cracks a smile when she and Ellie laugh over something about Tate.

She fits.

My missing piece.

I found her, but I don't know how to tell her.

Chapter 11

Skye

MY THUMB RUBS ALONG the blue flowers on the china teacup. A hot blur of tears takes me by surprise. I blink, ignoring the salty drop that lands in my passion fruit tea, then lift the cup to my lips.

"Hey, baby." Dad walks into the kitchen, a big grin on his face, as he scrolls through morning emails on his phone, no doubt. At the first glance my way, he halts. His smile fades. "Skye, what's wrong?"

I wipe the tear and hold up the cup. "Just thinking of her."

My dad's face scrunches up when he studies the teacup. A wistful, longing sort of look takes hold. "She loved this china style, and I thought it was hideous. Now, I can't stop looking at it."

"The wedding china came out every morning. Be it hot chocolate or tea. I don't think I ever got tired of hearing how you tripped on her train."

"I did not." He chuckles and rubs a hand over his chest where I'm ninety-nine percent sure his wedding ring hangs on a chain.

Divorced parents who were still crazy about each other. I know, it doesn't make much sense, but life is strange sometimes. I was glad they loved each other, glad they were friends, but sad my grandpa was pretentious enough to drive a wedge between them.

"Do you ever regret it?" I whisper.

Dad looks at me with those stormy eyes. He knows what I mean. "My dad was not gracious with your mom. He wanted me to marry a senator's daughter and when I didn't, he took my betrayal out on her."

I furrow my brow. "You've never told me that."

"Didn't think you guys needed to know." My dad takes a seat on the barstool next to me. "I never stopped loving your mom, but hated how miserable she was becoming. I regret allowing it to happen."

"You guys never considered getting remarried after Grandpa died?"

"Can you keep a secret, Skeeter?"

"Probably not."

He chuckles. "We sort of got used to being friends. But at the end" –he clears his throat – "I was ready to try again. So, my greatest regret was waiting too long."

"Dad." I rest a hand on his arm and tilt my head. "Don't regret things. She loved you too."

He blinks a few times, then waves it away. "Doesn't do any good to hold onto regret. But take it from me, kid, when you find that guy—don't give him up."

My cheeks heat when the first face to fill my head is Parker Knight's.

I'm not here for the deep, tragic love story of my parents. I'm here to begin anew. A fabulous job, a new house, a new take on Skye Anderson.

"I think I'll put finding my Romeo on hold."

Dad pours himself a mug of coffee and snorts. "Fine. Whenever you do, though, make sure it isn't Oliver Thackery."

"Um, excuse me. I thought you liked him."

"I did. At first." He takes a sip, peering at me over the rim of his mug. "Until he behaved like a toddler after he found out he wasn't getting moved up to the Kings. When he took the offer from Utah, it was more a slight than a career move."

"Dad, can you fault a player for taking a position on a major league roster?"

"No. Not at all. It's how he immediately tossed the best woman alive aside to take that position. I can read between the lines as well as you, Skeeter."

It's a shot to the heart, but we Andersons don't beat around the bush. And Dad isn't wrong. My ex was the starting pitcher for the Scorpions. Because, of course, he was pitcher. It's like I'm walking around with a sign calling out to all the pitchers in the Vegas Kings' organization.

The second he learned the Kings' closer was being advanced through the bullpen, not the starter from the minors, he changed.

An attentive, albeit overly jealous, boyfriend went cold, distant. Critical. After he reacted so harshly, with verbal assaults at the coaches, team, and . . . me, it was not surprise he jumped at the offer from the Utah Gulls.

It isn't hard to deduce the odds were high that Oliver dated me because my father owns the teams.

With Mom gone, and Oliver moving on, the offer to join my family here was like fate intervened and gave me a hand up.

"So," Dad says as he places his mug in the sink. "Moving day?"

"Yep." I'm grateful for the subject change, and a rush of excitement runs through my veins. "I'm about ready to head to the storage unit."

Dad checks his wristwatch. "If you wait until this evening, I'll be around to help."

"No worries. I have help, and don't have a lot of stuff anyway." Most of my furniture was sold when I left California, and the rest is being delivered today before three o'clock. "I better get going."

"Nope. No one leaves. Not yet." A female voice echoes through the entryway and carries with a cheerful hum all the way into the kitchen.

"Hey, Alice." I smile as my cousin blasts through the door. A fitting word. She's a force of reckoning wherever she goes, be it Burton Field, PTA meetings, or the Anderson kitchen at eight in the morning. "Thanks for coming."

"I'm amazing at moving and completely efficient." She waves her hands and takes a step closer. "But my shiny kitten, I have so much to talk to you about."

I don't know if it's motherhood, or just words that slip out of her mouth, but Alice will give a person more pet names in an hour than most couples do in their entire relationship.

My cousin is the equivalent of a honeybee. She keeps things running at the field and at her home. Mother of six-year-old twin boys, blonde pixie cut that is spiked to perfection, about the size of a toothpick, and feisty like a tiger.

My dad has one sister, my Aunt Helena. Since my grandfather had some archaic issue with females in business, she was bequeathed their old mansion with no foothold in the Kings' organization, nor the millions that come with it.

Since my dad does not share his father's sentiments, he immediately brought Helena in as a board member and the head of all marketing and merchandising. Alice and my cousins run the department and they're incredibly talented. If not a little pushy when they want everyone to participate in some marketing gig.

"What's up?" I ask, reaching for my purse

Alice hurries to the counter and snags a bran muffin, grimacing through the first bite, but she keeps eating it. "You're going to die. I got off the phone with Kathy Witstock, the content director for *Sport Nation*

Magazine. Ready for this? She told me they want to run a feature on the Vegas Kings' new head, *female,* trainer as part of their women in sports section!"

Alice squeals and does a funny little bounce on her toes.

I don't have the same thrill. My blood drains out of my face, and I think I might vomit the entire cup of tea back up. All at once my right hand wants to curl into a fist. I stretch the fingers, wincing against the ache.

"Why are we not jumping up and down? This is amazing." Alice has that look, something narrowed, but playful. A clear sign she's about to try to convince us to do something, then spin it as the only way to keep the Vegas Kings from going bankrupt.

We all cater to her, even if the Kings and the Scorpions brought in more ticket sales last season than any of the previous seasons in eleven years. I think it was due to it being Jovi Green's last year on the mound.

This year, since my Viking is a fan favorite, I expect much the same by way of sales. Which is great, but I'll leave it to the guys to do all their sexy posing for billboards, commercials, and magazines to bring crowds to the field.

"Being in a magazine isn't my sort of thing," I tell her.

"But it could be."

"It's pretty neat, Skeeter," Dad says, but he gives me a look of understanding.

"I don't know," I say. "I don't think I'm all that interesting."

"Skye," Alice says and drops her hands onto my shoulders. "This is for the Kings. New season, new players, new trainer. The perfect year to get a truckload of free publicity for our guys. Our *family*! This could be exactly what the season needs to start off right."

Wonderful. If I refuse, the season will be doomed, and the entire Anderson bloodline will be out on the street.

It's a talent with Alice, she has a way of brightening a room, then placing the weight of the world on your shoulders if you question her ideas.

But a spread? In *Sport Nation*? I think I'd rather pull my fingernails off than have my face blasted in a magazine for everyone to see.

"She's hesitating, Uncle Dal."

My dad shakes his head, gives Alice a kiss on the temple, then does the same to me. "You two work it out. I've got a meeting. Let me know what the final decision is, okay? And Skye, if you need help with the storage unit, I'll be home around four today."

"You run the empire, Uncle Dal, I'll take care of my shy little sparrow," Alice calls to his back. Once we're alone, she fixes me in her purposeful stare. She's here for a win. "This is huge, Skye, and you deserve it." Alice returns her hands to my shoulders again. "I know you don't like being front and center, but I'll be there with you."

"Can I think about it?"

"Yes. If you promise to really, *really* think about it." Also meaning, think about different ways I'll agree. She picks at the rest of her bran muffin. "We have until tomorrow to get back to Kathy."

"Okay. I'll let you know."

My cousin pats my cheek. "You're a babe and deserve to be recognized for all you do for these smelly guys."

I snort. "Thanks."

"Okay, I'm going to hit the bathroom, then we'll get out of here and into your new palace!" With that, Alice takes her whirlwind out of the kitchen as fast as she arrived.

My weak leg sort of trembles as adrenaline abandons my system. I plop onto the barstool again, considering the idea of being posed, beautified, and interviewed for a nationally ranked magazine.

Alice isn't off about the publicity being wonderful for the Kings. It's more that the subject would be better suited being someone other than me. I'm not all that interesting, and knowing me, I'd blurt out something weird that would go down in historic baseball infamy.

I peek at my phone to check the time and smile. There's a text on my screen I didn't notice.

Parker: *Bad news. I've been Googling and it looks like the consensus is . . . Jack could've fit on the door.*

My laugh is a gurgling mess, and I have to grab a paper towel and wipe under my nose. Who is this guy? He actually Googled my heartbreak ending? I love it.

Me: *I KNEW it. My rage is justified.*

Parker: *I've got to say, though, I think I'm still on Jack's side of being manly and self-sacrificing for the woman he loves.*

Me: *And I maintain Rose was being a baby. Move. Over. For. Your. Man.*

Parker: **laughing emoji* What are you up to today?*

Me: *Moving day! I'm about to head to the storage unit now.*

Parker: *Sounds busy. Need help?*

Oh, I'd take his help if I didn't have a total of maybe twenty boxes in the tiny unit. If I invite him, he'll know it was because I like to see his sexy face. And I mean sexy in the friendliest of ways.

Me: *No. I'm covered, but thank you.*

Parker: *Okay. If you're sure, I'm going to hit the gym and meditate.*

Me: *I think I just fell in love with you.*

Parker: *Mission accomplished.*

I smile and tuck my phone away, ignoring how every time I speak to the man he adds a new rapid thud to my pulse. Ignore. Avoid. And the truth will go away. The truth being I have a tiny crush on Parker. He's fun, sweet, gorgeous. The trouble is his rap sheet is extensive. My sexy new friend is not a guy who settles down.

To each their own. I'll never judge him for playing the field.

I smile, wishing he was here, so I could say pun intended just to see him roll his eyes. See, therein lies the problem. I already know things about him, already feel comfortable, already think of ways I can make his day better.

I could fall for Parker Knight should I allow it.

He's swiftly becoming a piece of my life. We text, we tease. He takes me to rock concerts, I take him house shopping. He has my back at the field, making sure the team is showing me respect and helping me settle into my new position.

I'm not willing to give all that up because I can't keep my head on straight.

Like with Oliver, I fall too quickly, and deeper than the other party. Before Oliver, it was Luke. His name was Sanderson. I basically thought it was meant to be, dating a guy with such a similar last name. Until he told me, in the nicest way, I was a little much.

Never did get more details than that.

Before Luke, the first guy after the incident was Bryan. He was nice, sweet. But he was nice and sweet to more than just me.

Parker has seen a bit of my muchness and still stuck around.

He's nice and sweet like Bryan. He's sexy like Oliver was, but this time I have a grip on my head. I'm holding the reins, not the overreactive thing in my chest.

If I fell into a guy like Parker, the crash at the end would be worse than the others before it.

I'd rather be friends than brokenhearted.

Chapter 12

Skye

"Skye." Mike smacks my arm when I drive around the corner in the storage facility. "Is that Parker Knight?"

My grip tightens around the steering wheel. No mistake, straight ahead, leaning against the steel door of my unit, is Parker. He's not alone. Griffin Marks, Ryder Huntington, and Dax Sage are all standing around in the sun, baking for no good reason.

"Ah, there are some of my favorite McHotties," Alice says, lifting her eyes off her phone screen.

"Does Pierce know his wife ogles baseball players?" Mike asks.

"Boy, please," says Alice. "My white knight is ogling right along with me. You have to be a little head over heels for our guys to be in the family, you know this."

"Okay, but what are they doing here?" I haven't blinked. I'm not sure if he can tell from this distance, but I'm locked and loaded on the hulk of a man in the middle.

"I don't know, but the day got better," Alice says with a wink.

At the sight of my car, Parker waves and takes a few long strides until he's at the driver's window.

When I roll down the glass, he leans on the edge and a wave of his sweet spice fills my car.

"Hey."

"What are you doing?" I shield my eyes and give him a pointed look. "Are you following me, Knight? I know I never told you where my storage unit was."

"I could be."

"Do it, Muscles," Alice says. "Follow her."

I scoff. "Parker, this is Alice Hunt, not sure if you've met her. She's my cousin and in charge of all the merchandising and marketing for the Kings."

Parker reaches in and shakes her hand. "I think I've met your mom."

"Probably," Alice says. "She loves to hang out in the clubhouse."

I roll my eyes. "She does not, but I'm going to reel back to my question. Should I be worried that you are somehow here, Knight?"

"No. But what I've learned in life is when people move into new houses, they usually need help. So, when someone is asked if they need said help, but says no they're going to be good, usually it means they could use extra hands but don't want to ask for them."

"You've given this some thought."

"I really have."

"So, do you have some storage unit radar and you guessed which one belongs to me?"

"Unfortunately, not one of my many talents." He smiles and it's a delightful shock to my system. "We asked your dad. We're not scared of the big boss, Skye. In fact, I think we just won points in his book. He'll probably add another million to my contract."

"Ah, the plot thickens. That's why you're here. Mountains and mountains of money."

"Obviously."

"You guys are weird," Mike mutters under his breath and slips out of the car.

Alice chimes in with a soft, "Completely adorable" then follows my brother to the other guys waiting at the door.

Parker gives me a look that is rife in something playful, like he set out to accomplish what he wanted by making someone feel uncomfortable. Maybe Mike is right and we're both a little weird.

"You don't need to do this," I say. "I'm not lying about not having a lot to move."

"Then we'll be done quick," he says. "We've got all day. Off-season, and all. Plus, our trainer isn't making us do group workouts today."

I grin. "She will be on that in two days."

"Looking forward to it."

His hand drifts to the small of my back when I step out of the car. I bite down a ridiculous sigh and pray he can't feel the way my body reacts to such simple touch. I'd like to scream at my body and its intrinsic reactions to this man's touch. Reel it in, there is no shuddering, prickling, or longing needed here.

"This is nice of you guys," I say, "but I only have a few boxes."

Griffin steps forward, a sly grin on his face. "Skye, you're leaving out the part where you have two couches, a bed, and a desk being delivered today."

Griffin is tall, not Viking tall like Parker, and he has one of those smiles that makes you feel like the world revolves around you when he uses it. He reaches down once the door is unlocked and tosses it up with a clang of steel and squeaky wheels on the track.

Ryder steps forward, gives me a smile, then dips into the small unit. Dax is the somber one. He's polite, but says little as Ryder pulls him into the space. Alice does know how to move. She barks orders in her chirpy way, organizing us through dishes, bathroom supplies, a few small pieces of furniture, and most of my clothes.

The boxes of my belongings are loaded in my car and Parker's truck within twenty minutes.

"We'll meet you at the house," Parker tells me before we pull away.

Mike glances at me once the ball players are gone. "Is something going on with you two?"

"Oh, yes queen. Yes." Alice practically groans. "Please tell me there is. I live for this sort of thing. I told you my friend from college writes sports romance books, right? She'd eat this up."

I have no idea what friend she's talking about, but I'm more focused on my brother.

"Parker and I are friends."

Mike scrunches his nose. "Knight isn't the guy I'd peg to be friends with a woman."

"Then you've misjudged him."

"We'll see." My brother drapes his arm out the open window. "Based on past behavior, statistically it's unlikely he has no interest in you."

"Statistically? He's not a math equation, Michael."

"Oh, we're all equations and algorithms. We just need to find out what triggers each of our individual code."

Let's talk weird. Kettle meet pot.

"We met off the field. Did I tell you that?"

"Um, you didn't tell me." Alice leans forward between the front seats. "Sir Grumpsalot here might doubt the schmexy pitcher, but I am here for it."

"I'm not doubting anything, Skeet." Mike holds up his hands. "Past behavior is a predictor of future behavior, that's all."

"When did you meet him?" Alice asks.

"The weekend before my first day. He was at the Titanic expo."

"No." Mike scrubs his face. "He's not a fan like you. Tell me my pitching hero is not fangirling over—"

"Chill out," I say with a laugh. "He thought it was the baseball expo. But we clicked. I didn't recognize him, of course. And he had no idea who I was."

Alice draws in a breath through her nose, causing a deep snort. "Wren would devour this. I'm texting her."

I'm assuming Wren is the romance author, and I've officially lost my cousin to a text.

I flick my gaze to Mike. "Parker and I got to be us at the first meet, so when we saw each other again, there hasn't been any need to hide the real us, you know? We're friends."

My brother frowns. "There isn't a reason for you to hide the real you, but Parker isn't known for his openness. Has he shared anything about his life with you?"

"Yes." Why do I sound so defensive? "He's told me about his sister, his famous brother-in-law."

"Well known by everyone. I know you've been in California for most of his career, but Perfectly Broken rarely misses a home game. They're basically part of the stands now."

I pull into the driveway, blood heating, and I don't know why. "He told me a bit about what it was like to grow up here, how he's also lost a parent—his dad. He's told me about his nephew."

I'm stretching it a bit. I know he has a new nephew. That is the extent of my knowledge on the subject.

"But nothing about him."

"Michael, hush," Alice snaps without looking up from her phone.

My brother ignores her. "All I'm saying is I bet he knows more about you and what makes you tick than you do about him."

"He doesn't." I close my eyes. "I haven't told him details about the accident, or my background. He knows I get heated over a movie, our mom is gone, and I have an ex who played for the Scorpions. Frankly, I don't know why you're so invested in what he knows or doesn't know about me."

Mike chuckles. "Habit. I'm looking out for you. You've got a big heart, Skeeter. Don't want to see it get broken again. Knight is a good guy, but he's not the one to hang your dreams of growing old with the love of your life on. If you really are friends, great. Just don't expect him to go much deeper."

"Because his stats are against him, right?"

My brother shoots me with his fingers. "Exactly."

"We're friends." My voice is soft, a little broken. I follow Parker's movements as he and his teammates pull up beside me and immediately set to work unloading boxes. I pocket my car key with a touch of frustration. "Nothing more."

I get where Mike is coming from. He's been at Burton, interacted with the team, for two years longer than me. He knows more about each of these guys than I do. No doubt he's simply wanting his sister not to be played by another player.

I know this too. I've checked and rechecked if I'm looking at Parker through rose colored glasses.

From the deepest parts of me, I don't believe I am.

We've connected, and I think it's because he might be as desperate to find someone who accepts him for him as much as I am. Apart from his teammates and his family, who has ever taken the time to really talk to him without the glamor of his position in the MLB?

Our meeting was a gift. An opportunity to meet without the flashy lights of a family name and a prestigious position on the field.

If anyone has a shot at the seeing the real Parker Knight it's me. And I can do it without falling for him.

A few hours later my house is stacked in unpacked boxes. Alice and Mike are setting up the patio with fresh plants Alice bought. My new couches are placed, and a scattered mattress is in my room where Dax and Ryder are fumbling to put the bed frame together. In the back is a rhythmic thud where Griffin has been working on hanging a massive mirror in the guest bedroom.

Parker places a stack of my mom's wedding china at the top of a cabinet. The man doesn't even need the stepstool.

I grin and hand him another few plates. "I appreciate this, Parker."

"Anytime," he grunts out, stacking the final plate. "I don't know how it was with the Scorpions, but the Kings look out for each other. You're part of the Kings, Skye."

Heat prickles up the back of my neck. "Thanks. It's been a little bit of a whirlwind, but the team has been welcoming. I've got to be honest, I sort of expected more pushback."

Parker gives me a sheepish look. "If *I'm* being honest, we planned to pushback since most of us were . . . hesitant about a new trainer."

"Nice way of putting annoyed."

"Not annoyed, but we don't like change." He leans back against the counter. "I know your dad doesn't give handouts, but I guess I didn't expect you to be so qualified."

"Well, I'm glad my qualifications won you over to give me a chance."

He smiles and moves onto a box of silverware. "No, that was all you. Qualifications had nothing to do with it."

I'm not sure he even realizes what he said. Parker keeps placing forks and spoons in the drawer as if he didn't melt at least three major organs with one sentence. I can't not touch him, and reach out, resting a hand on his forearm.

He stops, eyes falling to our touch, then he looks to me.

"Can I be honest?" I whisper.

"Always."

"You've made this move a hundred times easier than if I'd been at this alone."

A muscle tightens over the hinge of his jaw. Shadows splash over the blue and green in his eyes, deepening the color into something dark and smoky. Like hot coals. Parker adjusts his arm, so my hand slips into his. He takes a step closer. Silent. Deliberate. I don't dare blink, afraid to miss whatever he has planned.

For a breath I forget my resolve not to tangle myself in the strings of this man, in the heartache that will surely come. The way he's looking at me, I guarantee it'll be worth it.

"Perfect!" Alice's pitchy voice squeaks through the tension.

My heart catches in my throat and I whip around. Parker startles and takes a step away from me. I wasn't imagining it, then. We both were caught up in an electric charge just now.

Alice stands in the doorway, beaming at both of us. "I just had a vision."

"Should we call a doctor?"

"Funny." My cousin holds up her hands, framing us between her palms. "Yes. They'll love it. My sweet treat, I've solved your problem about the magazine spread. Let's be honest with each other. The idea of posing all by your lonesome is what intimidates you."

"What magazine?" Parker asks.

Alice ignores him and sashays across the kitchen, gripping Parker's arm. "You, my lovely little bird, are not the only new thing about the Vegas

Kings this season. The second I walked in here, I saw the most beautiful spread of delicious photographs with our two newest hot shots on the team. The beautiful new trainer, and the incredible rise of our closer to starting pitcher. They. Will. Love. It."

"Hold on." Parker holds up one of his giant hands. "What are we talking about?"

"Alice made an appointment with *Sport Nation Magazine.* They want to do a shoot with me as the new trainer for publicity purposes."

"And to honor you," Alice corrects, but her hungry eyes are on Parker. "If you both do it, we'll have so many eyes on us. Not to mention, you look beautiful side by side."

I glance at Parker. There probably isn't a way for me to get out of this shoot. Not when a woman like Alice is at the lead. To have him there, I don't know, it gives me a bit of relief. But would he want to be glamorized with me is the question.

"Well, what do you think, Hot Shot?" I nudge his arm.

Parker's mouth is tight, but the corner tilts in a small grin. "I'm not big about magazines."

"Me neither."

"We can make it awkward in equal amounts then."

"That's the attitude," Alice says, "except it will not be awkward. It'll be stunning."

"Are you really willing to do this with me?" I ask.

Parker shrugs. "It's for the team, right?"

"Yes," Alice says before I can respond. I'm not sure this is for the team or for her, but if that is what gets Parker to take the step. No doubt she'll spin this shoot as the saving grace for the Vegas Kings until he begs her to let him be photographed.

He turns to me. "I'd be game. You good with it?"

With him there. Yes. "I think I could play ball for one day."

"Pun intended," we say at the same time.

Alice claps her hands and squeals. "Yes! You two precious pearls will be so hot the pages will *ignite*. I've already sent Kathy the email."

"Alice." I scoff. "We agreed two seconds ago."

She gives me a dubious kind of look. "Um, but you would've agreed no matter what. This is me we're talking about, lovely."

She spins on her heel, chin lifted with a heap of smug victory, and leaves us in the kitchen to manage her wake.

"Did that just happen?"

Parker laughs. "I think so."

"I've never been in a magazine," I admit. My hands stiffen in thick tension as, unbidden, I tangle my fingers like they're boneless.

Parker leans his face close to mine. "It's not so bad, and I'll be right next to you. The whole time."

When he should pull back, he doesn't. Parker hovers there, tormenting me with an unnerving rush of heat in my belly. Oh, the things blazing in my skull right now would cause my mom to sit up in her grave and ask for all the details.

Does he know how perfect his mouth is? Wholly kissable, and I'd like to take a test drive without a thought for the three baseball players in the back room, my cousin—to be fair, Alice would encourage it—and my brother.

I hold my breath to keep my mouth from running off with something horribly embarrassing. Like all the things I'm imagining with his Norse biceps, and smug mouth, and those talented hands.

All I manage to choke out is a raspy, "Good."

This is a disaster.

If I don't get a grip, despite my best efforts, I will undoubtedly fall for my handsome, endearing, baseball playing Viking.

Chapter 13

Parker

"OH, COME ON, BUDDY." I groan and gently ease baby Garett off my shoulder. He puked again. "Bridge, where is that cloth thing?"

Bridger scrubs his sleep-deprived face and rummages through the overpacked diaper bag at his feet. I choke back a laugh when he tosses me a burp cloth, but there is still one on his shoulder he didn't notice.

"I'd apologize for your shirt," Alexis says, slurping juice off a popsicle she found in my freezer, "but I really don't care. I'm basically bathing in spit-up at this point. Only fair all the rest of you do too."

"Ah, it's all right, isn't it buddy?" I cup the back of my nephew's fuzzy head and adjust him against my shoulder again, gently patting his back. "Just means you're eating good, right? We'll get you plumped up and on the field in no time."

"The stage. Lights. Guitars." Bridger makes a weak 'rock on' sign with his hand. Alexis and I share a bemused look. He's only half here. Doesn't even have his eyes open.

"Baseball, Gare," I whisper to the baby and slump back in my couch watching the rest of my impromptu guests play *Call of Duty* in my living room. Griffin sits between Rees, and Mason Walker, a future King if I ever saw one. Mason isn't even seventeen, but it's been a long time since I've seen such raw talent on the field.

The kid has been on the varsity team since he was a freshman and has a killer arm. I thought I was obsessed with the game—no, Mason Walker bleeds baseball.

"Mase, when do your parents get back?" I ask.

"Uh . . ." He draws it out, flinching as he takes a shot in the game. "Tomorrow night. Then, Rees'll be off b-babysitting duty b-b-because every guy with a driver's license needs a sitter."

"When they're you, yeah," Griffin says, elbowing Mason in the ribs and starting a deeper virtual war on the screen.

I love how the kid doesn't even try to hide his stammer anymore. He's come a long way since we met almost three years ago.

He'd been a different kid then. Barely making it with Jazzy, his cousin and legal guardian. Until Finn, the producer for Perfectly Broken, and Jazzy got married. Mason was adopted by both, has a few sisters now, and smiles like every day is the best gift we can get.

"You're hardly at my house," Rees says. "And I wouldn't call it babysitting. Jaz gave me the bare minimum: give you a place to sleep, make sure you don't do drugs, and don't sneak girls into the house."

Mason's face flushes as Alexis snickers and Rees's girlfriend, Vienna, makes a joke about locking the guest room window to keep out a girl named Chloe. I don't know who they're talking about, but I like tormenting my teenage protégé all the same. Mase is a centerfielder through and through, but since he works out with me at the field, I call him my protégé and no one can tell me differently.

I love nights like this. These people are my family. We're only half full since the rest of the band, including Mason's family, is out of town for a Hawaiian vacation. Get nominated for another music award, the label CEO sends you to paradise apparently.

Mason hung back for baseball clinics, Rees and Vienna had a previous thing with her family, so they stayed to be chaperones, and obviously Bridger and Alexis just had their world flipped upside down.

I'm not complaining. Spring training will be here soon enough, and I want to spend as much time with my family as possible.

"Park, did I tell you Mom texted me?" Alexis says, pulling me out of the bliss that comes from the baby smell of Garett's head under my chin. "She wants to start having family dinners once a month."

A hot bite of resentment stabs my chest. "I hope you let her know we do have family dinners once a month."

We do. Rock stars and baseball players feed each other at least once a month at varying houses. But my voice is rife with bitterness, and I almost feel bad for putting that out there with Garett on my chest. Like he might absorb the negativity or something.

"So, I'm going to take that as you're not interested in trying?" Alexis tilts her head, studying me.

"I'm not sure why you are? She's mostly ignored me, but you, she's criticized everything you've ever done."

"I know," Alexis says softly. "But I do think she's trying—not to make up for anything, but to just try."

Bridger takes her hand and kisses her knuckles, then looks to me. He was there through it all. He gets how dysfunctional our house was. "I don't think she's pushing anything, man. She just put it out there."

"Well, I'm good," I say.

Alexis gives me a sad little nod. She won't push this. We've always respected each other and our stances on the house we grew up in. Still, I can see something in her eyes that hints to a bit of disappointment. Maybe it's motherhood that's making her more forgiving. I don't understand it. Alexis was mistreated. My mom never encouraged her to reach for any potential, more to not get pregnant in high school and find a guy who could support her even if he didn't love her.

Life goals.

A knock at the door kills the conversation, and I'm glad. To dig deeper into this will bring up old resentment I don't want to deal with on a day like this.

Maybe not ever.

Bridger holds out his hands and takes Garett from me, so I can answer the door. Probably Ryder or Dax. Chill, easy nights with video games and food are the best ways to pull Dax from his bat cave and into the light of society.

I open the door and my voice makes a stupid noise in the back of my throat. Sort of like I gag on my own tongue in surprise. "Skye?"

She offers a small arching wave, smiling. "Hey, Hot Shot."

"What, what are you doing here?"

With a playful smile, Skye leans in and whispers, "I stalked you."

When I don't move, I'm not even sure my face twitches at all, a furrow pulls her brows together, and she lets out a nervous chuckle. "Kidding. I mean, I definitely had to bring a Kit Kat to Lauren in my dad's office for her to give up your address, but that's not the point." Skye adjusts and holds up a large cardboard box. "I have the outfits for the shoot tomorrow. Hand delivered from our merchandising department, aka Alice and her vision board."

After another awkward, silent heartbeat, a smile breaks over my mouth and I forget I'm supposed to be uneasy. "Here. Let me take them."

I maneuver the box out of her hands and expect her to wave goodbye. I don't want her to go, and I do all in one weird emotion. The hair lifts on the back of my head. This is such new territory for me, I have no idea where to step.

"We're friends, right?"

A random thing to say. But Skye starts to shift on her feet like she's discomposed.

"Yeah," I say. "I can make a friendship bracelet to prove it if you want, Anderson."

"Weird, but I'd be so down with that." She grins. "I'm asking because I have something even more uncool to ask."

"I'm nervous."

"You should be." She bounces her knees a little and steps closer. "Can I use your bathroom? Awkward? Don't make it weird. All humans do it, Parker."

"My bathroom? Inside?"

"Um, unless you have an outhouse."

I blink and swallow a scratch in my throat. "No. Yeah. I mean, yeah, of course."

I'm letting her inside. This house is my safe zone. The place only people who know everything about me enter. Here, I don't hide behind personas or a good front. Inside my house, I can let down the barriers I put forward; I can be me in all my dorky, uncouth glory.

I've hesitated too long.

"Oh." Skye covers her mouth and lowers her voice to a breathy whisper. "You have company, don't you?"

"Yeah," I say before I realize my family and friends are not the sort of company she means. There is a flicker of pain in her eyes, and I hate that I put it there for even a second. "I mean, no. Not like that."

"Okay. Is your bathroom dirty, or . . ."

"No." I laugh. It's all wrong, too high and pitchy. "Sorry, come in. No problem."

Skye gives me a look, one a little too focused, as if she might see right through my skin and catch sight of the insecurity boiling beneath the surface.

"You do have company," she says when a woman's laugh trickles up the hallway.

I shouldn't, but I take a bit of pleasure knowing she's acting jealous. "It's my sister and Vienna."

She gives me a confused expression. Does she not remember Vienna from the concert?

"Rees Hayden's girlfriend. Remember her from the concert greenroom? Former schoolteacher, blonde, kind of shy?"

"Oh, right," Skye says, a wash of pink crossing her cheeks. "Day with the girls?"

"Do you need to use the bathroom, or not, Anderson?"

"Fine. Yes, I do. I just have so many questions. I feel like I've crossed a forbidden line here. No one knows what the great Parker Knight hides behind closed doors." She jabs her finger in my face. "I've read rumors, big guy."

"Don't move the big bag of cash in my bathtub and we won't have any problems."

She snickers and follows my directions down the hallway. My fists tighten. All I can do now is hope she doesn't snoop around. It's not a big deal. At least I shouldn't make things a big deal, but she was right. I have an image on the outside, and things I keep in here are personal. I don't trust a lot of people with my quirks like books. and building, and pictures, and all of me.

I stand alone in my hallway, holding the box, still unsure how to step here. Do I introduce Skye to my sister? Will she leave? Want to stay? Conflicted as I am, there is a sense of rightness having Skye Anderson around.

I like Skye. Not as a friend, although she makes a great friend, I like her as a woman. As someone who makes me think things like texting her just to let her know I was thinking of her. Of dinners at sports bars, not five-star restaurants. She's the face I see when I think of future days, of clear nights, of holidays with family.

When I let myself, I imagine holding her hand in public, kissing her senseless against a wall without a thought for who sees. Then doing it over and over again until we're gray and wrinkled.

"Who's here?" Alexis rounds the corner, munching on a handful of nuts. According to her, she's always hungry and depends on the rest of us to give her healthy snacks instead of the candy she really wants.

"Uh, our new—"

I stop midsentence because Skye steps out into the hallway. She flips off the light to the bathroom, then turns around with her bright, addicting smile.

Alexis starts to groan until it must hit her too. Her brother has shoved more than one woman in her presence, but Alexis knows—none of them ever stepped foot in my house.

She looks at me, entirely obvious she's surprised, but she likes to pretend she can mentally communicate with me.

"Lex," I start, shifting the box in my hand. "This is Skye Anderson. She's the new trainer. We're doing the shoot together tomorrow. Skye, this is my sister Alexis."

It takes another half a second, but Alexis relaxes. "Oh, right. Bridger mentioned you after the concert. She's also the one who shut you down, right?"

"I'm going to murder Griffin." My voice is low and rough.

Alexis beams. "It was too good a story not to text out, Park."

It only gets worse when Skye laughs. "He's so hard to look at, I didn't know how to let him down easy."

"Thanks." I roll my eyes and start to walk away.

Skye curls a hand around my bicep and pulls me back. My body must react because Alexis gives me one of her annoying sister-looks. Like she knows how much blood is rushing to my head right now.

"I'm teasing," Skye says and looks to my sister. "It really wasn't all that dramatic, and what was left out is the way I'd basically sobbed in his lap over the ending of Titanic at that point."

"I'm going to make it dramatic because it is my new favorite story." Alexis faces me. "Invite Skye to stay for dinner. We're ordering in."

I glare at my sister. Not because I don't want Skye to stay, but I'm the older freaking brother and somewhere along the line Alexis turned into the bossy one.

"Want to stay and have dinner with us?" I ask, sickly sweet to irritate Alexis.

Skye stretches her hand. I'm starting to wonder about it. A clear nervous tic and I want to know where it comes from. I want to know everything about her.

"I don't want to be in the way," she says. "I didn't come to crash your family time, or—"

"I'm here, too, Skye!" Griffin's voice echoes down the hall.

She flushes. "It is a party."

Alexis clicks her tongue. "Eh, a few rock and roll enthusiasts, baseball dweebs, a teenager who thinks he's an adult, and an infant who just blew out in his onesie. We're pretty impressive."

"Congratulations on the baby. Parker mentioned he's an uncle now."

"Yep," Alexis says. "The proof is all over him."

My face heats. I forgot about the white spit up stain. Awesome.

"Well, this is going to be fun," I say. "Let me go put this stuff away and we'll get food while you all make fun of me in my own house."

"Perfect." Alexis sneers. Not a smile, no, a sneer. She has plans. This is one of the few times I wish my sister and I weren't as close as we are, because she's picking up on the vibes and torment I'm trying to hide when it comes to Skye.

"If you're sure," Skye says to me.

My face softens. "I'm sure. You'll regret hanging out with these people, but I'll be there to save you in a second."

She laughs and hurries away with my sister.

So, this is how the night will go. Skye Anderson in my personal space, with the people who matter most to me, and I'm supposed to pretend we're just friends the entire time.

Awesome.

Chapter 14

Skye

For the briefest moment, I had a twinge of hesitation following Alexis Cole into the living room. I'm not so out of touch not to know I was about to spend an evening with people made of fame and fortune.

We chatted at the concert, but here, in such a casual setting, I'm not sure why I wasted any time worrying about meeting them again.

They're funny, unintimidating, and they don't care that my dad comes from Las Vegas royalty. To them, I'm just Skye, Vegas Kings trainer.

Alexis's husband and his bandmate start clearing the table from our takeout boxes and taco bags. I'm not sure I've ever eaten so many hard-shell tacos. I might've lost myself a bit, but they were delicious, and I wasn't the only one.

Griffin had no less than twenty, so did the kid. Mason Walker. He wants to play baseball, so I've been using that to repeat his name in my odd way of learning names all night. Mason is a King in the making and doesn't miss when it comes to catching the balls. So, Mason isn't missin' and is makin' the right plays. A King in the making Mason.

I wish I could say I didn't have to do the same thing for the people I've already met, but here I am rememorizing the names of faces I saw, talked with, got to know at the concert.

Bridger Cole. Best friend of Parker, the husband of Parker's sister. He's a bridge between them. Bridger.

Rees. How did I recall his name at the concert?

I glance at his eyes and grin. There it is. Two different colors, a brown eye and a blue. Peanut butter and chocolate are two different flavors, but both make a Rees's Peanut Butter Cup. Two different colors. Two different flavors. Rees.

It's a wild ride up here in my head.

For some reason Alexis sticks, and finally, so does the girlfriend, Vienna. Mostly because I've been to Vienna, Austria, and I have it locked in there since I nearly made a fool out of myself when I didn't know who she was when Parker first said her name earlier.

Baby Garett wasn't hard to memorize because Parker has been babbling with his nephew, calling him Gare-buddy, all night.

I'm not saying my body melts at the sight of my Colosseum Viking with a baby, but I'm not, *not* saying it either.

"Hey Park," Alexis says as she starts to pack up Garett's diaper bag. "Did you ever get those special editions of *Wicked Darlings*? I promised Rees I'd read them."

"They're good, Lex," Rees says. "And you'll break my brother's heart if you don't."

Oh, yeah. Rees is also a twin. Two flavors, two of him. His twin is famous too. Some up and coming actor who scored the lead in a Netflix series based on the *Wicked Darlings* book series. Funny enough, I've seen a few episodes, and now I intend to dive back in since it makes it so strangely exciting to know people who know the guy on the screen.

"They're on backorder," Parker says. "After I read them, I'll give them to you."

"I asked for them first," Alexis says.

"But I actually read the genre." Parker wiggles his brows and takes a plate from Griffin.

"Do you not typically read high fantasy?" I ask, helping clear the water glasses.

Alexis shakes her head. "Nope. I stick to classics mostly. *Jane Eyre*, things like that."

"Hmm. I always thought *Jane Eyre* was kind of a rip off of *Beauty and the Beast*."

The room silences but for Bridger bursting out in a laugh. He looks at Parker. "What have you done?"

I don't get it until I look back at Alexis. I will swear until the day I die, this nice, chatty, new mother cracks her neck side to side like some sort of gangster about to strike.

"You think *Jane Eyre* is a rip off of a fairy tale, huh? Let's have a chat."

"Lex," Parker warns. "No one meant any harm to your precious Jane."

"Oh, I did," I say, rolling my shoulders back. "Beauty will win every time."

"Is this the no-filter thing you warned me about?" Parker whispers. "I don't think you know what you're getting into here."

"Back up, Parker," Alexis says, one hand shoving against his chest. "I've waited for this debate since the day Bridger made me be his roommate. We're doing this."

"I didn't make you do anything," Bridger calls over his shoulder. "You practically begged me, Al."

"Not the time, Cole! I'm busy." She hasn't dropped her eyes from mine since I made the comment. I wasn't imagining the gangster-look. Alexis stretches out her fingers, cracks two knuckles, and it begins.

For ten minutes we mark similarities between the two stories. Lonely, moody men locked away in a big house with a staff that is afraid of him. I weave in the way the secret Mr. Rochester keeps is like the curse for the spoiled, ill-tempered prince in Beauty and the Beast.

Alexis disagrees. Like the night I met Parker and our swift debate on the ending of Titanic, my competitive nature rears to the surface. I swing back with timeline. Beauty and the Beast was first. Alexis sighs and rubs the bridge of her nose, explaining time doesn't matter because they are wholly different genres. Gothic classics compared to fairy tales.

In the end, I think we call it a draw.

Unexpected, debating Parker's sister on literature, since deep inside I want his people to like me because I like him, and I can't stop myself from liking him.

But Alexis beams, cheeks red, and squeezes my hand. "You are such a book freak."

"With broken heroes and romance, yes."

"I love it." She practically snarls, then squeezes me in a tight hug. "Thank you. I was starting to slip into a haze of no sleep. Now, I'm fired up."

"Great," Bridger mumbles.

"You love it." Alexis winks at her husband. When Garett starts to fuss in his car seat, she sighs. "We better get going. Skye, it was good to meet you."

"You too."

It's a slow procession of everyone leaving. Who knows if I intentionally ended up as the last by the door, but here we are. Parker, me, and nothing but night ahead.

He rubs the back of his neck. "Thanks for appeasing my insane sister. Don't know if you noticed, but Bridger literally has a tattoo of Jane Eyre on his arm. It's his version of having Alexis's name in ink. She's that obsessed."

"It was fun. They all were great. I mean, I knew Griffin was fun, but everyone else."

"I know what you meant."

"Right." I take a step back. "Well, I guess I'll see you at the shoot in the morning then." Ugh. Why is it so hard to leave? All it'll take is a step and I'll be off the porch. A few more strides and I'll be at the car. But I'm as stone, planted, unmoving, and stubborn.

"Unless . . ."

My attention goes stark still. Unless what?

"You want to stay for a little longer." Parker's voice grows husky, a low rumble in the back of his throat.

My heart squeezes. "Oh? Want to debate books with me too?"

He grins and steps a little closer. "No, but my sister did bring an entire sheet cake and we didn't touch it before their eight o'clock curfew hit. If you promise not to tell my trainer, I think it needs to be touched."

The word *touch* has never been this tantalizing and I'm embarrassed to admit I'd like his hands to touch me. Doesn't seem fair I'm the only one who gets to touch—as his trainer—when my skin is boiling for this man to hold me tightly.

There's something wrong with me. I'd be wise to call it a night.

"I'd love to stay. For cake. I mean, I'd love to stay for cake."

Parker's eyes brighten like green glass in sunlight. With one arm open, he makes way for me to step back into his house. I don't know what I'm doing, probably all the wrong things, but sometimes the wrong things turn out to be beautifully right in the end.

Chapter 15

Skye

I DON'T WANT TO stay just for cake. How did I let this happen? For a few weeks now, I've been satisfied keeping this guy at arm's length, as a friend. Tonight, the ground tilted. I'm still trying to pick who to blame. Probably Garett Cole. Baby scent, baby babbles, and a sexy, single uncle fawning. I'm a goner.

Or it could be I've always wanted to be closer to Parker Knight since he stuck around at a Titanic expo, watched me overheat, and still wanted to know me.

I had one job to do when I moved to Las Vegas, and falling for another baseball player was not in the description.

In my hands is a plate of white sheet cake, but I've hardly touched it. If I move the fork, no doubt my muscles will tense up and I'll drop it, make a mess, then end the night by scrubbing his spotless carpet.

I steal a glance at Parker as he puts the rest of the cake away. There is something about the man that sparks a bit of warmth inside. One of those attractions that builds at a deeper level, forming roots, and finding the person underneath the surface.

Except I know little about the heart inside the man.

My fingertips trace a framed photo on a wooden table against the wall. Looks like it was taken in someone's backyard. Everyone who was here tonight, except Vienna, is in the picture, with a few faces I didn't meet.

Everyone is in a swimming suit and holding up cupcakes.

"Where is this?" I ask, holding up the frame.

"Tate's house about three years ago."

"Ah. I was going to say, Mason looks quite a bit younger."

Parker wipes his hands on a towel and leans back against the counter. "Yeah, that was right after we met. His dad, there, he adopted him after he married Mase's cousin. We call her his momsin."

I lift my brow. "Sounds like he's had a rough go of life."

"Yeah." Parker strides out of the kitchen and stands beside me. "He's a good kid though."

"Cool that you guys on the team have been mentoring him."

"I keep telling him he'll be a King someday, so he better get used to Burton Field."

I snicker. "I'll be sure to let my dad know."

"Do that."

I study that picture again. My brother's voice is in my head. Parker knows about me. Well, most things. But he gives up very little. I want to know everything. Another good thing about having a standing friendship. Most people aren't as wary to give up shortcomings to their friends.

"So, are you going to give me the tour?" I point my fork down one of the hallways leading to the rooms in the back.

Parker's mouth tightens. "A tour?"

"Yep. Fair since you've been in every room in my house, unless you really are hiding a pile of cash, in which case, I think it's better if I'm left in the dark." He holds my stare, face like carved marble. "No, my jokes are already falling flat?"

"No. It's not that." He scoffs.

Oh.

Oh.

Parker is uneasy. This is the exact reason why I shouldn't have allowed myself to get wrapped up in anyone's strings. His in particular. They're too intoxicating, too tricky to maneuver.

He doesn't want me to see too far into his life.

A wash of painful self-doubt rams into my stomach. What if he's been nice because of the same reason most people show me respect—my father owns their careers.

I feel sick.

Am I so desperate for acceptance, for someone to want me around in the same way I connect to people that I completely duped myself into believing a man like Parker Knight would be my friend without an underlying motive?

Of course he'd cater to my weirdness. He doesn't want to get on my dad's bad side. When you're on the bad list for Dallas Anderson, it's difficult to get off. Parker would probably do anything I asked if it kept me happy, while inside, doubtless, he's cringing.

"Skye."

My eyes kick to his. I hadn't realized my stare had gone blank and hard on the untouched sheet cake in my hands. "Sorry. I zoned off."

"That wasn't a zone," he says, coming closer. "That was some major thinking going on."

"No, not a lot." I hold out the plate of cake for him to take. I'm jittery and can't get my own assumptions out of my head. "Um, I think I better go, actually."

"What, why?"

"We have a busy day and—"

"You don't want a tour anymore?"

"No." I shake my head. "Not when you don't want to give one. Thank you for this. Your friends and family are . . . they're wonderful, and your nephew is adorable. He doesn't look like a prune, and—"

My words dry up when Parker traps one side of my face with his palm. It's warm, callused, rough, and gentle in the same touch.

"Hey, what's wrong?" His voice is so soft. I could revel in the sound for hours.

My mind is holding steady on an unbreakable track of perseveration is what's wrong. Once the carousel begins, I have trouble getting off. I can't lie to him. Not when he's holding me close, not when his thumb is gently tracing the ridge of my cheek. Not when his eyes are nothing but concerned.

"You seem very uncomfortable with me being here," I admit. "So, I think I might've made this friendship into something more than it is. I hope it has nothing to do with my dad and you impressing him. If it does, I'd rather be honest about it and go back to being colleagues. No hard feelings."

"Skye, stop." Oh, goodness. His second palm is on the other side of my face. His eyes are narrowed. "Where is this coming from? I'm not faking a friendship because your dad is Dallas Anderson."

"Okay."

Parker closes his eyes for half a breath before leveling me in a hard stare. "I am uncomfortable, but not in a bad way. I've never let anyone in my house who is not my sister, my closest friends, people dating those friends, or married to them. My own mother hasn't even been here."

I draw in a sharp breath. "You're not close with your mom, I take it."

"Not even a little bit." His grip tightens on my face. "If I let you see these rooms, let you see anything I keep here in my space, it means letting someone in, and I don't do that."

"Okay. We don't need to—"

"No." He interrupts me. "You're misunderstanding. I *want* to let you in. Because it's *you*, and to be honest, I don't know how to handle it."

He could start by kissing me. I'll leave that to him.

For now.

This is a bit of vulnerability and the way he holds tight to me, like I'm his ballast in a storm, I'm going to venture a guess that Parker doesn't do these kinds of confessions often.

"I want to see you," I admit, my hands go to his wrists. "I want to know about you, Parker."

"I'm weird."

"Where have you been all my life? So am I."

He smiles, but there is caution there. "Okay."

"Yeah?"

"Yeah."

He takes my hand and leads us down the hallway to the first door after the bathroom. A bedroom that serves as a tidy office with a computer, file cabinets, all the basic things one might find in an office. The difference is the walls are plastered in photos of him, his friends, and his sister.

Some are from childhood, others more recent. There are posters of Perfectly Broken.

I grin, looking at their stony faces. Funny to see Rees and Bridger in their styled rock star clothes—black, a lot of black—and eyeliner when we were all guzzling tacos an hour ago.

I smile at a toothy photograph on the corner of the desk. A lanky Parker wears a little league jersey, and is engulfed in big, bulky arms with a few tattoos. A man with dark, trimmed hair has Parker's back to his chest, and is lifting him off the ground, laughing.

I smile and touch his boyish face. "Who is this?"

"Garett Cole," he says. "Bridger's dad. Gare's namesake. He was my dad, too, in every way that matters. That game was my first homerun and first time I struck out a batter. It was the luckiest game, and he was there cheering me on the entire time. It's also the last one he saw before he died."

My heart cramps. He's lost two fathers and there aren't words to make it okay. "Parker, I'm so sorry."

"I miss him," he admits. "He's the one who told me I'd make it to the big leagues. My mom would laugh at me, but Garett would tell me to keep pushing. He's why I'm here."

The sting is almost too much. Anger and sadness collide; I grit my teeth, turning away from the photo. His mom would laugh at him for dreaming? Why? Yes, statistics are not in favor of most people making it to the MLB, but to laugh at him for the dream?

Every player had to have the dream, or they wouldn't be here.

I turn over my shoulder. He's studying a picture that looks like him, a little Alexis, and probably a young Bridger tucked in a makeshift tent with books stacked around them.

Parker traces the edges of the frame on the wall. "We'd hide out, Lex and me, in this fort we built behind the Cole's house. They lived across the street from us. I think Bridger's mom took this, and we didn't even know she was there we were so lost in our own world."

"Hide out?" I'm almost afraid to ask. "From what?"

"My house." One fist clenches at his side. "My mom brought home a lot of men. Nine times out of ten they were horrible. I didn't want Lex in the house with them." Inadvertently he touches the scar through his eyebrow. "They were cruel, angry, abusive. To keep Alexis distracted, I'd buy cheap books from the library. You know, those sales they have sometimes where they sell books for a quarter. I'd read to Alexis to keep our minds off things. For some reason the cheapest books were always the classics."

"*Jane Eyre*," I whisper.

He nods. "I'd read to her until she could read on her own, then I'd listen and toss a ball around. I knew she was safe as long as we were in that tent."

I touch his arm, sliding my hand to his palm, and slip my fingers into his. A soft smile pulls at his mouth.

"Our neighborhood looked out for us," he goes on. "Mom never let guys stay if they hit us, but she couldn't pick good ones either. It's like after my dad died, she broke and stopped caring."

"But you cared," I say. "All you thought about was your sister and letting her escape. What about you? How did you escape?"

A bit of color paints his cheeks. "Well, that's the next room. I warned you, I'm not as cool as *Sport Nation* will try to make me look tomorrow."

I laugh and keep hold of his hand as he takes me out of his memory room and into a spare bedroom. There isn't a bed. Only tables and a small couch. Parker hangs back in the doorway as he releases me. He shoves his hands in his pockets and stares sheepishly at the ground.

"Oh, my gosh." I take in the room. "Did you build all these?"

Models of sports cars, airplanes, fighter jets, and Legos. Oh, the Legos. Set after set lines the tables. Some in disarray, others pristine and intricate. There are pirate ships and *Star Wars*, jeeps and *Jurassic Park*, airplanes and cities.

I pull my bottom lip between my teeth, and whip around. "You are a Lego nerd? This is your deep, dark secret?"

He folds his arms over his chest. "Yes. I'm obsessed with building things, okay? I drew the line on Lincoln Logs when I was eighteen, but I fully plan to buy some now that Gare is here."

I love everything about this room, and he looks ready to vomit. "Tell me about it. Why do you build things? What does it do for you?"

He studies me for a few breaths, no doubt searching for any hint of teasing, then gives in. "Calms me, I guess. Forces me to focus on that thing instead of whatever I'm worried about. Don't get me wrong, I love to go to the batting cages, or throw a ball as hard as I can, too, but there is something about the stillness of building things. It's always been my thing. Lex gets me a set every Christmas and birthday. So do all the guys."

Parker gestures to a stack of unopened boxes. At least fifteen sets are in a tall stack.

I laugh. "You better get working on them, Knight."

"I know it's weird to have a room dedicated to toys, but—"

"Did I say weird?" I squint at him. "I don't think I ever said weird. Therapeutic is the word you're looking for, I believe."

I abandon the Legos and drift across the room to a collage of black and white prints. Simple images. A bee on a flower petal. A single dandelion in a sea of grass. A lizard sunning on stone. Interesting choice in photography. Pretty, calming, but not the sort of thing I'd expect on Parker Knight's wall.

"I took those." His voice is soft.

"You?" I point at the lizard. "You took these pictures?"

Parker rocks onto his heels, unsettled. "I like to take pictures of things people might overlook."

The photos take on a new meaning now. "They're happy. I like them."

Parker comes to my side, his shoulder brushing mine. A magnetic tug demands I lean into him. Why resist? I'm hooked, and he has no idea how deep his claws have gone.

Parker's palm opens on the small of my back. With a gentle tug, he pulls me into his side. "You don't need to talk up my weird hobbies."

"There's that word again." I pin him with a glare. "To quote a sexy Viking I recently met, you're weird, Parker, but I like your weird. I'm not stroking your ego. I, in fact, am very bad at ego stroking. It goes right over my head." I reach for one of the unopened Lego sets—the Bat Cave—and shake it so the pieces rattle inside the box. "If you must know, I happen to be an expert at Lego sets."

"Don't lie to me, Anderson. You might not be real if you know baseball and build with Legos."

"Sometimes perfect is found in one body, yes." I wiggle the box over my figure. "You're lucky you found it before someone else came and snatched all this up."

Alarms sound off in my head. I let it slip, the insinuation Parker has staked any sort of claim on me other than platonic affection.

Then again, the way his eyes simmer in a dark, delicious heat, I'm not so sure he minds.

"Trust me," he says, voice rough. "I know."

He's close, *so* close. My brain is ping-ponging with a thousand things I want to have happen, a dozen more things I'm afraid to let happen, and every tendon on my right side seems to curl in on itself until I stumble.

The Lego box falls, and his arm catches me around the waist.

"Sorry," I breathe out, stretching my fingers until the tone in the tendons dies down.

With his arm still hooked around my waist he looks at my fingers. "Why do you do that? Stretch your hand."

This could crash and burn like the last guy who knew. Funny, but any of the former men I thought I wanted to give my everything to don't measure up to the sting that would come if Parker looked at me differently, or thought differently.

How is that possible? We have never crossed a line to anything more than friends.

Until now. This feels important. Like a new page is being flipped, and I'm not sure if I need to put a bookmark in or keep reading.

I can't let the past dictate the future. I can't put what others have said or done on Parker's shoulders. It isn't fair. Besides, the man who is supposed to be a vault has spent the last thirty minutes cracking the glass shield over his heart for me.

I hold out my right hand. The tips of my fingers are curled slightly since my heart is about to crack a rib. "It's involuntary—the tight muscles, I mean. When I get nervous, or excited, or uneasy, the muscle tone on my right side sometimes tightens and cramps."

He looks at me as if he knows there is more to come.

"I'm not good at telling people this."

Parker brushes a wisp of hair off my brow. "Neither was I."

"I told you I was in a car accident." My body stiffens at the memory. "I hit my head on the window so hard my . . . brain started to swell. Gave me a traumatic brain injury."

The words hang there in the open, empty silence.

"And?" Parker finally says.

"And there it is." Blood rushes to my face, words fly out unhindered. "I'm not blunt because that's my personality, I'm blunt because my filter was bruised. I-I-I didn't argue with your sister over books because I love to debate. When my brain gets too hung up on something it's hard to shut off. Titanic being a perfect example. This is why I told you if I let myself get tangled up in you, oh, I would tangle up so good, and wouldn't know how to wade out."

I pull back, fingers in my hair, tension gathering in my joints and limbs like a rope growing taut with each breath.

"I struggle to recall faces. Like tonight. For two hours I was mentally memorizing and re-memorizing the names of your friends and family. I recall long term facts about the Vegas Kings, right? But ask me what happened last season, and I'll need to Google it with everyone else. I mean, I didn't even know your face, Parker. How many times have I seen you on ESPN, or at a game? I still didn't recognize you.

"There are reasons I know what I'm talking about as a trainer—I've lived through it. I've learned how to regrow pathways in my brain and how to form new ones. I built with Legos, Parker. Helped me get my fine motor skills back in my hand. There were moments we weren't sure if I'd get any function back in my right side. So, there. That's it. I'm a lot to handle, and it will likely be a forever thing."

My hands go to my hips, I pace. Avoid his eyes.

The sound of his even breaths is deafening. I want to scream at him to speak. Say anything, just don't look at me like I'm broken.

"And?" is all he says. Again.

One word in his deep, rich timbre is enough to split me in two. "And? What?"

Parker chases the space between us, his hands trap my face like earlier, only this time there is a possessive gleam in his gaze, a silent look that says *mine*. Everything about his body, the way he cages me without being overbearing, the way his hips, shoulders, chest skim against mine sends a shiver of desire through my veins.

His.

Parker's thumb tugs on my bottom lip. "What part of this story is going to make me not want you?"

I don't have time to respond before he smashes his mouth onto mine. Nothing sweet, or gentle. It's hard, needy. Almost dirty. He uses the weight of his body to press mine against the wall. One of his palms glides off my cheek to my throat, holding there for a few breaths before falling to my hip, keeping me in place as he kisses me. And kisses me.

He kisses me until my knees quake, until my entire arm starts to curl inward.

"Parker." I pull back trying to get my hand and elbow to cooperate.

He grins with a touch of wickedness, then gently eases my thumb out of my curled fist first—like he knows exactly what to do. With the thumb out my fingers start to relax.

Parker threads our fingers together, one by one, then meets my eyes. "Hold onto me. Tight as you want."

The world tilts.

I narrow my eyes. If I'm his, he's mine.

No need to wait. I take the lead, arching my chin until our mouths meet again. He tastes like mint and sweet heat. I'm lost in a frenzy. My body wants to contract, but Parker is there, holding me steady, keeping my fingers spread, my arm down.

He's holding me like he was designed to hold me.

His teeth trap my bottom lip, a small nip, but the sly grin against my mouth is enough to turn my body inside out. My free hand grips his T-shirt, pulling him closer until not even a hairsbreadth remains between us.

He's assertive, demanding. The man exudes a ravenous confidence, as if all that he wants is all I am, and he is ready for the taking. One hand in my hair, tugging and tilting my face to the angle he wants. Next his palm moves to my jaw, my neck, my waist. Every touch spins my head until the room is an underwater dance of passion, desire, something like love.

Maybe I'll get my heart broken by falling for baseball's biggest heartbreaker.

But I think all the pain will be worth it if, even for a little while, I get to have Parker Knight.

Chapter 16

Parker

MY STOMACH IS TWISTED up all because I'm going to see a girl.

I think I've either reverted to junior high, or this is the anticipation, the excitement, the thrill of catching a glimpse of someone who holds a place in your heart Alexis and Bridger told me about when they were in their nauseating phase.

With women, I've always been confident, maybe even cocky. But only because when they spent time with me, I was Parker Knight the MLB pitcher with a big old paycheck. Our conversations consisted of small talk, the Vegas Kings, any luxury vacations they dreamed I'd take them on. For a few, I was merely a way to weasel closer to my brother-in-law and the band.

This is new and terrifying.

With Skye, she knows I'm not the suave, arrogant pitcher. No. Behind closed doors, I'm the guy who only hangs out with a select few people, takes pictures of dandelions, and has a room dedicated to building blocks.

And she wants me.

I scrub my hands down my face, idling in the parking lot of the field. The shoot will be in one of the rooms in the clubhouse, then some out on the field.

I'm two minutes late, and I still haven't left my truck. There is no reality where I'm going to walk in there like some hormonal d-bag who can't talk around a woman.

Skye knocked my world off its axis last night. I'm not inexperienced, but this, this is something new. There is a tomorrow. Hopefully many tomorrows. I want more, and more. Whatever Skye Anderson is willing to give me from that heart, I want again and again.

Tomorrows have never existed for me before, and I don't know what it all means. Where do we go? Are we dating? Friends with benefits?

With a groan I let my forehead fall to the steering wheel. I'm an idiot.

One deep breath, I try a few of the mediation exercises Skye taught us and it doesn't work since she taught them. My head is locked on her touch, her taste, the way she held me close in a way that was intimate and perfect. A closeness I never knew I wanted before.

I'm now five minutes late.

Rolling my eyes, I slip out of my truck, a duffel bag with some clothes in hand, and head toward the field.

The clubhouse is quiet, only a few staff members wander around. I return waves, muttered hellos, and try to forget the constant thrum of blood in my ears as I wait for Skye to pop around the corner at any moment.

She doesn't. But one look in the team room and my breath catches in my lungs. One corner is arranged as a makeshift dressing area. At a full-length mirror, Skye stands inspecting her reflection.

She's stunning.

Athletic pants, staged to fall just above her ankles, showing off brilliant white tennis shoes from one of our sponsors (naturally). A black Kings jersey that sort of drapes off her shoulder. Not in a sexual way, no mistake, it's sexy, but it looks tasteful and bold on her.

They have her ponytail high on her head, and she keeps touching her temple, tugging at her hair.

Any hint of reservation for seeing her after last night fades.

There is no possible way I can hold back and not step closer to her. The photographer is busy with his equipment set up at the front of the room, Alice is chatting with two women in lanyards and pencil skirts. No one has noticed me.

With careful steps, I hurry to the corner. A better man might announce his presence, but I've found a great deal of satisfaction making Skye gasp. My hand slides across her middle, smashes her back to my chest, then I press a kiss to the curve of her neck.

She jolts. At first. Two seconds is all the time needed before she sighs and melts against me.

"You smell good." I draw in a deep lungful of her summer sweet skin.

Skye threads her fingers through my hair on the back of my head, holding me close. "I used my special perfume with pheromones designed to attract sexy major league pitchers who look like Ragnar Lodbrok."

I let out a growl and wrap both my arms around her, hugging her close. "It's working."

Skye wiggles around, so she's facing me, her fingers still touching the hairline on her temple. She pecks my lips. "How are you today?"

"Honestly, I was nervous to see you."

She grins. "Me too. I felt like I was in middle school again."

"Well, we're going to say that's a good thing then." She touches her nose to mine as I pull her hand from her head. "What are you playing with?"

"Oh." She lowers her voice. "They pulled my hair up so high it's showing my scar." There is something awesome about the way she doesn't hesitate, not like she did last night, and shows me a faint, shiny scar that disappears beneath her hairline. "From surgery after the accident. I'm self-conscious about it."

I hold her face, turn her to the side, then press a kiss to the scar. Skye draws in a sharp breath, her hand gripping my shirt like she did last night. My new favorite thing. The way she tugged at me, it was like she wanted to crawl into my skin. I'd never felt so wanted, so needed.

"You better get ready," she whispers and takes a step away.

I scoop up my bag with the list of outfits we're supposed to wear. First up is my home jersey with a glove and bat. No hat for this one, and I'm not to smile. The only good thing about this will be posing next to Skye and getting her recognition for how she's handling a bunch of stubborn guys like a boss.

Knowing what she's gone through to get here makes her even more impressive. The world of sports should know it.

Once I'm dressed, the photographer starts snapping his fingers, to summon us, I guess. Skye bites her bottom lip, and keeps finding funny reasons to touch me.

"Shouldn't I wrap my leg around his waist?" or "What if I spread my palms over his chest like this?"

Not sure the photographer is amused by our wandering hands, but Alice looks like she's about to implode with giddiness. Truth be told, I'd do just about anything to keep Skye's hands on my skin, so his scowls mean nothing.

We're arranged in stern poses. Me with my glove, or shots of the bat tossed over my shoulder. Skye stands in a superhero pose with a fan blowing her hair around, I have a fist pounded in my glove.

"Let's try one more. Miss Anderson," the photographer says after we've been prodded and placed for the better part of an hour. "I want you to prop your elbow up on his shoulder. Then, Mr. Knight, your arm will go around her waist."

"Done."

"No." The photographer pushes my hand back when I basically engulf her in my grip. "No, I don't want to see your hand, just so it looks like you're standing close. We're creating a united front. Believe it or not there are still plenty of teams in the world who don't like women in charge of any department. Miss Anderson is shaking up your world, and you're going to show you're good with it."

When the photographer turns away, I draw my lips next to Skye's ear. "I'm definitely good with it."

She shudders under my hand. "Stop saying things like that, Knight, or I'll kiss you in front of everyone, and I like this lipstick."

"Later then, Anderson," I whisper. "Don't get too attached to that lipstick."

A soft moan hums from the back of Skye's throat and it takes all my grit to focus on the photographer's instructions. The end of the shoot finally wraps everything.

"I'll have the prints by next week, but *Sport Nation* will have the final say."

"And the article will run before spring training?" Alice asks.

The guy nods. "It should be out in the next edition, but again, I don't have any say on what is written. They'll be calling for interviews, I'm sure."

We get the chance to look at a few shots at the end. I'm not all that impressed with me, but next to Skye—we look pretty incredible together.

But the few glimpses of her body staged with mine has me ready to get out of here and find a place where we can be alone.

Skye must be capable of reading my mind because she pinches my side, waiting until I look at her. With a nod she gestures to the dressing area, a devious little grin on her lips. A second later, I'm pulling her away while the staff from *Sport Nation* packs up, and Alice takes a call from her kids' school.

I shove Skye behind one of the shades and waste no time putting my mouth on hers. It's a strange kind of desperate that comes out when I kiss this woman. Possessive, greedy, filled with more heat and pure affection in a way I've never known.

Skye smiles against my mouth, a little breathless, and breaks the kiss.

"I've wanted to do that all day," I whisper, holding her face in my palms.

"Parker?" Skye draws soft circles up my chest with her hands. "Can I tell you something?"

"Always." My lips hover above hers in a cruel torture forcing me to wait patiently for the next taste.

"Your strings are the best ones I've ever gotten tangled up in."

My heart jumps. If she's tangled in me, I'm devoured by her. What freaked me out twenty-four hours ago, now feels warm and right.

"I plan to keep you there, Anderson. Don't even try to cut loose."

"What if I did?"

I take her weaker hand and press it to the center of my chest. "Feel that? You'd take half of it with you if you did."

Skye's smile fades. For a minute I think I might've said something wrong. Until she digs her claws into my neck and yanks me against her lips, like staking a claim, making it clear to anyone who might see, I'm off limits.

Being tied to one person used to turn my stomach, now the idea of it is like the thrill of falling. I'm not certain of the outcome, but I would not miss this chance to see it all through for anything.

Chapter 17

Skye

"I FEEL LIKE I'M breaking a rule." Alexis looks over her shoulder at the empty doorway. "Maybe gaming the system."

I laugh and tickle baby Garett's feet where he wiggles on the therapy mat. "It's fine. This is my domain, and no one shall enter without my permission, nor tell us what we may or may not do with this little one."

Yes, my voice is basically Gandalf from *Lord of the Rings*, but by now Alexis is used to my weird, the same as her brother.

If I'm being honest, Alexis Cole is plenty weird on her own. And I love it.

Parker has been mine a few days shy of a month. It took Alexis about two of those weeks to get accustomed to seeing a repeat face with her brother. I'm not oblivious to the truth of Parker Knight, playboy of the Vegas Kings, but it is a truth I try to forget.

Especially when the man has me wrapped up in his arms, his mouth on me like I'm the only thing worth having in the world.

I worried how the team would treat me when the other Kings noticed their pitcher spent a lot of time in the therapy gym. No one seems to mind, then again, I'm also the owner's daughter. I doubt a player would be vocal to my face if they had any issues.

My dad—he's not a guy who keeps his head in the sand. Never straight up asked, but I'm positive Dallas Anderson is aware of what goes on with his players.

Mike is worse. My brother holds a level of mistrust, I think. We're not fitting into his algorithmic logic, I suppose. By all mathematical statistics, Parker Knight should've moved on long ago.

I give little Garett's neck a gentle nudge to the side. The muscles are tight and he's favoring one side too much. I pointed out the torticollis—a slight tilt to his head—over a week ago since one side of his soft skull has flattened a little too much.

I offered to help work the muscles to avoid a baby helmet. Although Parker already has a baseball themed one picked out if Gare needs it for a few months.

The baby whimpers.

"I know buddy," I coo at him. "It's not easy, huh? But guess what? You're finished for today."

I scoop him up and hand him off to Alexis.

"Thanks for doing this, Skye. Really, I feel like we need to pay you, or go somewhere else. I know you're probably insanely busy getting ready for spring training."

"It's busy, but he's the cutest thirty minutes of my week." I touch the fluff of hair on Garett's head. I can't stop, it's like silk and plush cotton all at once.

"I'm competing with my nephew? Not a fair fight."

Mmm. That voice will never grow old. I tickle Garett's tummy without turning around. "Great, big Uncle Parker is jealous, buddy."

An arm scoops around my waist, a kiss goes to my neck. A proper Parker greeting. Then, he's onto the baby. The big Viking can't resist his nephew, and he practically snatches him out of Alexis's arms.

"How's he doing?"

"He's still tight," I say, cleaning off the mat, "but it's not quite severe enough to go the helmet route yet. Check with your pediatrician if you want, but maybe a little more time and he'll be looking both ways. Oh." I snap my fingers. "Lex, I promised you a print-out of things you can do at home with him."

I hurry into my office alcove and grab the packet I'd made earlier and come back to Alice huddled between Alexis and Parker.

"Skye it's printed! The piece on you two."

"You guys are fire." Alexis beams. "Seriously, if I didn't already know you're making a wise man out of my brother, these pictures would have me convinced."

"Lex," Parker says, a bit of heat in his face. "Come on, they're professional."

"Some kid is going to hang this picture of Skye on his wall." Alexis points to a page in the magazine.

Parker scowls. "Maybe this was a bad idea."

I snicker and loop my arm through his, leaning my head on his shoulder. The pictures are beautiful. I'd been worried, but they're done in such a way, my heart is racing. My favorite is the one of Parker standing sideways, his taut jaw pulsed, fist in his glove, and me standing off his shoulder like I'm about to lead a rebellion.

He looks fierce. I look powerful.

The article doesn't give anything about my accident, and I'm grateful it focuses on my achievements more than some rise-from-the-ashes story. Parker is featured as the plot twist of baseball. It goes on for two paragraphs about the rarity of a relief pitcher vying for a starting position on the roster.

My man is amazing. Simple as that.

"I've got to head, but I wanted you to see the article," Alice says, then blows the room a kiss before she runs out the door.

"Well, I love these. I'm probably going to frame them," Alexis says and starts loading Garett into his car seat. "Park, did you talk to Skye about tonight?"

"Lex," he warns.

I scrunch my nose. "What?"

"Sorry," Alexis says in a lazy tone. I don't think she's all that sorry. She loops her arm through the handle of the car seat. "I thought you'd already said something."

Parker grunts. "I bet you did."

"What?" I squeeze his arm a little tighter.

"It's nothing."

"Are you holding out on me, Hot Shot?"

He faces me, and his shoulders slump. "Our mom wanted us to come over tonight, but I made sure to let her know we were busy."

"Are we?"

"We can be."

I let out a sigh. "I have thoughts, but I'm going to leave this between you two."

"What thoughts?"

"No. This is up to you." I turn back toward my office, but Parker is nipping at my heels.

"I want to know what you're thinking. You think I'm being stubborn? Think I should go?"

"Park, I'm not going to be the influencer here. This is your decision. I wasn't the one raised by your mom."

"Skye." He takes my arm, voice low. When I look at him again, his face is a little more broken. He dips his forehead to mine. "What do you think? I

. . . I don't know where to step here. I don't know if I should let things go or keep her shut out."

I'm one hundred and one percent in love with this man.

Once he let me in, he let me in. We laugh, joke, but there are these moments when he is so raw, I can practically see his bones.

I rest a palm to his cheek. "My thoughts are: life is short. We both know that. If you have unsaid things, I hope you face her and say them. If things can be repaired and healed, I hope—for your sake—you can find healing."

"One dinner isn't going to fix anything."

"Maybe not." I give him a quick kiss. "But you're a little torn, so maybe that's your gut telling you it might be time to find out if it's worth fixing or to walk away."

"Will you come with me?"

"Don't even need to ask."

He kisses me, slower, deeper. "Want to know something, Anderson?"

"Something is my favorite thing to know," I whisper.

"I'd give up the door for you."

A tight knot lodges in the back of my throat. I refuse to cry. The door, a nod at my unsubtle addiction to a sinking ship. No one has said anything so perfectly perfect to me before.

My fist curls in his T-shirt over his heart. I tug him closer. "Sorry to tell you, but it wouldn't happen. Not a chance. Because I wouldn't stop fighting until you were on the door too."

Parker chuckles. "This battle will never end."

"Not until you agree with me."

He shakes his head and leverages one hip on the edge of my desk. "Well, I concede. For now."

"Wise man."

Parker kisses the tips of my fingers. "I made you something, the reason I came here before I was distracted by the cutest baby and sexiest trainer." From inside his pocket he removes a small Lego figure.

I laugh and take it, stroking the long brown hair and Vegas Kings jersey. The Lego girl has a mini clipboard in her hand.

"Who is this?"

"That is a custom figure." He laughs a little nervously, like he might be embarrassed. "She's you."

"You made me a Lego?" I hold the figure to my chest.

"Well, she's one of a kind. Like someone else I know."

"Parker," I say as I peck his lips. "And you brought the sappy lines out too. I'm getting spoiled tonight."

He scoops his arms around me, and buries his face against my neck. "Don't forget how lucky you are, Anderson. You've got a guy who buys you Legos."

Parker is subtly self-deprecating, a habit I've learned he does when he's feeling insecure. I laugh with him, but inside, he's stolen my heart all over again with a tiny, simple gesture. He's my one-of-a-kind.

He's becoming everything.

WE DRIVE SEPARATE FROM Bridger and Alexis. They have plans to visit Bridger's mom across the street after this dinner.

I have no idea what to expect.

All I have are stories. Alexis corroborates what Parker told me; their upbringing was not easy. I don't know if I did the right thing by encouraging Parker to make peace or not. I'm out of my element here. Sure, I grew up in a broken home, but my parents were involved. They loved Mike and me more than anything, and they loved and respected each other.

Parker was ignored. When he wasn't, he was laughed at. Belittled.

For him to be as gentle and thoughtful as he is, in my opinion, is a sort of miracle.

We're still in his truck when Bridger and Alexis enter the small, single floor house. It's run down with age, red and pink rock in the yard, and a few knotty trees. My fingers lace with Parker's over the center console, and we sit in a nervous silence.

"How long has it been since you've come home?" I ask.

"Last Christmas. Stopped by for a few minutes. Not a lot was said before she had to go to work."

He doesn't look at me as he speaks. His eyes are trained on the house like it might disappear if he blinks. No rush. I make grand plans to sit in this truck as long as Parker needs me to sit in this truck.

Another minute, maybe two, he shoves his key in his pocket and mutely gets out of the truck. Parker hurries to my door, opens it, and reaches back for my hand. Not a word spoken. I have a thousand thoughts splattering across my brain, but he needs to take the lead here.

I bite the inside of my cheek to keep my mouth from running wild.

Parker grits his teeth at the door, takes a breath to the count of three, then leads me inside.

It's tidy inside, the tang of marinara sauce in the air, but burrowed in the walls is tension. From Parker's unyielding grip on my hand, or if disquiet is merely part of the skeleton of the house at this point, I don't know.

In the kitchen, Bridger and Alexis are already seated. A woman with hair that reminds me of a watercolor sunset, a little washed out in a mix of orange and red, but vibrant at the same time, hovers over Garett. She tickles his growing double chin, but at the shuffle of our feet, she turns around.

Her pale eyes drift to Parker first. Hesitation is there, and her smile is forced. Clearly, his mother is hiding her own unease.

"Hi, Park."

"Mom." He's gruff, and I think I might lose a finger if he doesn't loosen his grip on my hand. I'll go to nine fingers if he needs me to. No question. Parker clears his throat and nudges me forward. "This is Skye Anderson."

"Hi, Ms. Knight." I hold out my hand.

"You can call me Lila," she says and shakes my hand. The way she looks at me, then to Parker's hand in mine, I get the feeling she doesn't trust a hair on my head.

The feeling is mutual.

I'm putting on a friendly face, but rabid protectiveness reared up the second we walked through the door. If anything unkind is said, I'm ready to jump in front of Parker. Heck, I'm ready to leap in front of Bridger and Alexis too. I know things have happened with them, they're simply ready to put the past in the past.

If Parker doesn't get there, well, I'm on his side.

"So, you're . . . Parker's girlfriend?"

She must think I'm a jersey chaser, but the thing is, Parker and I haven't defined our relationship. I'm at a fork in the road and don't know which way he wants me to take.

He doesn't make me decide.

"Yeah," he says, sharply. "She's my girlfriend, and also the head trainer for the Kings."

I give him a small smile. He misses it since he's too busy scowling at the table as he plops into a chair, but I'll thank him later in the sexiest ways.

Lila lifts her brows. "The head trainer. That's a big job."

Parker scoffs under his breath—his mom doesn't hear it, but Alexis kicks his shin under the table.

"It is," I say. "But the team has been welcoming. It's helped with Parker having my back. They respect him a lot. I could do just about anything, and if he said do it, they would."

"Skye, please," Bridger groans. "Don't make his head bigger."

It brings a few stiff laughs. Even Parker smiles at his brother-in-law. His mom looks at ease, and places a boxed lasagna in the center of the table.

"Well, I'm glad you all could make it," she says. "Um, let's eat, I guess."

Things are . . . uncomfortable. For the first five minutes we pass around serving dishes, a pitcher of lemonade, and dish up our plates without a word. I'm sure nothing can make the pressure worse.

I'm wrong.

"Parker, do you not want pasta? Lasagna's your favorite," Lila says.

Parker's jaw flinches. He meets his mother's eyes straight on. "No, Mom. It's not. I actually don't eat red sauce and haven't since third grade when I puked it up in the lunchroom."

"I remember that," Bridger says, clearly trying to draw the boiling point back to a simmer.

Parker makes a fist with one hand under the table. "Lost my taste for it and fell in love with white sauce."

"Oh." His mom looks confused. "Must be Lex's then."

"Nope." The word rips out through Parker's teeth.

"Park," Alexis whispers.

He ignores her. "Alexis's favorite food is Holly's homemade tamales. Have been since her sixth birthday. Did you notice Holly made them every year to celebrate?"

I rest a hand on his forearm, give him a reassuring squeeze. His skin is hot, and I wish I could take the hurt from his voice.

Lila stares at the dish. "I swear someone loved lasagna."

"Maybe an old boyfriend. You paid attention to them plenty." With that, Parker slides his chair out and storms out of the kitchen.

As I said. Pressure can absolutely get worse.

Chapter 18

Parker

THE AIR HAS A bite to it, a desert chill that cuts. I close my eyes and breathe it in, filling my lungs until they can't expand any more.

In what universe did I think coming here would be a good idea? I'm too bitter. One trigger and I turn into a bear. No doubt, I've probably given Skye a glimpse into a guy she doesn't want. Who wants the baggage?

I'd take hers. The thought slaps me in the back of the head.

No mistake, if the tables were turned, I'd take all the baggage Skye could give me. She matters, and I don't want her to question us because I can't get rid of my prickly attitude toward my childhood.

"Hey." Bridger's voice makes me jump.

"Hey."

"You good?"

"No."

He steps to my side and stands quietly, waiting. The best part of Bridger Cole is he won't ever push me, not about this. I can be pigheaded. The only time he forced me to talk was when I flipped out after I learned he was secretly dating my sister. He had to bribe a staffer at Burton Field to get me to talk to him.

"I shouldn't have blown up like that," I admit.

Bridger shrugs. "Park, you shouldered everything in this house. No judgment here, man."

He never does.

I rake my fingers through my hair and stare at the darkening sky. "Not exactly the impression I wanted to give Skye. Think I scared her off?

Bridger snorts. "She's why I'm out here. I think you might want to go look at what your girl is doing in there."

My girl. I like the sound of it.

He doesn't need to say another word before I'm beelining it back into the house.

"Al is feeding Garett in her old room," Bridger whispers at my back. "I'm going to check on her."

"You're going to hide."

"One hundred percent." He claps me on the shoulder. "Oh, and listen—if you don't marry that woman, you're an idiot."

With those parting words, he abandons me to hide in a comfortable room with his peaceful little family while I face the fire out here.

From the sound of it the flames are starting to grow.

"I just think you're missing where he's coming from." Skye's voice. The sound trembles a little. From what I know of her, I have no doubt she's trying to keep it steady, but is feeling a great deal. Her fingers are likely tense, and she could use a guy to hold her hand to keep those fingers extended.

I'll pretend to be the hero, but the truth is the second I glance in the kitchen, I'm more the guy-damsel and she's the hot white knight.

My mom shakes her head, a familiar expression of frustration painted on her features. "He'll never give it a chance. Should've known. He's too stubborn."

"He is stubborn," Skye says. "He'd have to be to make it as far as he has, but I feel like you're making that into something negative. It's one of my favorite things about him."

"It is negative when he won't try to fix our family. Alexis is trying. I think he came here to be cruel intentionally."

Skye hesitates—no—she pauses and takes a deep breath as if calming her temper. She's going to battle for me, and I'm captivated.

"Lila," Skye says, voice low. "The problem with what you said is that you just placed fixing your family all on Parker. The way I see it, this isn't his responsibility."

"What are you saying?"

Skye breaks all my expectations and reaches out, resting a hand over my growly mother's fidgety palm.

"I'm saying, acknowledge him," she says with nothing but kindness. "Be honest with yourself about the things that happened while he was growing up. Things that, for him, might've been difficult and painful. He has responsibility for how he behaves now as a man, but he does not shoulder the things childhood and . . . adults in his life forced upon him."

"I can't change the past."

"You're right, you can't. But don't pretend like those scars aren't there. One nice gesture, because this dinner is a nice gesture, isn't going to blot out those parts of him that hurt."

"So, I'm supposed to do all the work to fix everything; my kids don't need to put in any effort?"

"Lila, Parker showed up. Maybe you thought he and Lex could put big smiles on and let bygones be bygones, but that is rarely the case. The fact that he came at all, well, that is him trying. He didn't have to."

Skye is amazing, but she's fighting an impossible war. Lila Knight will never budge in her obstinance. I know where I get my own bullish head. But maybe Skye has a touch of magic because my mom slumps in her chair.

"I don't know how to even begin," she admits, softly. "How do you fix so many years?"

"Oh, you don't," Skye says. "You move forward. Start by acknowledging your son is a wonderful man despite things that have happened to him. And please don't downplay his past hurt, or it will create a new scar."

"I did try, you know. I kept them fed, kept a roof over their heads."

"You did, but I think you know those aren't the things behind the hurt."

"I know." My mom sighs and scrubs her face. "I know I get defensive. I'm sure it comes from guilt and . . . a lot of disdain for things I've allowed to happen."

"I get it. It's hard to be presented with our wrong moves, but we need to look them in the eyes, memorize them, so we never do them again, you know?"

"You must think I'm horrible."

Skye takes a sip of lemonade. "No, we just met. I take a little while to form opinions, but I have an insanely high opinion of your son, so I'm going to have his back. Doesn't mean I won't have yours someday too. But you can't hurt him, or I'm not even going to come close to your side of the line." She winces. "Was that rude to say?"

"No." My voice is rough as sandpaper. Both my mom and Skye whip around. My pulse won't stop racing. I reach for Skye's hand and bring her knuckles to my lips. "I've never heard a rude word out of your mouth."

"Give it some time, Knight," she whispers, concern written on every surface of her face.

I smile. "Do you think I could have a second alone with my mom?"

"Of course." She jolts to her feet, but takes time to tell my mom thank you for letting her come. Skye pecks my lips. "I'll be outside."

When we're alone, I lean my hands on the back of a chair, burning my stare at the table. I'm not sure how long my mom and I stay in silence, but my body is exhausted from clenching by the time I speak. "Mom, I appreciate the gesture. I do. But I think, for me, maybe we should start smaller. Meet for lunch. Coming here, acting like we're all good, is too much for me right now."

My mom's lip quivers. "Was it all so bad that you hate this house, Park?"

I close my eyes. "It wasn't always bad, no. But there was a lot of bad, Mom. A lot."

Where I expect her to argue, she doesn't. My mom nods and stares at her hands. "So, what do you want to do, Park?"

What did I want? For years, I've convinced myself this door was closed, but Skye called it. There is a piece of me that does want to see the fractures in this family healed. I don't know if it'll be worth the risk, but maybe it'll pay off to find out.

"How about we meet, just you and me, before I go to training."

My mom nods again. "I'd like that."

Anger still burns, heady and thick under my skin. A large part of me wants to shout at her, tell her all the things that are burned in my memory, but the softer part is content to leave it there.

"I'm going to take off if that's good," I say.

"Okay. I'll, um, I'll call you."

"I'll answer." I stand, pausing at the front door. "Thanks for . . . trying."

You'd think I told her she was the best mom in the world, the way she looks at me. I can wade through the walls of bitterness to notice there is a great deal of remorse in Lila Knight. Whether she can prove she's turned a new page or not will be determined, I guess.

My shoulders aren't weighed down when I step outside. A good thing because I have plans for Skye Anderson.

To see her fight for me unlocked a heat, a need inside I can't quite grapple with, but if I don't do something this tightness in my chest is going to explode.

Skye leans against my truck. At the sight of me, she smiles. "Are you o—"

I don't let her finish before I have my hands on her and I'm pulling her mouth to mine. I kiss her. Hard. She takes everything, digging her fingers through my hair, tugging on the ends.

I don't know what I'm doing. I'm terrified. Excited. A collision of emotion balls in my chest until, like her, my filter breaks, and the racing thoughts spill out. "I've fallen in love with you, Anderson."

Skye gasps against my lips. Her glassy eyes lift to mine. Fingertips stroke the stubble on my jaw. "Oh, you have no idea how much I love you."

I kiss her again. And again. I'd be content to stay like this all night. I do have some consideration for her need to draw a breath and dip my chin, breaking the kiss. My brow rests against hers. "So, you're good with my strings?"

"Knight, tangle me up. I'm yours."

The smile pulls at my lips. There isn't bitter anger rushing through my blood anymore. There is only her.

Chapter 19

Skye

MY BED IS COVERED in clothes ready to be rolled and folded. We're off to Arizona in two days. spring training for pitchers and catchers is officially beginning. To be the one who gets to watch over the team while they strut their feathers for fans and fellow teams is half the reason I wanted this job.

I love the intensity, the anticipation of the season.

To be in the thick of it, working on their aches and pains, stretching their limbs, is a thrill only nerds who love a good anatomy lesson will understand.

With the Scorpions, I only traveled at the end of spring training. This time, I'm going to be there from the beginning. The rest of the training staff will hold down Burton Field with the rest of the team until they join us in a few weeks.

What the beginning of spring training means is Parker.

True, the rest of the pitchers will be there, along with Griffin and the two other catchers from the Scorpions. But Parker is front and center in my head. A few weeks of working side by side, day after day. My stomach tightens in excitement.

With a quick glance at the clock on the wall, my heart speeds up. He'll be here soon.

I'm anxious to ask him how it went today. Parker decided to meet with his mom one-on-one at a small café. It could go either way, and I want to know what side of the line I'm standing on. Open-arms toward the woman who gave him life, or in front of him like his own personal shield-maiden.

My phone rings and I fumble across my bed to snag it, anxious to hear his voice, and don't even glance at the screen.

"Hi!"

"Hi." A non-Parker man's voice returns. "I didn't expect you to sound that happy to talk to me."

I groan when it registers. There isn't even a concern about whether I'm being rude or not. "Oliver. I thought you weren't you. Trust me, I would've answered much differently if I took the time to read the name."

"Come on, Skye."

"Come on, Skye." I mimic him and roll my eyes. Ugh. Why do I allow the man to get under my skin until I'm petty as middle school? "What do you want?"

He pauses. "Look, I know you're probably hurt by what I did."

Nope. I haven't thought of Oliver Thackery in nearly two months. That is the power of Parker Knight and those delicious hands of his. "Really, I'm fine. Is there something you need? I can't imagine why you'd be calling me otherwise."

"I saw the *Sport Nation* spread." There is a smile in his voice. "You look good."

"Amazing what a professional makeup artist can do. Thanks for the call, Oliver."

"Skye, please. I want to apologize for how I acted. I sort of lost sight of things, and I don't want to go into spring training with bad feelings."

My chest pinches. The Utah Gulls are in the Cactus League, and . . . I close my eyes. Oliver will be there. With the pitchers and catchers.

A black cloud blows over my head and devours all the excitement I had two minutes ago.

"I shouldn't have reacted the way I did when I was traded. I guess I didn't know how we'd make it work when you bleed for the Kings, and I was moving."

"See, that part I can understand," I say softly. "It's the other things I'll never get. Things no one should ever say to someone they supposedly care about."

Parker has scars. But so do I. Some I've never mentioned. If he knew, I have a feeling there would be no friendly rivalry between two pitchers.

"Maybe I came off harsh, but I really was trying to look out for you."

"I see." My voice is flat. Unbidden, a sharp pain tugs at my heart as forgotten insecurities try to leech into my head. Try to take over. "Is that why you told me no one in the MLB would make me the head of anything with my deficits? No one except my dad, of course. Is that why you tried to ruin my chances before they even started?"

"I wanted you with me. With my contract you wouldn't have needed to work; we could've moved here together and had a life without the umbrella of your family."

"So, you did things to hurt me because I wanted to reach my goals? You called the Commissioner of Baseball, Oliver. What was that supposed to do?"

His voice takes on a hard tone. "Don't raise your voice at me."

"I'll do as I please. You don't have a say anymore."

This is not a man I should antagonize, but time apart has strengthened my resolve, reminded me of worth I forgot I had.

"I spoke with the commissioner to ensure he understood everything if you took the job," he says. "The leagues deserve the best staffers, including trainers."

"Naturally, I couldn't possibly be one of the best." A bite of angry tears threatens to rise. I refuse to give him the satisfaction. "Why did you call today? What is the point of talking about this?"

"I didn't want to talk about it," he snaps. "You brought it up. I just wanted to clear the air before spring training. I hoped we could, I don't know, get together. Be friends again. I thought some time apart was the best thing and . . . I care about you still, Skye. I thought maybe we could start fresh."

The thing about my hopelessly romantic heart is once upon a time it fell for the slightest attention. I know, it sounds weak minded. But for years I battled with the notion that I was somehow broken. Then spent years in counseling trying to unlearn those thoughts I'd shaped.

Still, when a man, handsome, successful, and talented like Oliver said he wanted me—I fell hard.

I ignored comments from others on the outside. Warnings from my mom, my dad, even Mike who is the most black and white thinker I know. Those bright, blood red flags I can see clearly now that a gentle, kind man worked to earn my heart sincerely.

Oliver controlled me. Dictated my life, and I didn't see it.

I smile with a touch of relief, tears in my eyes, grateful that tonight I will be in the arms of a man who thinks I could rule the world if I wanted to.

"I don't think we can, Oliver."

"Skye, don't be immature, you know I hate that. It's just one dinner."

"I'm seeing Parker Knight."

This will hit him hard. Parker doesn't know it, but Oliver holds unwarranted resentment for him. The closer was never supposed to move up from a relief pitcher when Jovi Green retired. Scorpions anticipated they'd be pulled to the major leagues, and Oliver was the first in line to be considered.

What he needs to realize is Parker earned his shot. He's worked for this, he's doing something rather unprecedented, and deserves a chance to be a starting pitcher.

As expected, a thick silence takes up the line. A shuffle on the other side paints a picture in my mind. No doubt Oliver is sitting up, fists clenched, jaw tight, the burn of his temper in his gaze.

His words are tight and scrape out like rusted nails. "Well, don't you get around."

It's a slap, but there isn't a sting. Not anymore. "Goodbye, Oliver."

I hang up, toss my phone aside, then flop onto my folded clothes. Deep breaths calm the ache in my chest. Exhales soothe the burn in my blood. Oliver doesn't deserve my energy. He certainly doesn't deserve the opportunity to crush me. If I let him, only I lose.

I'm repeating all my inner mantras when the front door clicks with a beep, announcing someone with my code is here.

I know exactly who it is.

Scrambling off my bed, I dart for my entryway. Parker has barely closed the door behind him by the time I leap into his arms.

"Oof." He stumbles back against the wall, hands running up my spine in slow strokes. "Hey to you too."

I pull back, then kiss him. Parker seems a little taken back by the force of it, but like a good boyfriend he's all-in half a breath later.

My arms curl around his neck, holding him closer as he opens the kiss, goes deeper. His hands dig into my hair, his mouth finds my jaw, my throat. When he pulls back for a short pause, his eyes are green fire. Parker scoops his hands beneath my thighs, carrying me to the couch in my front room. I pull him over me and hold him like letting go will leave me stumbling toward destruction.

Time is irrelevant. All I know is when we pull back his hair is on end, my breaths are shallow, and my lips sting.

I hold his stare as my fingertips trace the smooth line of his chin. "I love you. It's real with you."

A soft smile tugs at the corner of his mouth as he presses a gentle kiss to my nose. "It's real, Anderson. I'm not complaining or anything about being jumped in your entryway, but are you okay?"

I smile. "Ready for my cheesy line?"

"Always."

"I'm good now that you're here."

"Mmm." He growls against my neck. "Dirty talker. But you need to let me go."

"No."

"You need to."

"I refuse." To prove my point, I hold him tighter.

"If you don't let me go," he mumbles against my skin, "then I can't set up my epic date night. Trust me, you're going to want this date night."

"Fine." I release him. "Go. Be free. Wait! I didn't even ask, how did it go with your mom?"

He shifts on his feet. "Uh, it was . . . weird."

"Bad weird?"

"No." Parker scratches the back of his neck. "We sort of caught up on basic things. It's weird I have to tell my favorite food, my hobbies, my likes and dislikes to my mom. But, I don't know, it didn't feel bad at the end of it."

I smile and drape my arms over his shoulders. "You're amazing."

"Because I had lunch with my mom?"

"Yes. A lot of people wouldn't even make the effort, and I would not blame them. But your heart is big, Viking. You want to fix things, and I just think you're amazing."

He pulls me close and buries his face in my hair. "You're making it hard to get this date night going."

"Fine." I nudge him back. "I won't distract you, at least not for the moment. What am I supposed to do while you set up?"

"You are in charge of ordering food. Get whatever you want, then meet me in the backyard. But don't look until food is ready, got it?"

I lift one brow. "Knight, what are you up to? I thought we were going to a movie. Are you throwing a changeup here? Pun—"

"Intended!"

This is how lame we are. We officially try to out pun each other, and I love it.

"Just trust me," he says. "Order food. Meet me outside. Get your world rocked."

"Sold." I kiss him again. "You should've led with the world rocking part."

He laughs and swats my backside as I scurry away. If I don't leave, I'll be tempted to peek at whatever grand plans he's creating in my backyard, and temptation is too much, so I opt to pick up the food. All to get me out of the house.

Once I'm home, bags of curry in hand, dusk has settled. My house is dark, the only proof that Parker is still in there is his truck in my driveway.

"Park?" The kitchen is empty, but soon I bite my lip between my teeth.

Candles form a pathway leading to my sliding glass door at the back of the house. My skin tingles. I quicken my step and hurry out into the backyard.

Once there, my breath catches.

"Oh, good." Parker pokes his head out from behind a white projector screen. "You're back."

"What is this?" In the twenty minutes I've been gone, he's set up a bed of sorts with pillows and blankets. Two buckets of theater-style popcorn, candied nuts, and wine. It's all set up in front of the massive screen.

"Dinner and a movie," he says, clapping his hands as he backs away from his set up. "And . . ." Parker presses the button on the projector. The image of the title pops up and I'm not even embarrassed when I let out a little squeal.

"Are you sure you want to do this, Knight?" I go up on my toes, grinning. "It could get scary."

He laughs and wraps me up in his arms. "I've been waiting for this since I met a sexy trainer at a Titanic expo."

I kiss his cheeks at least five times, his lips at least ten, then plop myself onto the pillows and blow-up mattress. The screen is paused on a shot of the slow waves in a dark ocean, the word *Titanic* spread over the screen.

Parker settles next to my side and takes one of the boxes of food.

I wiggle a little bit until I'm nestled right next to him. "Everyone else avoids this movie with me like it's a disease."

Parker presses a kiss to my temple. "It's your favorite. I want to do all the favorites with you."

My heart swells. I rest my head on his shoulder. No question, he owns every piece of my heart.

Chapter 20

Parker

I MISSED BASEBALL. THE scent of dirt and grass, sweat and leather. On the field with Spring fans screaming out names—I belong on this field.

This year's spring training has been incredible for a few reasons. My pitch speed bumped up a mile an hour, my accuracy is up, and after every practice I have a gorgeous trainer to chastise me for not warming up right, or about my inflammation.

She might gripe at me, but each visit ends in her arms around me, and her kiss mine to take.

To have Skye here has been the frosting on a perfect cake. But tomorrow is when the last part of the fun begins. The rest of the team will be here, and the idea of scrimmaging together again is keeping a dopey smile on my face.

"Food." Griffin moans and basically salivates as he takes the carton of falafel from the street cart. He inhales again and lets his head fall back in a sigh.

"You're making too many sounds over that food," I tell him and pay for my own order.

"I can't help it. Got to get used to all the up and down since you don't pitch straight."

"You're not talking about me. I know you're not."

Griffin chuckles and follows me down the sidewalk back toward the field. "I'm going to get serious on you this once—Park, you're on point out there. I don't know what changed, but—oh, wait—yes, I do. You've been meditating."

"I have. Among other things."

"Nice." Griffin smiles. "Honestly, I *have* been doing Skye's stuff. I'll probably tease her until the end of time about incense and mind work, but dude, it helps. I'm more focused."

I know the team is sold on Skye Anderson as our trainer, but it means something to hear from one of my best friends that her techniques are not only being implemented, but they're respected. She'll want to hear it, and I plan to tell her before we hit the field again for the afternoon.

"She'll be glad to hear it."

"So, how is it with Dallas?"

I shrug. "Honestly, I haven't seen much of him. He's been friendly whenever we see each other. I don't think he has an issue."

"Did you fill out any paperwork?" Griffin asks. "Isn't there some form when Kings employees get together?"

"Yeah." I rake my fingers through my hair. "I didn't hear from him directly, but his signature came back on it, so I guess he's good with it."

"What can he do?" Griffin goes on. "It's not like she's his little girl. She's almost thirty."

True, but I had anticipated a few more glares from the man. Maybe a one-on-one. For all I know he's biding his time. "I'll take it as a good sign that I'm still on the field and not buried behind his massive house."

"Way to think positive. What about Mike?"

"He's cool," I say. "But I've got to be honest. He looks at me like he's always trying to figure me out. He's sort of gone off radar. You know how the math guys are, they're tracking draft and scout reports right now. Maybe this summer he'll come up for air and we'll get to know each other better."

Griffin takes a huge bite and talks with his mouth full. But it's just us. Who cares? "It's weird to hear you talk long-term relationship stuff." My teeth clamp tightly, but Griffin barrels on. "Hey, I don't mean it bad. I'm happy for you, man. Skye's great. She passes the Alexis test, she's not star-struck by Bridger and the guys, and she told your mom off."

I'm starting to worry about how much Griffin, Bridger, and Alexis share about me. I'm almost positive they have their own group text.

"I love her, Griff."

His brows kick up. "Wow. The big one, huh? Good. Get off the market. Maybe the magazines will start posting my pretty face as baseball's bachelor."

"They already do."

Griffin sobers too quickly. "Speaking of all that, you know eventually it's going to get out. Think there will be blowback? She is an Anderson. People could cry favoritism."

To be honest, I've worried about the same thing. "It might happen, but my track record should speak for itself, as should Skye's. Neither of us are rookies, you know. And it only matters what our team thinks anyway."

Griffin takes another massive bite. "No worries there; she won everyone over with Zumba."

I laugh. More than one image of the Kings' dance-off made it to the internet. I think we even became a meme.

My shoulder hits another body. I hold out a hand. "Whoa, sorry." Three guys pause on the sidewalk, ballcaps on with a fierce looking seagull on the front. Players from the Utah Gulls. My back stiffens, my voice lowers. "Sorry about that."

The man in the center looks at me with an arrogance I don't like. "No worries, Knight."

I know exactly who he is. Not because I recognize him from his time with the Scorpions. I searched out the draft picks like I promised and was promptly reminded of the Scorps pitcher who signed with Utah last year.

"Thackery."

"Wow. Didn't know the Kings' ace would know my name."

What a douche. "Not the ace. Yet. But I make it a point to know the names of people I think I should keep an eye on."

Griffin slaps my bicep. His face is hard. "Let's get to the field, man."

"Yeah," Oliver says, crossing his arms over his chest. The guy is probably two inches shorter than me, but he's not small. Clearly, he's flexing, and he looks like a fool for it. "Run on back, boys."

I scoff. "Really? Is that your version of a burn, Thack?"

"Parker," Griffin warns. "Come on."

Oliver steps closer. "Not a burn. We just know how much you need to impress old man Anderson."

"What's that supposed to mean?" Now, I'm taking a step for him. Griffin grabs my arm, one of the Gulls grabs Oliver's.

Oliver has a smile I want to smash off his face. I knew he'd be here, but Skye and I have managed to avoid the Gulls and any of their pitchers. It's like he sniffed me out.

After a few tense seconds, Oliver chuckles and returns to his teammates. "Nothing, Knight. Means nothing." He turns around. Should've known a jerk like this guy couldn't let it go, and before I have a chance to follow Griffin, he's back around, running his mouth. "Oh, before I forget—enjoy my leftovers."

Red. That's all I see. I'm on him in two seconds. In three, Griffin has me in a bear hug, pulling me away.

"Parker," Griffin says through a grunt. "Leave it."

"Don't talk about her," I snarl, pulling against my friend. One swing. I'd have his nose cracked in one swing.

It'd feel amazing.

Griffin somehow maneuvers between me and this psycho, hand on my chest, scowl pointed at the other Gull players. "Keep your dog on his leash. We don't disrespect your team, especially not your staffers. If you want to go there, find a different league, boys."

"Thackery," a Gull—the one who seems to have some reason—says as he tries to pull Oliver away. "Walk away. What's with you?"

Oliver shakes off his teammate and aims his stupid face at me. "My bad. That was too far."

"Yeah." I spit out the word on the sidewalk, glaring at him.

With Oliver pulling back, the two Gulls turn toward the parking lot of food trucks. Griffin taps my shoulder, a signal to keep moving, but Oliver calls my name again.

"Parker, wait. There is something I think you should know."

I give Griffin a look. His jaw tightens and he sticks to my side.

Oliver wears a cruel grin. "One guy to another, you think your girl is all into you because she acts like you make her world spin, right? Don't fall for it. It's part of her issue. You're like a shiny new toy, and when she sees a new one, she moves on."

"You need to walk away."

"She did the same with me," he hurries on. "I didn't drop her, she did. Just likes to tell people she's the jilted one. Squashed my future with the Scorps and the Kings with her lies. Made it so my contract didn't get renewed. If the Gulls hadn't made the offer for the trade, Dallas would've seen to it I was kicked out of the league."

I don't believe it. Even if Skye did end things first with this tool, I'd give her a freaking high-five for doing it.

"Thanks for the warning, but I'm going to need you to stay out of my relationship with my girlfriend."

"I almost believe you care about her, Knight. I always took you for a hit it and quit it type."

"That's enough," Griffin says.

Oliver holds up his hands. "I don't like being disrespected, you get me? And the Andersons, they disrespected me, in the game, and in Skye flaunting her new plaything for the entire league to see."

This guy is a piece of work. He's a replica of the men who filtered in and out of my house growing up. Cruel. Vindictive.

The hair lifts on the back of my neck.

"Be aware," Oliver says, "I tend to lash out when I've been disrespected."

My chest smacks his. "Are you threatening Skye?"

"I know things," he says. "Things Skye showed me, gave to me, back when I thought she was it. Things that might cast doubt on the beautiful new trainer's ability to do the job."

"There is nothing about her that would keep her from doing her job."

"I doubt everyone will see it the same. It'd be a shame if she was viewed as incompetent."

"You need to know this about me," I say, voice dangerously low. "You lash out at disrespect, I lash out when people I love are threatened."

"My contract with Utah is a year, Knight. They'll renew, but I want options. Tell Dallas Anderson to buy me back, and put me on the mound, I might forget to go to the League about how the Kings' trainer is a liability."

"He's joking." Griffin holds a new anger in his eyes. "I know this douche pickle did not try to extort you."

I barely register what Griffin says. My eyes are locked on Oliver. There isn't light in his eyes. They're empty, a little wicked. Honestly, I believe he's messing with me, but his threat churns my gut.

"You better walk away, Thackery," I spit out through my teeth. "*Now.*"

He laughs. "Thought you were smarter, Knight. Maybe Skye is rubbing off on you. You know, because she's, uh, well she's not all there."

He taps the side of his head.

Griffin curses under his breath, but his hands fall away from me. Almost like he's giving me permission.

With the gatekeeper gone, my fists curl around Oliver's shirt and I have him pinned down in three seconds. I've never been a brawler. One or two fights in high school with bullies who tried to harass my sister. I'm not the one who resorts to violence.

Unless you mess with those who are locked tightly in my heart.

Skye has the largest real estate in this thing in my chest. All I feel is hot, red rage when I hit Oliver Thackery in the face. He swings, striking my shoulder. It burns. Then, he strikes it again.

He's hitting my pitching arm intentionally.

The Gulls wheel back around. They must notice his direct hits because they both start shouting bad form. He's crossing a line, and I'm allowing it because I can't shake the fight response.

Blame it on a rough home life, I don't care. Skye's face is the only thing in my mind right now.

Somehow Griffin manages to pull me off. Oliver's nose is soaked in hot blood. He spits on the sidewalk. We're surrounded by cell phones. The clicks of cameras are everywhere. I don't care. The Gulls grip Oliver behind the neck.

"What is wrong with you? You'll be suspended for that," one hisses.

"Park," Griffin says close to my ear. "Come on. Walk away."

I grit my teeth and force my steps to aim for the field. My body is on fire, and I can't remember a time when I was so angry. It isn't until we're through the security leading inside the field, once adrenaline begins to fade, that I feel the sharp jab in my arm.

It's swollen from the pummeling it took, and the nerves tingle in pain all the way to my fingertips.

"Griff." My face pulls into a grimace as I reach for my arm.

Griffin curses again. He doesn't need to say anything; he knows. "Come on. We've got to find Skye."

Right now I have to think of her as my trainer. This is my career. My arm is worth millions, and I need her to work her magic to reverse my stupidity.

Still, it doesn't mean I'm not terrified to face her. No mistake, this'll be my last spring training because Skye Anderson is going to murder me.

SHE HASN'T SAID A word. Skye keeps cutting tape, her mouth pinched into a tight line as she works. Shirtless, lathered in pain relieving cream, massaged, and stretched, I sit with my gaze pinned on the ground.

Skye's face said it all when she looked at my arm—I might've done damage. Possibly cut down the years I can be called a King.

Griffin and his big mouth blurted out what happened, then beelined it to safety outside the gym. From that moment on, Skye has been mute. Anxiety stacks like heavy blocks in my chest. From my girlfriend giving me the cold shoulder or because I might've screwed up my career, I don't know.

Skye returns and begins placing the rubbery pieces of kinesiology tape across the grooves of my ligaments and muscles. Soon a web of tape covers my entire shoulder.

"I don't want you moving it more than eating and showering for forty-eight hours."

"Skye . . ."

"Take Ibuprofen for swelling."

"Skye."

She turns her back on me. "Make sure you alternate between ice and heat and—"

"Skye!" My voice croaks, and I'm ashamed.

But she wheels around at the sound. I meet her gaze. My eyes sting and I don't even know why. All at once everything strikes me like poisonous darts, one after the other. Why was I so stupid? Why did I let him get under my skin in such a way that I'd get into a fist fight? To just let him hit my arm.

Skye's disappointment tossed into the mix is almost more than I can take.

But I don't know what to do. I don't know what I need from her, all I know is I need her. I'm ashamed to even ask, ashamed to show a bit of weakness when I've been the protector all my life. The one who didn't let wild emotions take over.

I grip the edge of the table, squeeze my eyes shut. My arm trembles from the damage done, but soon it stops when gentle fingers brush over the tops of my shoulders.

Skye stands in front of me. Her palm touches the side of my face, lifting my eyes to hers. She smiles softly, then with one smooth motion, she hugs my head to her chest. My body falls into her. Arms go around her waist, clinging to her like a lifeline. Skye rests her cheek on the top of my head, she kisses my hair, holds me tighter.

I shudder. No. In this instance there is no crying in baseball. It's the fear of losing all I've worked for taking hold. I let out a shaky breath, and Skye strokes the back of my neck. Soft, easy motions that soothe the muscles until I'm pliable in her hands.

"Parker," she whispers in my hair. "Why did you hit him?"

I smile even if she can't see my face. "I just wanted to take one for the team."

She lets out a wet laugh. If I had to guess, it's a reluctant one. Like she doesn't want to give me the satisfaction. Still, she whispers, "Pun intended."

"Please tell me I didn't ruin my career."

She pulls away and uses both hands to lift my chin. With a sigh, she presses her forehead to mine. "I will not let you ruin your career. Listen to me, follow my care instructions, and you'll be out on the field. And promise me, no matter what Oliver says, you will not engage him. Park, he gets a thrill off it."

At that, I lift my head, a narrowed look on my face. "Did he hurt you? Be honest with me. Did he put his hands on you when you were with him?"

She pecks my lips. "No. But now that I've stepped away, I do realize how controlling he was. That's all this is, Park. He's jealous you got the roster spot he wanted, and now you've got me. He can't manipulate me into giving him clout in the MLB and he's retaliating because he's feeling like he has nothing to control."

Her wrist is close to my face. I kiss her pulse point and pull her against me with my uninjured arm. "Don't go close to him, Skye. Not alone, at least. He puts off creep vibes, and I've known my fair share. Promise me."

She kisses me. "I promise. If you do the same and listen to me when it comes to that arm."

"You're being demanding." I tighten my hold around her waist. "I like it."

She rolls her eyes, then steps back to pick up the supplies at the same time the door swings open.

My blood chills. Dallas strides in like the world would stop turning if he simply gave the order. At his back is my pitching coach and Buck, the guy who seems to keep the field running across all departments.

Dallas has pure fury in his eyes. He's young to be an owner of a team, but I've seen him make older men stop in their tracks. Right now, I'm the one in his track.

"I want to know your side, Knight." It's a command. Not a request.

"Dad," Skye starts, but falls quiet when he flashes her the same harsh look.

I meet his eyes and nod. "Marks and I were out for lunch. We ran into some guys from the Gulls and I, uh, I took issue with some of the things Thackery said." I let my eyes drift to Skye. She's quietly picking up her workspace, but her face is a deep red, like she's holding her breath too long.

"So, you fist fight like a couple of wet teens?" Coach snaps, then curses my name.

My jaw pulses. "I should've walked away."

"But?" Dallas presses.

"There isn't a but, sir."

He narrows his eyes. "There is. You've been a King for years and have never had anything like this happen. Why *didn't* you walk away?"

I'm not going to tell a father the disgusting way Oliver spoke about his daughter. The threats he made. Dallas seems like a chill guy, but the way he's looking at me right now, if I had to guess, he'd be out for blood.

"Knight," he grits out when I keep quiet.

"It was because of me, Dad," Skye says.

I glare at her. "Skye, I made the choice."

She ignores me and faces her father and Coach again. "Oliver made insinuations about me and mocked my brain injury. According to Griffin, they tried to leave, but Oliver made the comment. Parker decided to let it get to him, which I wish he wouldn't have, but Oliver should never have gone after the golden arm. It's bad form and downright bad sportsmanship when he knows exactly what it means to mess up a pitcher's shoulder. That does not mean this guy" –she gestures at me – "did not behave idiotically. I'm just saying he was the lesser idiot."

It should sting that she's pointing to me, but I smile.

"But," she goes on, "if he listens to me, he should be okay in a couple days."

Through her entire spiel the three new men in the room have a few reactions. Buck chuckles and gives me a thumbs up. Coach mutters under his breath, but now I think his hostility is aimed at conversations he's going to have with the Gulls' pitching coach, and Dallas hasn't blinked.

He closes in on me. "On this team, we don't pick fights. Not for trash talk, not for anything, Knight."

"Yes, sir."

He flicks his eyes to my coach. "He's suspended from the first scrimmage."

I close my eyes, but don't even think of arguing. I know fighting is against the conduct agreement. Frankly, one game is more than fair.

"Now, on a personal note." Dallas wheels back on me. "I haven't spoken to the Gulls' trainer, but . . ." He pauses, lowering his voice. "I hope you broke his nose."

I fight a grin. "You and me both, sir."

Dallas puts his hands on his hips, nodding his fury at the ground. "All right. Take care of that shoulder."

He gives Skye a tight smile, then wheels back around, still on a warpath. Once we're alone, I breathe a little easier.

"Well, Hot Shot. What are we going to do tonight since you're not allowed to do anything rigorous, or I'll destroy you?"

"You're scary." I smile. "I just want to be with you."

She tilts her head, hand to her chest. "Ah, Park. Did you make that cheesy line just for me?"

"Anderson, every line I have to give is yours."

She laughs and wraps her arms around my waist when I stand off the mat. "Let's stay in and avoid people."

"Sounds perfect."

I don't know what I did to deserve her, but Skye is a perfect relief from the stress of life. She calls me out, then has my back when she's done.

I love her. In the back of my head, Oliver's threat is alive and well. Does he have something he could use against Skye? I don't know. I doubt it. Guys like him are bullies, and dish out empty threats to make themselves look bigger. When called on it, they cower and disappear back to the hole they scurried from.

For now, I'll push Oliver Thackery far out of my mind.

I wish it could've stayed that way.

Chapter 21

Skye

LEAGUE OFFICIALS HEARD OF the confrontation and kept the Gulls and Kings at a distance through the weeks. After Dad and Riley, the pitching coach, had a tense conversation with the Gulls, Oliver was suspended for the rest of spring training, and the first three games of the season.

I should feel a sense of satisfaction he's on thin ice with his team, but I know Oliver. He'll get revenge. Ominous, perhaps, but there is a side to him. Like someone different peels back the handsome, charismatic guy.

The second side is mean to the marrow. Words cut, actions hurt.

When I think hard on it, I saw things on the Scorpions. Things I must've brushed away like a fool.

When he disagreed with a teammate he'd cut them down, create a divide with them and the team. There were a few times he beamed a few players—insisting a bad pitch was to blame—but Oliver is accurate. I'm starting to wonder if he threw balls that broke a few fingers and chipped the kneecap of another player on purpose.

Why didn't I realize these things back then?

Dad always told me something was off with Oliver. My gut tells me those reservations were behind his insistence the coaches never call Oliver up to the Kings. He'd never admit it, but I'm starting to wonder.

Mike never liked him. I'm certain my brother and my ex have said a total of ten words to each other.

I've tried to keep the confrontation with him and Parker out of my mind. This spring training was supposed to be special, and Oliver cast a shadow over us.

"You're doing it again." Parker's voice is warm against the curve of my neck.

There is something magical about the way he can chase worries away with a simple sentence. His Norse arms wrap around my waist from behind.

I grin and lean into him. His shoulder took longer than forty-eight hours to straighten out again. That inflammation a certain trainer warned him about did not need a few punches thrown at it. For nearly four days I babied that shoulder until it was fluid and back at full range.

"What am I doing?" I ask, turning around to face him.

"Looking over your shoulder." He kisses the tip of my nose. "He's not here. He's been hidden away in his little hole for weeks, baby."

I close my eyes and lean my forehead to his. "I'm letting him get to me and it's ruining this."

"Impossible to ruin a thing when you're there, Anderson."

I nuzzle into his neck. "You're getting good at those lines, Knight."

"Food's up!" Ryder's voice carries over the crowd.

Music blares around us, the air is rife in butter-grilled onions and fries. Couples dance and laugh, players surround billiards and karaoke machines at the front.

We're at the tip of our last week at spring training. Some of the guys insisted we go out, let loose, and enjoy ourselves off the field.

In all honesty, I was a little worried when the rest of the team arrived. Would they be bothered their guy came with a plus one on their ultimate bachelor getaway? Soon I realized it was a foolish thing to worry about.

I've met a few of the baseball wives who travel with their children to watch their guys train. Even went to a ladies' night. But the Kings Parker is closest to, they've taken me in as part of their posse. When my TV in my temporary apartment broke, I called Dax. Tech genius that he is, the man had it up and running in point five seconds.

When I need honest opinions on treatment techniques, I ask Ryder. The man is gruff and seems incapable of sugar coating. He's the sort of guy who, if a woman asked how she looked, he'd tell her honestly.

Griffin is charming and charismatic. He's Parker's righthand guy, and since he had my back and Parker's with Oliver, I trust him.

At the table a few women laugh with Griffin. He winks and scoots over in his chair for one to sit beside him. Such a flirt, but if I had to guess, I'd say the guy has more layers to him. Sort of like another playboy ball player I know.

I take Parker's hand and squeeze. He glances at our touch, then kisses my knuckles.

I'd take the guy every statistic said would be a heartbreaker every day.

Ryder mutters about Griffin's new fan club crowding over the food. When a girl tries to touch Dax, the first baseman looks like he'd rather be anywhere else. He looks to his phone, starts typing, and we've lost him.

I'm not sure who Dax texts all the time. At first, I thought it might be one of his sisters, but I don't think a sister would draw out the funny grins he gets when he thinks we aren't looking.

"Parker Knight."

Parker looks over his shoulder. My stomach tightens. A woman with two friends, I assume, stands behind us. She's stunning. Long silky hair, a perfect hour-glass type. Listen, there have been plenty of fangirls to come around my guy. But this woman, I don't know, she's locked on him like he's dinner.

The worst part of it all is the way Parker stiffens. "Hi."

She comes closer.

Griffin clears his throat and throws a fry at my head because that is where our friendship has taken us. Throwing food at each other.

He shakes his head and whispers. "Hang on, okay? Don't let her get to you."

"What?"

He clamps his jaw tight. I understand. Silky Hair has inserted herself at our table. No. Not the table. She's inserted herself halfway between me and Parker.

I can tolerate the dismissal. No doubt, the way I've been chatting it up with all the guys, the way I wander the field and Arizona Trailblazer clubhouse, people assume I'm merely part of the team.

What I cannot tolerate is the way she fondles Parker's face and tries to sit on his lap. Are personal boundaries a lost artform?

"Do you not remember my name?" she croons.

"Yes," he says, trying to gently ease her back. "Revna, I do. Excuse us, we're—"

"I was told you'd be here, you know." The woman is relentless and tugs at the collar of his shirt. "I couldn't wait to see you after our time together last year."

My face heats. Oh. My. Gosh. She's one of Parker's, what do I even call them? Fling seems degrading to womankind, but there isn't really a better term for the way the guy ran through dates before . . . well, before me.

This is what Griffin meant. He knew who she was, and I'm not supposed to let it get under my skin.

I won't either.

Let her flirt. I know about the man's Lego room. I've met his mother. He's mine and I trust him.

"That's nice," Parker says. Under the table his hand sort of slaps around until he hits my knee. He squeezes around her intrusive body, holding me, reassuring me. Poor guy. He's looking for a hero to save him here.

I clear my throat. "Revna, is it? Hi, it's great to meet you. I'm so glad you're a frequenter of spring training, but Parker isn't alone tonight."

I make a sweeping gesture at my own figure.

"I know. I was told he wouldn't be alone." Revna flutters her lashes. "Figured he might want a choice." She has the gall to lean close to me. "Between a real woman, or one with a broken head."

Her words are boiling water splashed in my face. A rush of unfettered embarrassment, pain, and fear slaps me across the jaw. There will always be insecurities, times when I feel less-than. I wish I could say I had a grip on the nasty thoughts of self-doubt, but I don't. It's moments like this the ugly head of insignificance rears up and takes hold.

I stand, desperate to escape before I make it worse by revealing how painful her words were. To let a bully of a human see the open wounds is the worst tactic. It gives more ammunition.

I'm not the only one on my feet.

Ryder and Dax have moved in, Griffin tugs my arm away, and Parker is there to catch me.

"Get out of here, Revna," he snarls.

"Your loss, Parker."

"No." He pulls me into his side. "No, it really isn't."

From there, Parker weaves us through the crowds until we find one of the back doors in the grill. He pushes it open and lets me step outside first. He must have a Skye sense and knew my flight response was kicking in.

My hands are shaking as I hold my face, pacing.

In three quick moves, Parker has my back to the wall of the grill, his face burning in white hot fury. "Ugly words make people ugly, Skye. If you think I'd take you any other way than you are, you're wrong. Do you get me?"

A sting of tears burns my eyes. "She wasn't wrong, Park. I do have—"

"Don't you dare say it," he growls. Yes, growls. One of his big, deliciously callused palms holds the side of my face. "Don't you dare feed what she said. I would not take you any other way. This" – he touches my temple – "is what I fell in love with."

I meet his eyes, holding his gaze. "You went out with her."

Parker sighs. "You know that before you . . . Skye, I was different."

I kiss him. A quick, gentle kiss, but his muscles slump in relaxation. "I know. I was just clarifying her in my head—memorizing her—so I can avoid her."

"You trust me, right?" It's not so much a question as it is a plea.

"Parker Knight, I've trusted you since the day you didn't run away screaming at my rage over a movie."

"Good, because I would give up the door for you."

I groan. "No. Ugh. We've been over this. We would claw and fight to the death until your big body found a way to get on or we'd go down together."

He laughs. "Fine. As long as you know I would. I want it all with you, Anderson." Parker threads his fingers through my hair. "I think you've made me lose my mind because when I look at you I see it all." Parker touches his mouth to my forehead, his fingers trace my jaw, his voice goes low. "I see lace and vows and babies. All I see is you. I hope you know that."

My stomach twists in a delightful heat. I arch into him, holding his palm against my face.

"I do," I whisper. "I bet Revna never got a custom Lego girl from you."

A bit of color reddens his face, but he smiles, shaking his head. "Only you, Anderson. These hands build with blocks for you only."

I laugh until he swallows it with a kiss. A fierce, needy kiss. The sort that draws out embarrassing sounds from the back of the throat. Well, embarrassing to some. With every sigh and moan, Parker kisses me deeper, harder. I'm grateful we're behind the restaurant, or people might begin to clutch their pearls at the sight of us.

I kiss him, alone in the dark, with fried food and laughter and music swirling around us. I'd be content to stay here all night, as long as these arms are there keeping me safe and empowered.

He's mine. And I wish the nagging thought in the back of my head would leave. Revna kept saying she was told Parker was at the restaurant. She knew he wouldn't be alone.

She knew about my brain injury.

How?

One name stands out among the rest: Oliver.

Chapter 22

Skye

WE HAVE THREE DAYS left; the energy of the approaching season is heady in the crowds who braved the Arizona sun to watch the games, to interact with their favorite players.

I bite my thumbnail between my teeth, watching from the sides as Dax steps up to bat. Last inning, and I've hardly relaxed through any of it. Parker pitched six innings before his accuracy dropped. He's lucky his arm recovered so well.

Since the encounter with Revna, I hate to admit it, but Oliver hasn't been far from my mind. A place he doesn't deserve to be.

It feels off. Like she was a warning. A terrifying reminder Oliver hasn't forgotten about what happened here.

Inside the dugout, Parker winks at me from the bench, an ice pad strapped to his shoulder. I force a smile, hating how being on the field makes me so uneasy. I don't relax until scrimmages are over and we can escape to dinners with the team, or nights alone with Parker.

Today is even worse. A strange foreboding keeps the skin on my arms speckled in goosebumps, and I can't shake the uneasiness.

Stupid Oliver. His viciousness ruined this place for me.

A loud thwack shakes me from my rambling thoughts. The Kings' dugout erupts with shouts for Dax Sage. Bases will be loaded if he makes it to first. A rookie named Spence bolts off to second, and Ryder speeds to third. Dax is fast, but Ryder is ridiculous. He makes it to third before Spence reaches second, and before Dax's toe touches the bag. Dax snags first, then rounds for second, but skids to a stop when Trailblazers, Arizona's home team, gets a centerfield throw to the shortstop.

My pulse slows when I think players are safe, but the crowd roars as Ryder takes the steal from third to home when the pitcher fumbles with a bad throw. Dax aims for second. The Kings are screaming for Ryder to slide.

He does. In a plume of dust and catcher gear, the umpire hovers over the collision at home.

"Out!"

A collective groan goes through the crowd nearest the Kings' dugout.

The Kings were considered the home team this game, so it's over with the third out. Ryder strips his helmet, covered in red dirt head to toe. I snort a laugh when his squealing fan club in the front of the stands shrieks his name. He waves, like a good guy, but his scowl is still in place.

All the guys have their own chasers. Even Parker. Pfft. Especially Parker. Do they bother me? All the time, but our relationship isn't well known outside the Kings, so I can't hold it against all of them who ask him out.

I like to give my fellow women the benefit of the doubt that they might simply not realize he's taken.

The man is taken so far off the market, he can't even see it anymore.

I steal another glance at the dugout where the Kings celebrate with each other on a win. Parker must sense my gaze. He looks over his shoulder and mouths, *I love you*, then returns to the guys.

"And that's the game," the public announcer bellows over the field. "The Vegas Kings keep the momentum going. If they keep this pace, it'll be a wild start to the season, folks. But that's the name of the game."

I grin and begin packing away our bags and supplies with the rest of the training staff as *Take Me Out to the Ballgame* plays.

"Whoop. I don't know—" The announcer's voice comes on. My ears prick to attention, but I keep my focus on the cleanup. It's as if he's half talking into the mic and half talking to someone on the side. "Well, looks like we have some runners on the field."

The crowd starts to cheer. I roll my eyes. Field runners aren't a new thing. Fans always trying to get a feel for the grass of their favorite teams. But it isn't long before the cheers darken, almost like they're stunned.

"Skye." Brad, one of the interns, taps my shoulder.

I turn to the field. A line of people darts onto the field, their faces covered with hoods and masks. But it isn't the rush of fans that sets me on edge—security is on their tails—it's the massive posters they're holding.

Posters filled with images of me.

When the screens around the field flash away from the Trailblazers' logo, bile rises to my throat. Two screens are locked with a still frame of my face for the entire field to see. Another camera, covering the Spring Training, pans to an up-close shot of the posters, filling the screens with each image.

None of the posters are flattering. In fact, they're horribly personal. Some of my most vulnerable moments are printed on those posters, and the image on the screen is even worse.

Tears blur my sight as I study the brutal, gnarled photo of me in the hospital after my car accident. Over my face are the words: *Born to privilege, so even when you become this, you can be this.*

The image shifts into the photo shoot of Parker and me with *Sport Nation.*

My hand covers my mouth. The announcer insists their tech people are working to clear up the screens. The picture fades, but instead of making it better, now every feed comes from the cameras on the field, and every direction holds a shot of the posters.

I want to scream at the camera crew to get a clue and cut the feed, but they practically zoom in, curious to know what the invasion is all about.

One runner stops in centerfield waving a photo of me learning how to hold a spoon again, food on my chin as my therapist helps. No doubt the camera is holding the shot, broadcasting the picture to . . . where? TVs at home? The nation?

Another man darts toward right field with a picture of me half-dressed, struggling to walk in between therapy bars. Two, three, four more across the field. All intimate. All with the power to send me back to a nightmare.

Even when the security team snatches the runners at the back fence, all I can think is how the people in the stands now have glimpses of one of the worst times in my life.

The only place I kept these pictures was in my cell phone, possibly my mom's since she was there every day.

A new video begins on the screen.

"No, come on. Where is this coming . . . hang on, folks." The public announcer is agitated. Clearly, the people in the tech box are struggling to cut the link to the cameras.

A murmur runs through the crowd when a dim, but clear video takes over the photos of me. A stolen shot from the other night at the restaurant. My blood goes cold. Someone caught the heated kiss between Parker and me.

"Closer to ace?" One of the men, now in the grip of security, shouts at the Kings' dugout. "Favoritism! The Kings' play dirty and ignore talent!"

By now the rest of the field runners are shouting similar things, all about how the Vegas Kings play dirty and hide their favoritism and nepotism and all the —isms from the Major Leagues. The crowd is in a frenzy, confused, and stunned. Probably a little intrigued. But I hardly care. They all saw too much.

I choke on a sob when the video of our kiss finally shuts down and is replaced with the Trailblazers' logo.

"Sorry about that, folks," the announcer says, a new thickness to his voice.

"Skye," Brad tries again.

I wheel around, face boiling, and I run. My head is spinning, the ground is like a dozen peaks and valleys.

"Skye!" A voice shouts at me, it's muddled, but comforting. "Skye, wait." Parker.

My muscles are tight, and I can't stop shaking long enough to stretch the tension in my fingers. When Parker's arms swallow me whole, I break against his chest.

"I've got you," he whispers in my ear.

"P-Park, I can't . . . I can't breathe."

He kisses my temple, holds my head to his shoulder, and somehow manages to guide me out of the sun. There are voices around us, deep rumbles of anger. I don't pull my head away from his body, but I'm guessing some of the team is surrounding us.

"In here, Sweets."

More tears come when Alice's voice chirps with a strange crack underneath. My cousin and her family arrived for the last week of spring training, and now they've all relived my most vulnerable moments the same as me.

Parker doesn't release his hold on my body as he guides us through an open door. The air is cool, sound echoes, and when a door clicks shut behind us, I break.

There is a bit of shame that comes from hating those pictures.

I endured so much pain, fear, struggle, and I overcame it all. I'm proud of me, in so many ways, I'm proud. The trouble is those moments were shared with the people nearest to my heart. The strangers filling those seats today had no business seeing my pain.

Then, to have my progress degraded into nothing but my father playing favorites to his daughter, and to have Parker brought into it—it's too much.

I soak his jersey with tears. My knees tremble and I think they might give out.

"Baby, I'm sorry," he whispers near my ear. "I'm sorry."

"How did that h-happen?" I cry against him.

"Ah, sweet love," Alice says. I didn't know she was still there. She rubs my back. "The Trailblazer owner is going ballistic. Thinks it might've been someone in their tech box."

"B-But why?" I wipe my eyes. Have I offended someone in the technical department of the Trailblazers? I can't even remember if I've spoken with any of them.

"That or someone hacked their feed, but that seems far-fetched," Alice says in a soft coo, rubbing my back in the places Parker isn't holding me.

Why would they be so cruel? I realize we played against the Trailblazers. They're Arizona's team, but how could someone do such a thing? The thoughts are whirling until Parker's voice makes the situation even worse.

"I'm going to kill him."

My blood freezes. With tense, jerky movement I lift my head. "Who?"

His eyes are black. "This was Oliver."

Alice clears her throat, her constant smile fading. "We need to be careful with accusations. Like I said, they think it was an inside guy."

"Probably because of Oliver," Parker snarls.

Alice grips his arm. "Proceed with caution, love."

"It was him." Parker curses under his breath and looks to the side. I let out a groan. Griffin, Ryder, and Dax followed us, standing guard at the door. I assume we're under the stands. Parker narrows his gaze at Griffin. "This is what he meant."

A groove forms between my brows. "What he meant?"

Parker's jaw pulses with barely managed rage. "Oliver threatened to give up something personal about you unless I paid him off."

"What?" My voice is a dry rasp.

"He's a snake, but I thought he was full of—" Parker shakes his head. "I didn't think he'd do anything like this."

The pictures. Oliver has seen those pictures, had access to my phone library, probably my mom's before she died.

Would he be so crafty as to save them? For what? A way to keep me under his thumb? Or was it when he spoke with the commissioner, and needed proof to back up his claims I wasn't suited for a job with the MLB?

A dozen different thought patterns batter my skull, but I keep spinning back to what Parker just admitted.

After I was injured, at times, I struggled to regulate my emotions. It's been years since I've felt like I'm spinning in space without an end in sight. But I can't see straight. My heart stills in my chest. "You knew?"

Parker's anger fades. He looks at me with hollow concern. "I didn't know he'd do this."

"But . . . but you knew he might do something." I pull back. Breaths come too sharp, too quick. My mind goes hazy. "You knew he had something and didn't . . . you didn't tell me."

"Skye." Parker reaches for me, almost pleading.

I can't be here anymore. I'm off balance. Walls seem too tight. How could Parker not at least mention this? At least give me a warning? I know Oliver. His threats are not empty. The man takes vengeance to a wicked level.

"I need to go." I'm hyperventilating. Hand to my chest, I glance at Alice. "I need to go."

"Skye, if I would've known he'd hurt you, I would've stopped this," Parker says.

"We thought it was an empty threat," Griffin offers.

Their voices are tumbling into one muddled sound. Parker shouldn't have paid Oliver anything, he was right about that. But he should've told me, given me time to prepare, to watch my back.

I shake my head. This is a kind of pain I've not felt since the day my mom died. A deep, driving ache in my chest. I don't know how to wade through it.

"Don't walk away," Parker says. "I'm sorry, I should've told you—"

"You should've!" Tears fall from my lashes. "I don't need you being my white knight. I can fight my own battles, but you left me unaware there was even a battle to be fought." My fingers grip the sides of my head. "I-I need to go. I need to be alone."

I turn on my heel. Alice murmurs she'll follow right behind me. My cousin has seen when my brain overwhelms and I start to shut down. There are times when too much stimulation, too much emotion, breaks me until I can hardly keep one thought straight.

I certainly can't follow the thread to unravel myself from this mess.

"Give her a sec, sweetie," Alice whispers to Parker.

"Skye, please."

His voice snaps a piece of my heart, but I'm lost in my own vicious cloud of pain. I want to be alone, to hide, to fall apart.

I'm pushing him out. Somewhere inside screams at me I shouldn't, but the impulse to flee pulls me forward.

All I can think is to run, to escape this place where a knife went through my heart.

Alone.

Chapter 23

Parker

ALL MY LIFE, I'VE tried to find a bit of bright in the dark days. When Mom brought home terrible guys, I took it as an excuse to have more sleepovers at Bridger's house, to build forts with my friends and Alexis, to find more hours needed at a small fishing pond we thought was our secret place, but really everyone knew about.

When I gave up time with family and friends to train, I saw the sacrifice as a long game. The time when I'd get to claim the mound from start to finish in a game.

But this? I can see no bright light at the end of any tunnel if Skye Anderson fades out of my life.

We've been home for a total of twenty-four hours, but it's been closer to a hundred since I've heard her voice.

One text. That's all I've been given. A somber request for time and space to process what happened at the scrimmage.

I've never wanted to disrespect a person's request for space more than now. Truth be told, I never expected I'd be this way over a woman. If I ever wondered if I loved Skye—I didn't, but if I did—this would prove how much she'd come to claim every part of me.

"Hey, Parker. Did you see that catch?"

A vise wraps around my chest. I can't even focus. "Sorry, my guy. I missed it."

Mason Walker groans with all the drama of a teenager, and kicks at the turf on the indoor practice field. Tomorrow is opening day, but I promised Mason another session before we were locked in with practices, training, and games.

Dax chuckles and catches the toss from Mason. "You're getting pretty good at those long throws."

"Yeah, but he's got to work on that jump. When a ball is going over the fence, outfielders need to be able to jump." Ryder says, catching the ball when it comes to him.

Mason nods, taking all the tips any of us give him. He's a solid student and doesn't get red in the face if we give him criticism. He wants to learn, and he'll take anything he can get. Makes me love the kid that much more.

I call him my protégé, but the truth is all the guys have sort of taken Mason in.

Mason looks back to me. "Have they figured out any more about that stupid son—"

"Mase." I interrupt him. "Jazzy and Finn will kill me if you keep talking like that."

He snorts a laugh and starts tossing pop flies to himself. I wish I could say no one outside those who were at the scrimmage game knew what happened, but word travels. There were social media posts made, those reached my sister, my phone blew up with concerned rock stars and their wives.

End of story.

"I don't like bullies," Mason says through a grunt as he stretches for a wild ball. "Skye's cool and that was worse than b-bullying. It was cruel."

He doesn't need to tell me. I've been twisted up in angry knots since Arizona. It means something, though, to hear how people in my life care for Skye. For us.

"Wish I had answers for you, my guy," I say in a rough voice. "We haven't found out for sure if he was behind it."

I give Dax a quick look, unwilling to ask the exact thing. I've already bombarded him with a thousand questions about the hacked feed in Arizona. Like some type of super spy, Dax has been digging through the feeds, trying to trace where it began, what cell phone had the video, if there are any digital fingerprints.

"I'm doing everything I know how to do," he says. "The Trailblazers have given up everything. I'll find out where the feed came from, man."

"I know." My voice croaks. I can't help it. Since the night Skye walked away, a consuming pressure crept up my shoulders and took up space there, weighing down every step.

It pays to have a tech guy as one of your best friends. Helps even more knowing he cares about your girl too. Every guy on the team is furious. They came to Skye's defense in interviews, came out in condemnation for anyone insinuating I hadn't earned my place.

I was overwhelmed with Skye shutting me out. In a way that makes each sunrise a little grayer. But to have my teammates have my back—attesting to the training hours I've put in to reach this place, talking about Skye's work ethic, it means more than I can articulate.

Everyone suspects Oliver is behind everything.

But the Gulls responded with a typical *unless there is proof, they're doing nothing* response. Dax set to work trying to sniff out the truth through technology, Dallas Anderson took a more threatening approach, offering a reward for anyone who'd come forward with information.

As far as I know, it's been radio silence.

"Park," Griffin says, stripping the catcher's mask off his face. "I'm going to speak for everyone here, and give you some sound, tried-and-true advice. Go. Talk. To. Her."

Mason tilts his head and nods. "Dude, do it. Your head needs to be in the game."

I shove the kid's shoulder. "Oh, is this coming from all your experience with women?"

"Hey, I'm basically the reason Dad and Jay got together."

"You ever going to call Jazzy Mom?" Ryder asks.

Mason blows out his lips. "I can't just flip it off. She's always been Jay. Finn came around and they got together so quickly, I don't know, Dad was easier." He looks at me again. "I don't know all the details about what happened, but if she's mad at you, I've learned most girls like a good apology."

Ah, gotta love teenage naivety. An apology won't help fix everything. I should've told her about Oliver's threat. I pushed it aside and basically forgot about it. But I never intended for it to turn around and hurt her.

I can't shake the shadow of pain in her eyes. She looked at me as if I'd stabbed her through the back.

Then again, if I'd made someone aware, would we have been able to stop it?

My opinion, if Oliver wanted to hurt her, he'd find a way. Still, I get how she was blindsided, how it hurt discovering I had information and withheld.

I don't know where it leaves us.

And I've been wandering in a haze ever since.

"I think it's a little more involved," Griffin says, "but the kid isn't way off. Skye was embarrassed in front of hundreds of people right as she was finding her footing here; it might take a bit of time for her to feel comfortable again."

"But she doesn't want to talk to me," I say.

"Could be she just doesn't know what to say," Dax says, his voice comes in a soft pensive tone, like he's figuring something out in real time. "I mean, I like to be alone, right?"

"Yeah, we know," Griffin says, laughing. "Learned a long time ago solitude is your jam."

Dax rolls his eyes. "Doesn't mean I don't want people around. There are times when I just don't feel comfortable surrounded by other people, so I get more comfortable in my own space, you know? Skye is sensitive about her injury. She might not know how to take the step out of her own head right now."

"So, what do I do? How do I let her know that the things she's embarrassed about are things that make me love her more?" I shake my head and lower into a crouch. My stomach burns in sick. Mason did have a point—I'll pitch my worst game tomorrow if I can't get out of my own way.

"You grand gesture her."

A willowy voice breaks over the practice field. Near the offices in the back, a woman in a long T-shirt over maroon leggings stands near one of the doors. She adjusts her black rimmed glasses, and smiles.

"Sorry, I didn't mean to eavesdrop, but you seemed so upset I couldn't keep quiet." I straighten and crack a thumb knuckle. She steps forward and holds out her hand. "Hi, I'm Wren."

I shake her hand. She shifts on her feet a little. If I had to guess, she isn't comfortable, and probably wishes she'd kept her mouth shut.

"Griffin." My friend shoves between us.

Wren startles a little, then gives him a nervous smile, and shakes his hand too. "Hi."

"What do you mean grand gesture?"

A spot of pink fills Wren's cheeks. "I shouldn't have blurted that out."

"Well, now you have," Ryder says, his voice low and rough. "Might as well finish the thought."

Logical. To the point.

"Don't listen to him, beautiful," Griffin says with a wink. "He's in a chronic bad mood."

Wren's lip twitches, like she might want to smile, but thinks better of it. "I'm a friend of Alice Hunt. I'm going to be here this season doing research for a novel."

"Cool!" Mason says. "You w-write baseball books?"

"Uh, no. I'm a romance author." Wren waves the point away. "By grand gesture I only mean do something to really let her know how you feel. It's a plot point for a reason. Of course, they're a little out there in books, but the idea is still the same."

A romance novel. Great. My answer is to pretend we're in a romance novel.

"Thanks, but—"

"I know it sounds out there, but there is a layer of reality to it. Sounds like your girlfriend needs to be reminded you'd hang the moon for her, so a gesture to do the reminding might help."

"This is a little more complex, sweetheart," Griffin says with his cheeky grin. "Serenading her isn't going to fix the actions of others."

The wispy Wren starts to fade. She straightens her shoulders and locks Griffin in a stare, one rife in challenge. "I don't suggest serenading, and my name is Wren, not *sweetheart*. I'm merely suggesting if there is a way to overwhelm the emotions of hurt with emotions of unbending love, then yeah. Women tend to like that. Again, there is a reason it is a plot point in the largest genre, with a readership made up ninety percent of women. But what do I know?"

She's not really talking to me. Wren keeps her eyes on Griffin, and there is a fierce spark of fire in them now, where before she looked ready to sink into the earth.

"Okay," Griffin says, beaming like this is some new game for him. "I stand corrected."

"I don't think you do," she says.

"You're right. Because my buddy here is dealing with a real situation. Romance books are fantasy."

"True, but like any myth there is truth to be found at the heart."

Debating the merits of romance novels versus real life is the last thing I want to be doing. I open my mouth to thank Wren for trying to help, maybe save her from Griffin who is about to put on all the charm, but stop when the office door opens again.

"Oh, Wren Bird. Good, you've met some of the guys." Alice pops out of the office. How many people have been here listening to me sob and moan over my broken heart? Alice flicks her eyes to me. "This is my darling Wren. You'll be seeing her face around. She just came to pick up her pass."

"Right," I say. Being around Alice is digging the knife deeper into my chest.

Maybe she realizes it because she sidles up to me, grips my bicep, and gives it a reassuring squeeze. "How are you holding up, big bear?"

"Not talking is about killing me." I shake my head. "How is she?"

Alice gives me a sympathetic look. "It rocked her. But to be honest, she's not really talking to anyone. She'll give us signs of life, but that's about it."

An ache blooms behind my eyes. "I messed up by not telling her about Oliver."

"Lessons learned," Alice says. "Honey bunch, at the heart of this, I don't think Skye blames you. Frankly, I think what happened drew out an army of old insecurities. It took my girl a solid year to stop self-deprecating about being broken. Those words we tell ourselves, well, they come harder and faster than words we hear from others."

"She's perfect to me," I say. "All those imperfections she thinks are weaknesses, I think make her incredible."

Alice smiles. "A girl could use a good reminder from the guy who loves her sometimes."

"The grand gesture," Wren whispers. "Make it stick. Make it meaningful."

Alice's mouth curves into a grin. "Something so undeniably sincere, Skye won't have time to think the bad things."

Griffin lets out a groan, but my head is spinning with a new thought. Maybe it's not something Wren or Alice will think is wildly romantic, but I think, for Skye, it might mean something.

Truth be told, there is something to be said about this grand gesture crap. The more I think about it the more I realize my own brother-in-law grand-gestured Alexis at a rock concert.

"He's thinking," Mason whispers to Griffin.

My friend smiles. "Good. We're making progress and we'll be back to playing hardball."

If Skye were here, she'd say pun intended. I miss her light; I crave it. Over my shoulder I glance at Alice. She stares back with glassy eyes like she might want to start crying, or laughing, but can't decide.

"I know what to do," is all I say.

Alice lets out a little squeak and bounces on her toes next to Wren who keeps typing something into her phone. Notes for her novel, no doubt. I don't care. The idea is in my head now, and it won't leave. But I'll need some help.

This next step will either be amazing, or horrible.

THE ANDERSON HOUSE IS more a mansion than anything. A long driveway, with a stone fountain in the center. The front is immaculate with desert plants in pots and expensive looking vases on either side of the door.

My hands won't stop sweating. I swallow thickly, then knock on the heavy wooden door. With each breath, I rock on my heels. Unsettled and twitchy. Then, the door opens.

"Knight." Mike Anderson stares back at me, confused. One mark in my favor that he doesn't look like he wants to kill me.

"Hey, man." I step closer to the door. "I was wondering if Dallas is around."

"Why?" Mike is a nice guy, but he's protective of his sister. One hundred percent understood over here. Until Skye came into my life, Alexis was truly the only woman I really lived for.

"I might need some help with something at the game tomorrow."

"The game?" Mike scoffs. "I thought you might be here for Skye."

"I am," I admit. My chin dips, and I let out a long sigh. "She won't talk to me, Mike. But she'll need to be at the game. I just want her to know I'm sorry."

"Can't call her?"

"Mike, give it a rest."

My stomach backflips when Dallas appears in the doorway. He rolls his eyes at his son. "Let him in, you know Skye isn't talking to anyone."

It shouldn't, but I've got to admit it makes me feel a little better Skye has been avoiding more than just me.

"Thank you." I step inside. I've been here twice, and only stepped foot in the backyard where a Kings party was held. The inside is kept at a comfortable chill, with wide rooms and tall ceilings. The house is large on the outside, but inside feels like it might take a week to see every room.

"Come have a drink with me, kid," Dallas says.

He opens one arm, guiding me into a large office. Mike follows and takes a seat on a couch near the back wall. Shelves and the big mahogany desk are coated in Vegas Kings logos and pictures of past players. Dallas goes toward a drink cart.

"What's your flavor?" he asks.

"Water before a game for me, sir," I say.

He gives me an approving look and tosses a bottled water from a cooler under the cart.

"Sit down." He waits for me to find a seat in a leather chair in front of the desk before Dallas sits in his office chair. He takes a drink from his glass, then cuts his eyes to me. "What do you need from me, Parker?"

"First, I want you to know, I should've told you and Skye about the threat. I've been threatened by guys like Oliver since I was a kid. Most of the time they're blowing smoke. But I never intended for her to get hurt like this."

Dallas dips his chin in a slow, methodical nod. "None of us blame you for what happened, Knight. Even if we had a heads up, I'm not sure any of us would've planned for what went down. It was cruel, and even if Thackery is a jerk, I didn't think he'd go so far."

Part of the weight on my shoulders eases. "I know it isn't a secret Skye and I were together, but Dallas, I want you to know I love Skye. When I think of life from here on out, I think of her. She's everything that matters to me."

"Parker." Dallas hesitates. "I've had the privilege of getting to know you as a ball player for years now. I've never been more impressed with a King than you."

"Thank you," I say with a touch of caution. It feels a lot like there is a 'but' coming.

"I know my daughter, Knight. I've watched her in relationships, watched her think she was in love, and stood by waiting for them to end. They weren't the real deal. With you, it's different. You've brought out the confidence we missed. You helped remind her it's a good idea to be exactly who she is. You're her real deal."

I grit my teeth and stare at the floor. All at once the absence of Skye is a hole drilling through my center.

"Parker," Dallas says softly. "She loves you."

"She won't see me."

"I know. I also know this about Skye, emotions are difficult to process when they come so abruptly and harshly as they did in Arizona. Sounds to me you've come here looking for some help from us. You thinking up something?"

A curve cuts a grin over my face. "I had an idea. I'm told by experts, women like a grand romantic gesture from time to time."

Dallas chuckles. "I'm not sure I'm the best judge of what women want, but I'm interested to hear what you have in mind." He flicks his eyes to his son. "Both of us would."

Mike hasn't cracked a smile once. In fact, he's still staring at me like he can't decide if I'm a nightmare or not.

"Mike," I say. "Are we good?"

"I think so."

Hardly the sort of confident answer a guy wants from his girlfriend's brother. But Dallas laughs, and it gives me hope.

"Don't worry about Mike," Dallas says. "He's still trying to figure out how you broke his equation."

"Thanks, Dad," Mike mutters. "Look, you proved me wrong, okay? I'm not easy to prove wrong. You got with my sister, and after Arizona, I guess . . . well, I thought it might've been the straw that got you to run."

"Why?"

"You're not exactly known for your long-term relationships."

I tilt my head to each side. "Fair."

"But here you are, fighting for her. Like I said, you proved me wrong."

"Good thing or a bad thing?"

There it is. I knew the guy could smile. Mike chuckles and shrugs. "Knight, I'm all for it. Unless you hurt her, obviously."

"Obviously." I smile at my hands. "So, can I get your help with something at the game tomorrow?"

Dallas and Mike share a look. It's Dallas who answers. "We're with you. What do you have planned?"

Chapter 24

Skye

No matter how much I try, the rush of painful adrenaline is still there. I don't know how to escape it.

My head does not let go easily. Another reminder my brain is less-than perfect. Because of those reminders, because of the constant replay of those pictures, I can't escape this vicious cycle of wanting to scream and cry.

Somehow I manage to shower, but now I'm stuck in my Vegas Kings shirt, a pair of shorts, and dripping hair. The next steps are overwhelming. They'll put me back at a ballfield, my face will be forced to be around the team who saw me in some of my most vulnerable moments.

I'll see him.

How do I face Parker? What is he thinking? During a dark moment, I texted him to leave me alone. Now, I regret it. Parker is not one who gives his heart easily, and I have a feeling my dismissal of him has probably broken his, like mine has been broken.

Do I wish he had told me Oliver threatened to hurt me? Yes. Do I understand why my hot Viking didn't? Also, yes. To Parker, those threats would be words, nothing more. To Parker, he was likely shielding me from past hurt.

There isn't a part of me that believes Parker would ever intentionally hurt me. But I'm stuck. Embarrassed. Bruised. I'm giving into the easier desire to stay holed up in my house, and I'm not sure how to break out.

No sooner than the thought leaves my head, a knock comes to the door.

I want to be alone, yet want someone to force me out into the world at the same time. I snort a laugh at the irony.

When I open the door, I shake my head. "Lex?"

Alexis Knight-Cole stands on my front porch, decked from head to foot in Vegas Kings getup. She's wearing a jersey with Parker's number, a ball cap, even her leggings are made of baseballs and wooden bats.

"Hey, girl." Alexis doesn't wait for me to give permission, or even move aside from my doorjamb before she hugs me. "It's so good to see you."

"What are you doing here?"

"I thought you could use some moral support before you head to the game. I'm sure it hasn't been easy after what happened."

I close my eyes against the rush of heat. "It's a little mortifying how everyone knows."

"Welcome to the family. We're nosy, and your life will be known among rock stars and baseball players until you die."

I laugh, but there isn't much umph behind it. My heart cracks into a dozen pieces. "I'm not sure I'm part of the family."

Alexis sobers. "Because Parker said that, or . . . you don't want to be."

Unbidden, a sharp, burning rush of tears start to fall. In two seconds, Alexis has her arms around me again. "I don't know, Lex. How do I look at him again knowing he's seen all that about me, and after not talking to him, and . . . all this is a lot to take on for anyone."

Alexis strokes my wet hair. "Here's how you look at him again," she whispers. "You go to the field and look him right in the eye. Guarantee you'd have him falling all over himself with one sassy glance."

I sniff and pull away, wiping my eyes. "It doesn't feel easy."

"No," she says softly. "I'm sure it doesn't feel easy at all. I've never gone through the things you have, Skye, but I've been stuck in a place like this where I didn't know how my life would work out with the guy I loved."

I've never gone so deep with Alexis to admit I've fallen in love with her brother. A smile cracks. "I'm that obvious, huh?"

"You weren't. At first. It was Parker who gave it up." She squeezes my hand. "I never, *never* thought I'd see the day where I looked at that guy and thought, yeah, he's in love. But from the first night I met you, he's looked at you like you made his world stop spinning. I hope you feel the same, but even if you don't, I've got you. What happened to you was horrible and you did not deserve it."

"I was so hurt, and I blamed Parker for not telling me." I fall back onto my couch and cover my face with my hands.

"I know." Alexis sits on the couch next to me. "I guess you need to decide if it's a dealbreaker thing for you."

I have no idea what's happening here. Growing up in the shadow of a baseball empire, I didn't always have tight girlfriends. Alexis is Parker's sister, yet she sounds like she's not here for him, only me. It doesn't make a lot of sense in my head.

"What if it is a dealbreaker? What would you say then?" The words come out like a challenge.

She rises to it. "I'd be bummed, no lie there. But no one should ever feel like they settle for people who break their deals." Alexis squares her shoulders to me. "Skye, I'm here for what you need. If you need someone to let you know you're perfect for my brother, that he's completely head over heels for you, I'm also your girl. If you need someone to bake you all the cookies and cry over stupid men, I'll be here the second they're out of the oven."

"Why?"

"Because once you're part of the family, you're part of the family."

Not the answer I expected. My gaze lowers to the floor. "Parker would not be a guy I settled for," I whisper. "He checks the boxes."

"Is there a reason you don't want to talk with him then?"

My chin quivers. "I have trouble turning off certain thoughts sometimes. It's like my mind latches on and keeps them turning in a cycle. For a few days I've replayed what happened; now I can't turn it off. Those moments were so personal, and I was mortified so many strangers were forced into my experience. I don't know how to talk about it yet."

Alexis tightens her grip on my hand. My fingers curl around her, but she gently strokes the tips, as if understanding my muscles are growing taut. She probably does, and it doesn't even phase her.

Such a simple thing strikes me to my core. Oliver rolled his eyes whenever I asked him to help me massage out my hand. He wasn't the first to get annoyed whenever excitement, or nerves, or tears caused my body to weaken and tighten.

Parker didn't even hesitate to tell me to hold him as tightly as I wanted.

Now, his sister is here for *me*. Not for him. Like I matter to her too.

There is a fierce loyalty with the people of Parker Knight, and it adds a bloom of warmth to my chest.

"I can't imagine how hard it was," Alexis says after a long pause. "But I'm here to tell you that you're not alone in this. Have you seen the outcry?"

"Outcry?"

Alexis releases me and pulls out her phone. "Girl, you've raised an army on social media and throughout the baseball world. Look."

She shows me a few threads from Twitter.

Queen Grit @queengrit1

Justice for Skye Anderson. Personal photos are personal for a reason. #survivor #fighter #TBIawareness #justiceforskye

Kendra Luv @kenny123

Blasting private images without the person knowing is dirty. This is in the realm of revenge porn and no one should have to accept it as normal #survivor #justiceforskye

Alexis scrolls down showing me a tweet from the Trailblazer's pitcher.

Martin Shaffer @therealmshaffer

What happened at our field was a disgrace. Known @Parkerknight for years. Hardest working pitcher in the league. But those jabs he took come with the job. What is most

Martin Shaffer @therealmshaffer

Disgusting is how some SOB degraded an inspiring story of an incredible woman. To taint someone's miraculous recovery in such a way, there are no words #justiceforskye

There are more. Mostly from women, some from other ball players, but I can hardly read them through the tears. Alexis shows me TikTok videos, some with clips from the scrimmage. There is one that caught me sprinting from the field, Parker not far behind.

All are similar, demands for justice for me, and punishment for whoever exposed me in such a way. There are those that offer support. Some from others with a TBI and their fury at the suggestion in the cruel video that they were not capable of having full lives.

I felt a bit of kinship with those people. A spark of realization breaks through the haze of my depression. Why did I allow myself to hide away in mortification like this? I ought to be proud to say I'm alive and I thrived.

There are challenges whenever a brain is injured in such a way, but those challenges do not make me a broken thing.

Yet, I've allowed myself to fall back into old thoughts, old beliefs, old fears.

There is a bit of disappointment in myself for giving so much power to cruelty when I could've been taking a stand against it.

I didn't realize Alexis had started rubbing my back as I scrolled through the support, the kind words, the beautiful side of humanity.

"This is amazing," I whisper.

"We've got you," Alexis tells me. "Whether you're with Parker or not, we've got you."

"Lex," I say through a crack in my voice. "I'm not sure how to face him. I warned him this happens, but still, I never wanted him to see how badly I get stuck sometimes."

She smiles. "That's the best part of loving someone, though. Knowing they see all the rough edges of you, and they still show up again and again. You want to know how to face Parker? Go to the game, do your job like the boss you are, and if you feel ready, talk to him."

"Is he mad?"

"I'm not supposed to say anything."

"What?" My stomach sinks. "He is mad."

Alexis chuckles and stands. "Go to the game, Skye."

"You're just leaving me with that?"

She glances over her shoulder. "I've got to feed Gare before we party with the Kings. But I'm not a total jerk. You rocked Parker's world. I knew the woman who stole his heart would need to fly in like a whirlwind and snatch him up. You did that and he's not just going to go down without a fight. Trust me. Go to the game."

Alexis doesn't give up more before blowing me a kiss, winking with a bit of slyness, then slipping out my front door again like she's plotting something.

My staff offered to handle the opening game if I wasn't ready. I appreciate the gesture, but Alexis is right.

I need to go. No more hiding. Not only do I have a job to do, but Parker is starting on the mound tonight.

Whether he's upset that I've shut him out or not, I have grand plans to cheer for his beautiful face.

Even if I'm terrified tonight won't end how I hope.

Chapter 25

Skye

BURTON FIELD HUMS IN the energy of opening day. Swarms of fans dressed in black and gold and red, all the colors of the Kings' rainbow, filter toward their seats in thick bunches. Across the sound system is a low chime of music, and announcers chat back and forth about players and the hope for the new season.

The seats behind home are filled with the entire band of Perfectly Broken, Mason Walker, his sisters, and his parents. I smile at little Garett. Alexis and Bridger have him dressed in an infant-sized Kings jersey, and a black baseball cap with a strap that's getting lost in his double chin.

The infield is packed with reporters and camera crews readying to set up for the pre-interviews.

My stomach turns in swells of desire and hesitation when Parker strides out onto the field. Confident. Almost like he is the king of the field.

Then it all sinks in dread when he doesn't spare a look in my direction. The team knows where the trainers set up, and he doesn't offer the slightest glance, doesn't even look as though the thought crosses his mind.

Maybe Alexis was wrong, and her brother didn't fall like she thought.

I turn away from the field. My job is still there, and it needs to be done for the sake of the entire team.

When most of the seats are filled, Tom Vince, our public announcer, blares his deep gravelly voice across the field.

"It's opening day at Burton Field. Seats are loaded, and I think our Kings' court is ready for opening day. To start off, the new ace hopeful, Parker Knight has a few words from the mound."

My heart spins. I clench my fists, desperate not to turn around and meet those eyes.

"We're going to get things started. Parker, it's all yours."

What?

The next seconds blur. The sweet, gentle tune of a flute overtakes the hum of the crowd. A familiar—much too familiar—song trickles through the stands, smooth, tragic, and too strange for a ballfield tune.

Celine Dion's, *My Heart Will Go On* fills every corner of the field. My heart bounces out of place in my chest and lodges in my throat. The fingers of my right hand begin to curl as I scan the faces on the jumbo screen nearest me. I'm not the only one confused.

Until a collective 'ohhh' and a few rogue cheers take over.

"Skye," Brad says next to my ear. He's pointing behind me.

My teeth dig into my bottom lip as I inch over my shoulder. I blink too many times when I take in the pitcher's mound. Parker holds up big white poster board with big, black letters over the front—completely *Love Actually* style.

At his side, Griffin sort of sways to Celine's voice, mouthing the words, dramatically holding out his hands for the posters when Parker is done, I guess.

Parker holds up the first sign.

Skye, you came out of leftfield.

He pulls down the next poster.

Pun intended.

I cough against a wet chortle. Not so much a laugh, something mixed with a sob and a giggle. The music picks up its beat, and Parker keeps pulling away signs to the somber tune, captivating more than me; he has the attention of the entire crowd.

But the night we met changed everything.
You showed me what I was missing.
I never knew I'd meet my best friend over a
Debate about Titanic.
But you became something more.

You're my safe place.

My hero.

My inspiration.

So, here I am telling you on posters

In front of everyone

(Because you deserve a baseball field redo)

That I love you.

Not 'I think' I love you.

The real, all-in love you.

When I think of tomorrow.

All I see is you.

Maybe I do dumb things

I'm sorry for those.

I'll probably do a lot of dumb things

But one thing will never change.

Me, loving you.

You were my changeup, Anderson.

...I'd give up the door for you.

Don't argue with me. I'd give it up.

No need for a debate.

A weird laugh-sob breaks out of my throat when the Kings dugout and bullpen explodes with the players cheers of agreement. Then, the crowd.

Griffin steps away with a show for their fans, waving the white poster for them to roar their approval at the odd opening day.

They're not in my focus. The only thing I care about is the unbreaking stare of Parker Knight. His crooked smile cuts across his face. Those hands that touch so gently open, palm up, like he's waiting for me to fill them.

I'm happy to oblige.

In another second, I sprint across the field and practically pounce in his arms. My legs wrap around his waist, arms around his neck. I hold him like he's a lifeline, a heartbeat, a fresh breath.

Parker doesn't embrace me—he swallows me whole. Those Viking-strong arms hold my body against his, one hand on the back of my head, his face burrowed against my shoulder.

My face turns into him, breathing in the clean air and sweet spice of his skin.

"No," I mutter. "No, Knight."

"Problem with what I said, Anderson?"

"Yes," I say, tightening my grip around his neck. "If we've been over this once, we've been over this a hundred times. There would be no giving up the door. Either we're both on it, or we're not making it out."

"No way."

My eyes flash with a growing passion as I pull back to meet his gaze. We're not in front of hundreds of fans, we're right back on the curb of that

Titanic expo because I will win this argument. "You are not going down. I'd force your big body up there with me and this point is now moot."

Parker curls his hand behind my head, pulling me close. "I'd give up every door, Anderson, if you need me to hold them up and remind you of anything, I'll do it. You feel like you're inadequate, I'll hold you up. You think you're not incredible, I'll remind you that you knock the wind out of me because you are. If you believe there is anything about this—" His gentle fingers brush over my head. "That would make me not want you, I'll hold up every door until you remember there is no one I want more. And if you think for one second, I'm not in love with every piece of you, I would do more than give up a door to prove it to you."

My pulse races in my skull. Parker allows my body to slide down his, then tucks a piece of hair behind my ear, his thumb tugging on my bottom lip.

"I love you, Skye." His brow falls to mine. "So much I can't think right without you; I can't breathe. I never meant to hurt you with—"

I stop him with my fingers to his lips. My voice can't be trusted, so in the next breath, I kiss him. I'm only slightly aware at the cheers from the crowd and team. All that matters is the way Parker holds me closer, the way his mouth glides with mine, the way everything about his arms feels right, and safe, and real.

I dip my chin breaking away, a little breathless. "I love you, Hot Shot."

He smiles and my knees want to give out.

"Hey, can we play some ball now?" Griffin, in all his catcher's gear, grins with a bit of mischief from the dugout.

I laugh and kiss Parker again, swallowed up in the boom from the stands, the whoops and hollers from the team. Pretty sure somewhere in the mix I catch Bridger Cole shouting something mildly inappropriate at his friend.

The woman sitting next to Alice in the front room gives Parker a thumb's up, a gesture he returns. Her hair reminds me of cinnamon and is sort of stacked wild on her head. I intend to ask him about their exchange when I get the chance.

But not now. Right now, I'm lost to this moment. A redo of catching the attention at a ball field. This time when cameras pan to me, when my face lights up the massive screens on the field, the tears in my eyes aren't from mortification. They're all for the play boy pitcher who stole my heart a long time ago.

THE CLUBHOUSE STILL RINGS in the boisterous cheers from the team. Even if they've cleared out, the walls seem to sing their victory. A win to start off the season. I'll take it. A seven-inning game for Parker before the relief pitchers were brought in.

A hundred people trying to speak to me after the training staff made our way to the clubhouse for postgame wraps or tape.

My heart is still stampeding in my chest. A high I never want to escape.

"Skye." Alice's chipper voice comes out like a pitchy hiss at my back.

Grinning, I whip around. My cousin leans into the room, beaming. I hurry across the space and give her a hug. "Did you know?"

"Oh, yes. I highly encouraged this sort of behavior."

Behind her the woman who gave Parker a thumb's up stands at her back. She hugs her middle, a recorder in her hand, reminiscent of the devices reporters often use if they're not keen on using cell phones.

"Hi," she says. If pixies were real, she'd fit the mold. A bit of gold sparkle in her eyes and a voice that's soft as a summer's morning. She holds out her hand. "I'm Wren."

"Hi."

Alice tickles my forearm. "Wren Bird is my author friend. She's here doing research for her new romance."

I arch a brow. "Have you met Parker? You gave him a thumb's up."

Wren shrinks a little under my scrutiny. I didn't mean it to come out brisk, but sometimes I'm intense. And for the first time, it's okay. Parker Knight loves me and all the layers of this intensity.

"We've met briefly," Wren admits. "All I did was introduce him to the idea of a grand gesture. I swear the idea was totally his. I just let some men know, women appreciate gestures of love from time to time."

Doubtless, she's worried her suggestion will in some way lessen the impact of what Parker did. It doesn't. Posters, a baseball field, Titanic. Those have Parker Knight written all over them.

"It was a good suggestion. I'm glad we'll see more of you at the field."

"Thanks. Looking forward to it." Wren's smile is as soft as her voice. "I've got to admit it was fun to watch a real gesture play out."

"Gave her ideas," Alice says. "We'll get out of your way, but I just needed to give you a hug!"

Alice gives two more hugs before she and Wren leave to meet Alice's husband and kids outside.

I'm packing up the therapy tape when another knock startles me. I half expect Alice is back for more to say, but I grin at the guy in the doorway. "Geez, Dad. You scared me."

My dad leans one shoulder against the wall, grinning. "Interesting game."

A flush prickles up my neck. "Yeah. Better than the last game I went to."

"I'd say." My dad crosses the space between us. At my side, he takes hold of my hand. "I've missed you the last few days, Skeeter."

A pang of guilt hits me square in the chest. "I'm sorry, Dad. I know I go inward sometimes."

"We want to be there for you, Skye." He leans against the edge of my desk. "Not just us anymore."

Heat gathers in my stomach. Parker wants to be at my side through the ups and downs. I believed him before when he said he loved me, but something about tonight cemented it in my brain.

"Are you telling me I can't go into a cocoon every time something overwhelms me?"

"Sort of." Dad chuckles and takes hold of my hand. "He's desperate to be there for you, baby. Let him."

My brows raise. "Dad, I never thought I'd hear you tell me to let someone else be my shoulder to cry on over you."

"No one else was worthy of the job." He winks. "I want you to be happy, Skye. That's all I want for both you and your brother. But that is my bit of advice I can give you—let him love you, in good and bad times. And love him equally in return."

"I plan to," I say, voice soft.

"Good." His face grows somber. "We're close to tracking down what happened in Arizona, baby. But I hope you know, I would never have hired you for this position if you weren't perfect for the job. I have full confidence in you. So do the coaches, so do the players. You belong here. Don't let cruel words change that."

"Thanks, Dad."

He presses a kiss to my forehead and backs up. "I didn't do anything but give a little advice to my daughter."

My head tilts. "Liar. Don't tell me the owner doesn't know his pitcher is going to blast Celine Dion on his opening day."

My dad's smile brightens his face. "Maybe I'm not that involved in the field anymore."

Biggest lie of all.

I roll my eyes. "Sly, Dad. Real sly."

"Hey, he asked for some help. I can pull a few strings."

"Thank you," I say. "For being part of it at all."

The door swings open and we're not alone any longer. My heart burns at the sight of Parker. Hair damp, dressed in his warm-up sweats, cleaned and finished with post game interviews and press conferences.

My dad winks at me. "I'd do it all again. Have a good night, sweetheart."

He gives Parker a firm handshake before clapping him on the shoulder and striding out of the training room.

Parker has his arms around me in the next second. My face burrows in his neck. I breathe his fresh skin, all the smooth spice and fresh air smell.

"Skye," he says, pressing a kiss to my neck. "I'm sorry. I'm sorry for not telling you, for all of this."

My forehead wrinkles. "Park, I don't blame you for what happened. I do wish I would've known, but once I started digging through where the pain came from, it wasn't from you. I'm sorry I disappeared on you."

His hands go to my face. "Do you know I love every piece of you?"

"Yes. Do you know I love every piece of *you*? Even your Lego room."

He laughs and kisses me, long, hard, desperate.

When he pulls away, his eyes are dark with desire, with a new, fierce longing. With love. "You're safe with me, Skye. No matter how many times you need to repeat an argument if it helps you work through it, no matter how many times we need to watch Titanic. You are safe with me."

I offer a wet smile, grip his sweatshirt with one hand, and pull him close. "I love you, Knight. I doubt a lot of things about myself sometimes, but I've never doubted that."

His quicksilver smile brightens the room. "I'll work my entire life to make sure you never do."

Chapter 26

Parker

MY STOMACH IS IN knots.

On the bench outside the boardroom office, Dax, Ryder, and Griffin sit on one side of me. Skye sits on the other.

Four months ago, three days after opening day, Dax and his tech connections—as in a cop brother-in-law—managed to track down the cell phone used to take the video. I don't know all the details of how it was done, only that techy people found the bread crumbs.

The phone belongs to Revna.

It took one call from Dallas Anderson with a hint that the league commissioner and police were aware of her connection to unlawful use of official equipment, and she started singing.

Revna vomited the entire plan.

The night at the restaurant, Revna had been told I'd be there. She'd been paid to harass us and embarrass Skye. Revna was filled in on Skye's TBI, with explicit instructions to use her injury as an insult because it would be what set Skye off the quickest.

I was disgusted enough to know she'd agreed, but the bile rose in my throat when she confessed Oliver Thackery had offered her five thousand dollars to do it.

The investigation became clear from there.

During his suspension, Oliver more or less stalked Skye, and planned to humiliate her into removing herself from the league completely. From a dream career she earned.

I've known all this for months and it still burns like lemon juice on a fresh papercut.

With the footage from Revna, with old photos he'd gained access to while they were dating, Oliver made the clips, and made his scheme. Bribe a staffer in the tech department for the Trailblazers, pay some fans of the Gulls to rush the field, replace the closing footage with his video, and watch as Skye was humiliated into oblivion.

The only good thing about the entire thing is how fiercely Oliver's plan backfired.

Scrutiny pummeled the Utah Gulls the second public vigilantes discovered it was a vindictive ex behind Skye's exposure. The mobs came in hoards, demanding a judge and the MLB throw the book at the guy.

Their loud voices caused enough of a stir, the Commissioner of Major League Baseball declared an investigation be conducted. With all the bribes and mishandling of private equipment, formal chargers were leveled against Oliver and those who helped him.

Now, we were nearly finished. I closed my eyes, letting my head drop against the wall with the hope this would be the last time we had to think about that awful day.

A door opens and a woman wearing glasses with sparkly purple rims sticks her head out. "We're ready now. Mr. Huntington, Mr. Sage, and Mr. Marks, you're first."

My friends give me reassuring looks, they give Skye quick hugs as they enter the room, adjusting their pressed suits.

Skye lets out a long breath. I thread our fingers together and ghost a kiss over her knuckles. "Doing okay?"

She rests her head on my shoulder and shrugs. "I'm tired of this. I'm ready to move forward and end this season on the right foot."

I grin. This has been the best season since I joined the Vegas Kings. Not only am I pitching with more accuracy, but Skye is there. She's with me every step of the way. From the moment I step foot on the mound to the second I leave the field, Skye is there cheering us on. Cheering me on.

She's incredible.

Falling in love was never in the cards for me. I never wanted it, so to want more—a lot more—with Skye is a little remarkable. I'd never change a thing. There is more added in my life. A woman who wants all of me, knows me, cares. A woman who loves me.

Too soon the door opens and the woman with glasses returns. "Miss Anderson, Mr. Knight. We're ready for you."

I give Skye a significant look and smile. "Almost done."

She pecks my mouth. "I'm ready."

Together we step into the large room used for councils around the Utah Gulls. Their owner, board, legal team, and coaches are seated on one side of the table. In the middle is the mediator for the case, then opposite the Gulls' owner is Dallas, and our coaches.

Oliver sits with his head down, dressed in a fancy suit, next to his lawyer.

My eyes narrow into sharp slits, beyond my control. The creep brings out the worst in me. For months, Skye has rehashed moments in their relationship, moments she wondered if they were red flags or not.

He'd laughed at her, belittled her, then gaslighted her by causing Skye to believe she was overreacting and too sensitive.

I don't hate easily. But I despise this man.

He must sense my disdain and lifts his gaze. At first, he meets me, glare for glare, but quickly I crack his glass wall and catch sight of the fear he hides. He knows what's at stake today, and if I get my way, it'll be his last time in this room, the last time he dons a jersey.

If the MLB means as much to him as it does me, it'll be the worst kind of blow to the gut.

"Miss Anderson and Mr. Knight," the commissioner says. "With the final testimonies from Mr. Huntington, Mr. Sage, and Mr. Marks, the board has come to an agreement. You both are permitted a final statement on the events of March twenty-sixth. Miss Anderson."

Skye straightens her shoulders and strides to the podium at the head of the table like she owns the room. I grin with a rush of desire when my girl looks nowhere else but at Oliver. He thought he'd crush her, and instead, he empowered her.

She's never looked so sexy.

"I have one thing to say to Mr. Thackery. You did not break me. I bent, but didn't snap. But you are a broken man the way you mistreat others. I hope you take this and become someone better for your sake."

Oliver doesn't have the spine to look at her, but Skye is unfazed. She steps back and curls her fingertips around mine, briefly, as we pass each other.

"Miss Anderson is more forgiving than me," I say. "All I want you to know is I think you're a disgrace to the league. There is no place here for spineless men like you."

I'm not eloquent, and don't pretend to be. Still, I don't mind the way Oliver shifts in his seat like I rammed a pin under his leg. Hopefully, the words stick. He deserves each one.

I sit next to Skye at the table, snatching her hand over her leg, and squeezing tightly.

The commissioner and a few of the other members of the league board look to an official-looking document on the table. The commissioner clears his throat. "Regarding player status for Mr. Oliver Thackery, a first-year pitcher for the Utah Gulls, this board has determined his actions in no way reflect the values and morals of the Major Leagues. It is hereby our decision to terminate his three-year-contract according to clause six, addendum five, stating dissolution of contracts due to player misconduct or illegal activity."

Oliver closes his eyes and drags his fingers through his hair, his shoulders hunched. Skye's expression proves she's a thousand times better than me. She looks almost sorry for the idiot.

I'm freaking beaming.

"For the improper use of Major League equipment," the commissioner goes on, "Mr. Thackery will be fined a sum of ten thousand dollars, to be paid within ninety days. All civil suits outside the Major League Commission will need to be brought forth through proper legal channels." He looks up at the room, sparing Oliver a quick glance, before closing the folder with the official agreement. "This decision was unanimous and concludes our investigation."

Skye lets out a long breath, her smile lifts to meet mine. The relief is there, bright and alive in her eyes. The first look I ever fell in love with the night I met her.

I kiss her, then spend the next few minutes shaking hands with Dallas, the guys, then our coaches.

Oliver avoids us. He speaks with his lawyer for a few minutes, takes the sheer disappointment from the Gulls coach, then leaves the room. No apology, not even a look of remorse.

My fists curl at my sides, and I must look ready to burst into flames since Skye wraps her arms around my waist from behind. "It's done, Hot Shot. Let's not look over our shoulders anymore."

"He disrespected you just now. Not even a look."

She smiles against my shoulder. "Hmm. But you respect me. It's my favorite thing when you respect me."

I can't stay angry when she's trying hard to dirty talk. She's terrible at it, and I love every time she tries. In a few movements I have my arm wrapped around her shoulders, tugging her against my side. I lower my lips next to her ear. "I will respect the heck out of you when we're alone later."

"You're still up for a date night before we head back home?"

"Don't wimp out on me, Anderson. We're having this date night."

She snickers and presses a kiss to the hinge of my jaw. "Bring on whatever you've got, Knight."

Chapter 27

Parker

Five Months Later

A THOUSAND BLOCKS OF bricks weigh down the pit of my gut. This is nuts. No, it's fast. Not nuts.

I glance at my phone for a little extra fire before Skye shows up.

Bridger: *You puking?*

Me: *Thanks for reminding me. Yes.*

Bridger: *We're cheering for you.*

I grin at the picture of Alexis, him, and Garett with a good luck sign. It's a sweet reminder I have people in my corner.

Sweeter than the texts flooding in from my teammates.

Griffin: *This is insane. Feels like just yesterday we were talking up our bachelor bromance and now look at us growing up so much.*

Me: *Who'd have guessed, right?*

Dax: *I didn't. I think Ryder and Griff even had a bet.*

Griffin: *I love everything about this. And bets, oh yeah. Ryd and I had bets about you. I lost. Hardcore, man.*

Ryder: *Big time. We're talking a four-figure bet, Park. Thank you.*

I roll my eyes. I don't blame Griff for betting against me ever finding love. Last year, I would've bet against myself too.

Griffin: *Dude, remember we still have standing date nights at Rocco's for nachos. It can't change man. It can't.*

Ryder: *Don't mess it up. That's all.*

I tuck my phone away and blow out a breath outside the expo center. Almost a year ago, I walked this curb, still on a high from Garett's birth.

To think how one night can change the course of someone's life is mind boggling. I'd never go back; not one second of my life before Skye tempts me to return to old times.

So much changed last season. We didn't make it to the World Series, but we were close. I started on the mound for one hundred fifty-eight games. My shoulder's inflammation has faded with Skye's help, and I have a feeling there will be more years left in my shoulder than I thought.

She's changed not only my career, but my family.

Skye settled in quickly with Alexis. There was a stop on Perfectly Broken's tour where we were in the same city. My sister and Skye spent the entire time together with the other band wives. There is something perfect knowing the two most important women in my life have become unbreakable friends.

Then, there is my mom.

Sometimes I don't know how to pinpoint my resentment. To have Skye's honesty, her unconditional love for me, has helped me finally start to unravel pains of the past. I've had several phone conversations with my mom, a handful of one-on-one lunches, and we've had two successful family dinners during home game series'.

Credit goes to Skye. She's not afraid to tell me when I'm being rigid, when I'm not willing to bend. Then, in the next breath, she's there, hand in mine, validating the hurt of my childhood.

She is a perfectly unfiltered light for me, and I can't go another day without telling her exactly that.

With a wave, I smile at the manager of the expo center, a silent thank you for helping make this happen. No small feat, buying out the space for the next two hours, but the people inside were more than willing to help out when I explained all the details.

Across the outside walls are screens with video clips of a rippling ocean. Blue, purple, and white spotlights create an ambiance, and somewhere deep in the storage rooms, the staff found a half-staircase on wheels, like it'd been part of a set for a production. Two wooden banisters on the sides, long wide stairs in the middle.

Not a close likeness, but it works as my pseudo-Titanic staircase.

Blood rushes through my veins in a sharp, short burst when a car pulls up to the center. The headlights flicker off. Skye opens the door, stepping out, eyes wide.

I press a hand to my chest. She's stunning. Dressed in a black dress, skintight, with a neckline I can get behind any day. Her dark hair hangs in silky waves over her shoulders and those lips are pouted, utterly kissable.

"Park? What is this?"

I curl one finger, gesturing her toward me, and descend the stairs, hand out. "I thought you might want to go to a real party."

She snorts and takes my hand. "Below deck?"

I draw her into my chest. "Wherever you want, whenever you want."

"Park." Her breath is soft against my neck.

Skye's chin trembles when I kiss her palm, then lower to one knee. "Skye, I will give up every door, I'll do anything you ask me, so long as it makes you happy. I love you. You are my every tomorrow, Skye Anderson. Will you marry me?"

She laughs when I crack the ring box and on the velvet cushion is a ring made out of Lego bricks.

"No one gets me like you do," I tell her, unashamed at the thick emotion in my own voice. I start to reach into my breast pocket. "You're my safe place, my bright spot." I remove a solitaire diamond ring from the pocket, and hold it out, a sting in my eyes. "What do you say?"

She glances between both rings, takes each one. The Lego ring goes on her right hand, and she slides the diamond onto her left ring finger. I press a kiss to the top, and look up at her.

"Heck yes, I'll marry you, Knight. You're the best piece of me." She places her palms on my cheeks, and pulls me up, taking my mouth in a kiss, deep and needy.

Where I once thought being single until my dying day was the life I wanted, now a day without Skye at my side is gray and lonely.

She taught me how to love, how to trust.

Skye changed my life with one debate about doors, true love, and sinking ships.

Chapter 28

Epilogue

Skye

Two years later

My shoulders ache from hunching over the table all day long. The rookie closer had to go and get himself a nasty tear in his rotator cuff during the final game of the season.

Instead of a restful off-season, I've spent three days a week at Burton Field getting Marcus's muscles up to par again. Parker loves the guy, insists he's better than he ever was. Maybe I'm biased, but I disagree.

As I walk into the door, Mason Walker steps outside. The kid keeps growing. He's almost a redwood tree like Parker Knight. Another year, some college ball under his belt, and he probably will be.

I have to agree with Park. The kid is a King in the making.

Unless another team snatches him up. I'm not sure I'll allow it. I do have some pull with the owner of the team and all.

"Mase," I say, startling him. "Sorry."

"Hey, Skye. Didn't even hear you."

"How's it going in there?" I jab a thumb at the door to our house. We moved after getting married to a place on a hill. About a block away from Bridger and Alexis. Seeing how my sister-in-law is basically my soulmate, and Bridger and Parker have a friendship unlike anything I've ever seen, it seemed right.

Mason laughs at the door. "I'm not even sure he knows I'm there most of the time."

I snort. "I can sympathize."

"Griffin is about to be the same way," Mason groans.

I grin. Ah, these ball players. How life changed for both charmers of the Vegas Kings.

"So," I say, crossing my arms over my chest, pretending the idea of Mason leaving doesn't ache. "When are you officially heading to Colorado?"

Mason's eyes brighten. "Wednesday. You guys'll come to the house, right?"

"Masey, I wouldn't miss my favorite ball player's college send off." I wrap the kid in my arms—basically an adopted son if you ask me—and squeeze him. "I'm going to miss you."

"I'll b-be around for holidays."

"You better. We'll make it to some games, I'm sure."

He pulls back smiling and leaves with a wave.

The moment I step foot into our house, instantly, a weight starts to lift from my shoulders. I drop my bag, use my foot to shove it in the laundry room, out of the way, and follow the soft, deep rumble of a voice coming from our living room.

It's an open room, no doorway, more a large arch between walls. I lean against one beam, an impossible-to-hide grin on my face. The man is my entire heart, and these last two months, I've fallen in love with him even more.

"You've got to follow each step, Ev," he whispers to the space in his left elbow. Then with his right hand he maneuvers the instruction manual open and clips together two pink Lego bricks. "If you follow each step to the T, it makes something amazing."

I sneak up behind him and press a kiss to the side of his face.

Maybe his attention is divided for the guys, or for Mason, but Parker will always give me his undivided attention. It's one of my favorite things about the man. He makes me feel like nothing in the world matters but me.

Well, me and her now.

I snicker when I glance at the sweet little face of our daughter in his arm. She's fast asleep, her plump cheeks puffed out, and her lips suckling as she dreams.

"Teaching her to be a master builder already?" I scan the mess of pink, white, and yellow bricks. The trappings of a Disney princess castle.

"Two months is the perfect time, baby." Parker maneuvers Ever from his arm and places her in the little portable bed we can take with us wherever we go, then he stands and has me in his arms in the next breath. "How was it today?"

His voice is tight in concern.

I snicker and wrap my arms around his waist. "It was fine. *I'm* fine."

"You should technically still be on maternity leave."

I tilt my head. "It's the first day I've been to the gym since Ev was born, and Marcus is still planning on coming here. I just didn't want to fill the house with a ton of extra people since everyone was coming over for Mason. I thought the other guys would be here."

"They were." Parker grins. "Rees and Jude left just a bit ago. The kid won't leave Ev alone."

I laugh. Rees and Vienna's little boy fell in love with our daughter nearly the moment she was born and loves to 'mother' her whenever he can. Since Mason is leaving for college, Perfectly Broken, Griffin, Dax, and Ryder had a day planned for the guys.

Apparently babies were invited too.

I hadn't wanted to miss out, and hadn't wanted to leave Ever to go to the gym, but Parker is the only who one out-does Jude Hayden with his obsession over our daughter.

He practically skips everywhere he goes, showing her off for everyone to see.

Warmth from my head to my heart blooms with how much I love this man. He's a true white knight.

Perhaps averse to commitment once, now Parker is gentle, devoted. He loves me and Ever with a passion I never believed existed.

"Hey," he says, stirring me from my thoughts. "I made you food. You need to eat, then sit on the couch and not move."

"You know I'm not pregnant anymore, right, Knight?"

He laughs. "I know, but I will be texting Marcus again just to let him know how disappointed I am he jacked up his arm since my wife is the one who needs to fix him."

I wrap my arms around his waist. "The last five texts let him know, Hot Shot. Trust me, he knows."

Parker kisses my nose and buries his face in my shoulder, breathing like he wants to absorb all of me. It's my favorite thing he does. "I made alfredo."

"Mmm. You're a master at alfredo."

"I am." He holds me closer. "Then, we can fight about the door if you want."

"Parker, you're spoiling me." I speckle his face in a few kisses.

Argue the door. Another way of saying he's willing to settle in for three hours and watch Titanic with me for probably the eightieth time in two years.

I love this man.

"Don't forget you have an amazing husband when the tiny dictator wakes up at two in the morning."

I laugh. "Ah, now I see. The motives."

Parker takes away my breath when he goes in for a kiss; I'm unprepared, but when his lips cover mine, I'm one hundred percent on board. He kisses me like it's our first time. Need and passion in every movement, every touch.

When he pulls back, my heart is racing in my skull.

"The only motive is I really love you, Knight," he whispers.

I smile against his mouth. "I love you, Knight. I'd give up the door for you."

He groans, and pulls me down over the couch, hovering above me. "Do you want to start this? Really?"

"Bring it on."

Parker grins with a bit of wickedness, a bit of competition. Then he leans down, ready to prove which of us wins this everlasting debate.

Thank You

Thank you for reading the first book in the Vegas Kings. For years I worked in Occupational Therapy departments involved in cognition and the brain. I tried hard to encapsulate some of the struggles that come after a brain injury. I love Skye and hope those I've worked with in the past, and those who deal with similar things, know how incredible they are.

The Vegas Kings have been stewing in my head for a long time. Since the very first rock star romance in my For Love and Rock series. I've been so excited to get them out into the word, but couldn't have done it without some people.

Thank you to Derek. You've been my number one fan since the beginning. And yes, all the book boyfriends are based on you. To my kiddos for being amazing and patient when I needed to get work done. You're my why.

Thank you to Sara Sorensen for smoothing out the rough edges of this book with your feedback and edits. Couldn't do it without you. Thank you to Clara Stone at Authortree.co for the cover. You never cease to amaze me with your skills. Thank you to the readers who love these sweeties and swoony heroes. I could not do this without you. I hope to bring many more happily ever afters to your hands for years to come. Thank you.

All the best,

Em

Also By Emily

For Love and Rock Series:

Our Secret Song

Our Broken Song

Our Lost Song

Our New Song

The Debutante Rules

Don't Marry the Mechanic

Don't Marry the Enemy

Don't Marry the Ex

Don't Marry the Boss

Want More?

Enjoy a free digital bonus scene with Parker and Skye when you scan the QR code below. By downloading you'll be signed up to Emily's mailing list and can keep up to-date on all new releases.

Made in United States
Orlando, FL
28 December 2022

27718620R00195